THE CHRONICLE OF THE VERSEMAKER

CRAIG C. CHARLES

NORTH COUNTRY PUBLISHING, LLC

ISBN: 979-8-218-53512-4 (Hardback)

ISBN: 979-8-218-53783-8 (Ebook)

DEDICATION

To My Loving Family-

Suzanne, Emma, and Alex

'You are my sun, my moon, and all of my stars.'

You are my light, I do not shine without you.

Epigraph

"A poem cannot stop a bullet. A novel can't defuse a bomb...But we are not helpless...We can sing the truth and name the liars."

– Salman Rushdie

"Every word has consequences. Every silence too."

– Jean-Paul Sartre

"I take from the left and from the right, and even without feeling guilt, a little bit from cunning life..."

– Anna Akhmatova

"Make people's lives better and do no harm."

– Joseph Orbeli

Acknowledgments

This novel has been ten years in the making and many people had a hand in its development. I would like to thank the following people and organizations.

Clarissa Yeo at the now defunct YOCLA Designs for another stellar book cover. She designed three book covers for me back in 2014 including the cover for my first novel *The North Country Confessional*. Support human graphic designers and pay them for their talents.

Kendra Langeteig, PhD at EdgeWise Publishing for her invaluable insights and editorial suggestions.

Author Jamie Ford for his inspiration and boundless patience in answering my never ending questions about writing and publishing.

Writer and Director Ernest Thompson for his wisdom and wit.

The NH Writers Project for giving me the confidence to dust off this manuscript, finish it, and let the world read it.

1

The Intelligentsia

State Hermitage – June 1941

Joseph Orbeli placed a trembling hand on the silver samovar; the ornate tea urn was the only heirloom that had survived the revolution. An overwhelming sense of pride in his once-noble lineage filled Joseph's tired body, but he knew that with pride came danger. Joseph despised the Bolsheviks and everything they stood for—even refusing to call his beloved city by its new name, Leningrad. He risked everything to keep the memory of St. Petersburg, Peter the Great's capital, alive.

Checking his pocket watch and adjusting his silk tie in the office mirror, Joseph tilted his head, eyeing the old man looking back at him. At only fifty-four years of age, he appeared at least a full decade older. His once thick dark hair had thinned and silvered, while his gray eyes had accumulated wrinkles like ripples on a pond disturbed by a thrown rock. Joseph's bones ached. Gone was the energy of his youth, sapped by tragedy and heartbreak, coupled with the endless worries of an unhappy man. "Why do I continue to do it?" he asked his reflection.

Hearing no answer, Joseph's thoughts turned to the clandestine gathering in the museum that night. The German military's astounding invasion had accelerated his plans. Tonight's impromptu assembly had been spread by word of mouth. Making his way down the long corridor and into the dimly lit throne room of the Winter Palace, Joseph stood among his fellow White Patriots, speaking in hushed tones about their once-great city. Speaking too loudly, even among friends, could mean a trip to a desolate gulag prison. The secret police, the Chekists, were always watching, waiting for any sign of disloyalty.

The Great Patriot War had finally begun and Joseph had been preparing for it, against Stalin's explicit orders to not engage in defeatist behaviors. In a room that once hosted foreign dignitaries courting favors from the Tsar, the chamber now only hosted fear. The Winter Palace and State Hermitage Museum found within was at risk, and all of its contents needed to be evacuated before the German hoard arrived. A blinding hatred coursed through Joseph's veins. Why were the warmongering fascists and the corrupt Bolsheviks putting his city through another ordeal? Wasn't the last war fought to end all wars?

In preparation for the worst-case scenario, Joseph had spent the previous year stockpiling straw, paper, and lumber, while at the same time amassing vital food provisions, he prayed they would never need. In secret, he stashed it all away in the cavernous vaults beneath the museum. The

Hermitage's subterranean chambers would be a refuge of last resort for the two thousand souls who worked in the museum. Everyone else would have to fend for themselves.

The city's Intelligentsia had gathered in the Winter Palace's small throne room. Joseph climbed the red-carpeted steps of the dais, attempting to calm his racing heart. Sweat ran down his forehead and stung his eyes as a throng of bodies pushed forward awaiting his words. Professors from the Academy, historians, poets, and artisans stood before him, looking for a sense of purpose. They were ready to do whatever was asked of them to protect the museum and their once-peaceful lives.

"We are at war with the most despicable of enemies," Joseph began, his voice laced with rage. "The German fascists aim to wipe our city and all its treasures off the face of the Earth. Make no mistake, they will surround us, starve us, and bombard us with every caliber of inhumane weapon and aircraft in their arsenal. So, I ask you tonight; do you have the courage to fight back? Are you willing to help me save our threatened museum and our last true bastion of Russian culture?"

The crowd's deafening roar provided the answer Joseph had come in search of that night. He spoke for over an hour, reviewing all the urgent tasks needed to be done. Although he should have been thrilled at the sign of solidarity in the room, Joseph reminded himself that many of these brave people had already suffered unimaginable loss. He looked around the room, taking in the faces of Russia's greatest living poets, composers, and artists. How many of them would still be among the living once this nightmare was over?

The poet Anna Akhmatova conferred with her young protégé, Olga Bergholz, in a dimly lit corner of the chamber. In another, the renowned composer Dmitri Shostakovich deeply conversed with an aspiring sketch artist. Stalin, called the 'Red Tsar' in people's whispers, conducted his purges and slander campaigns, killing many of their families and tarnishing their reputations. Yet, they were here, risking everything to preserve the last remnants of pre-revolutionary Russia. A time when they were celebrated and free to express themselves through their art. Living under constant surveillance and in perpetual fear, they knew the People's Commissariat for Internal Affairs, the NKVD, could come for them in the middle of the night. But the outbreak of war had granted them a rare opportunity to move throughout the city without a shadow, making their presence at the Hermitage that night possible. Their bravery was unparalleled.

Tears welled up in Joseph's eyes as he witnessed the courage of these brave souls of St. Petersburg, a city whose name they could no longer speak freely. They had no idea how much they would have to endure. Joseph had seen the fascists' legions in Berlin the previous summer and knew they would soon be unleashed on his slumbering city. Those who survived the coming months of darkness would undoubtedly have to write their own grim verse in the chronicle of history. They would also have to remember those who could no longer remember themselves. It was a cursed fate to cast upon anyone, but suffering and enduring meant being Russian. They would do whatever it took to survive.

As the room still hummed with the aftermath of the stirring speech, a silver-haired man leaned in close to Joseph. "That was quite an inspirational sermon," he whispered.

Joseph nodded, appreciative of the compliment, though his thoughts were already consumed with the tasks ahead. "It was a speech I prayed I would never have to give, Levon. Come, we have much to do." He grasped his brother's arm and hurried them out of the throne room, their footsteps echoing through the vacant corridor.

"You did what was required," Levon said, his voice rich with admiration. "Father would be most proud."

Joseph paused, his face ashen and tense as he gazed out a side window onto the Palace Square, sighing as memories washed over him. The midnight twilight of the White Nights bathed the Alexander Column in a faint golden summer light. Joseph had once dreamed of becoming a member of the Tsar's court, a life of privilege and learning. Now, he only hoped to preserve the memory of what had been.

He turned back to Levon. "How do you know he would be proud?"

Levon smiled. "Because I am proud of you, brother."

"But how can you serve in their army, Levon? They stand against everything Father taught us. This is not the truth we grew up with."

"The revolution was inevitable," Levon replied, "but Reuben, you, and I survived it because Father taught us well."

Joseph nodded his head, still staring at the illuminated square. "We should have died beside him."

"The militant atheism of the Bolsheviks took our father," Levon reminded him.

"Don't you think I know that? Our father was the most influential priest in St. Petersburg, making him a target for the Bolsheviks and their Red Army. Stalin was quick to accuse the Orthodox Church of siding with the Whites, giving him the perfect excuse to slaughter all the men of God."

Levon shook his head as sadness filled his heart. "And that is why I honored Father's memory by joining the Red Army."

"So, you serve the army of his killers? That makes no sense."

Levon exhaled, struggling to stay calm. "It makes perfect sense, Joseph. I understand why you despise the current regime; oppression breeds discontent. But remember, I was fortunate to study under Dr.

Pavlov. Stalin finds his theories of classical conditioning useful to the State. Therefore, I joined the Red Army for survival...yours and mine."

Joseph was silent for a moment. "The only reason our family survived the Great Terror is because we have roots in the Caucasus, like Stalin himself."

"You may be right," Levon said. "It seems our Red Tsar feels a certain connection to those who have breathed the same air as him. I also hear that Stalin holds Pasternak in high regard because he translated the Georgian poets."

Joseph rolled his eyes, his throat tightening with anger. "Boris Pasternak is a coward. I have no respect for poets. Pasternak failed to speak truth to power when it mattered most. He had the chance to save his friend, Osip Mandelstam, but chose self-preservation instead. They shot Mandelstam just over there," Joseph said, gesturing out the window. "He also died alone."

Joseph's words reverberated through the hall, and Levon felt the weight of his brother's disappointment. "I saw Anna Akhmatova in the hall tonight," he said. "I don't know how she found the courage to go on after Mandelstam was taken and executed. She loved him deeply."

"I doubt that," Joseph said with venom in his voice. "I heard she turned down several marriage proposals from him."

"Mandelstam was already married, Joseph. What would you expect her to do?" Levon countered, trying to reason with his brother. "Anna has suffered and lost more than anyone else in our forsaken city. She has buried two husbands, and her son Lev is rotting in prison as we speak."

"Perhaps Mandelstam was a source of comfort for her," Joseph conceded.

"Like all of us, Akhmatova deserves happiness. If not for her, there would have been no crowd in that throne room tonight. As her countless admirers say, 'One hundred million voices shout through her tortured mouth.' She has always had the power to rally the masses. The Bolsheviks still fear her despite everything they've done to her."

Joseph could not argue with Levon's logic and felt a pang of guilt for not doing more to aid the once-revered poet. But in these uncertain times, survival demanded difficult choices.

"One voice that was missing tonight was Reuben's. Have you heard from him?" Levon asked.

"No, but I believe our eldest brother is preparing to depart, setting his sights on uncovering underwater ruins along the shores of the Caspian Sea."

"I've never understood Reuben's fascination with searching for long-lost ruins or his new diving apparatus," Levon said. "He boasts it's of Leonardo da Vinci's design. Can you believe that?"

Joseph laughed for the first time that day. "If you ask me, Reuben is just looking for new ways to endanger himself. He should stay here in...ST. PETERSBURG!" he shouted at the ceiling. "The fascists' legions will soon arrive, ready to take his life for free."

Levon raised an eyebrow. "A spoken word is not a sparrow, Joseph. Once it flies out, you cannot catch it again. If you're not more careful with your words and continue to refer to our once vibrant city by its former name, I fear Marshal Zhdanov will hear of it and take pleasure in sending General Popov to reeducate you."

"If I have to keep living this charade, I just might end my own life after the art has been evacuated. But I understand your concern, Levon. Do not worry; I have a plan."

Levon's heart raced as he listened to Joseph's daring plan to protect their nation's cultural heritage from both the Germans and Bolsheviks. Though he knew the risks were high, he couldn't help but admire his younger brother's bravery and resolve.

"The Bolsheviks are fools," Joseph spat. "They only care about lining their own pockets, selling our priceless art to the highest bidder. But I will not let them get away with it. Together, we will save what we can and preserve our true history. Stalin's lies cannot go on unchecked."

Levon's curiosity was piqued. "But how will you keep your plan a secret? What if someone betrays you?"

Joseph's face softened. "I have chosen a few trusted allies with great care, those who share my passion for preserving our pre-revolutionary treasures. Tonight's gathering revealed others who may be willing to help us. We will need all the support we can get, but I trust those who share our cause."

"And where will you take the art? How will you keep it safe?"

"I have a plan," Joseph repeated, his eyes sparkling with excitement. "I will take it east into the Urals, to Sverdlovsk. There, I will establish a new branch of the Hermitage, where I can safeguard our treasures from those who wish to destroy them."

"But why so far east?"

Joseph lowered his voice to a whisper. "I believe the harsh Russian winter will be our greatest ally against the invading fascists. They won't reach the Urals before the snows fall, and our treasures will be safe."

Levon shook his head in disbelief. "But what about our Red Army? Do you not have faith in them to protect our city?"

"It is not the German fascists we should fear," Joseph said with conviction. "It is Stalin and the Bolsheviks. They are the most pressing threat to our city. Once the art is gone, so too will Stalin's resolve to protect..." Joseph's voice trailed off into a faint whisper. "St. Petersburg."

"Sometimes we must choose between the lesser of two evils, Joseph. The Bolsheviks will feed us, the fascists will not. Do you want to eat or starve?"

Joseph felt his pulse quicken as his head throbbed. He looked at Levon's serious face, which reminded him of their father's. How he loved discussing impossible scenarios and challenging his sons to make hard choices. Levon had inherited wisdom and wit from their father. "Come, Levon, let us have some black tea and discuss whom we should invite into our conspiracy. I would so hate to die alone."

2

THE POET

Anna Akhmatova was accustomed to men fawning over her. However, it was not Anna's physical beauty that drew men to her, but rather her intellect, passion, and the profound emotions she stirred within her countless admirers. In her youth, Anna had despised her aquiline nose with its prominent curved bridge, betraying her Middle Eastern descent. But as Anna grew older, she learned to embrace its elegance, observing how her nose shape had been celebrated since antiquity in the art and literature of the Greeks and Romans. It only enhanced her mystical aura.

As a poet, her words possessed intensity, a magnetic allure that captivated hearts. Men desired her, loved her, and endured the turmoil that accompanied her presence. However, there was one man - the Director of the State Hermitage Museum - who was immune to her charms. Despite Anna making a formal appointment with the museum's gray-haired and dreadfully serious administrator, Joseph Orbeli had forgotten all about their meeting, or perhaps he did not care about Anna's celebrity status, as most Russians once did. He made her wait.

Alone and feeling perturbed, Anna paced the confines of the Director's wood-paneled office. Running her middle-aged fingers through dark bobbed hair, she pondered what kind of man could hold such an influential position within Leningrad's ruling elite while at the same time working against the city's Bolshevik leadership. Joseph Orbeli was an enigma to her, possessing an unusual gift: the ability to inspire. Anna could recognize this rare talent, but what she could not discern was if the museum director could be trusted to keep her secrets.

Each morning, Anna wandered outside the rusty gates of Leningrad's Kresty prison, hoping to catch sight of her son or any news regarding his well-being. She joined hundreds of other heartbroken mothers and wives in the queue, all with loved ones who had been taken by the secret police. The arrests were used to control the city's most influential and dangerous population—the Intelligentsia. Since the revolution, the well-educated, those trained in the arts, philosophy, or politics, had been rounded up, imprisoned, or shot by Stalin or his Bolshevik counterparts. The Intelligentsia posed a threat to the Soviet state, and opposition or dissension would not be tolerated. Such were the conditions as Anna waited for the man who could either imprison her or set her free. The question lingered: could she trust him?

Joseph Orbeli drifted into his office like a thick fog. His demeanor was respectful, yet his coolness left Anna both annoyed and intrigued. His gray, ill-fitting suit was wrinkled, and reeked of vanilla-laced pipe tobacco. He strode past Anna perching himself behind an imposing oak desk. Lifting a yellowed sheet of paper, he began to read, ignoring her. Anna cleared her throat, preparing to launch into a well-rehearsed speech, but was halted by the Director's single finger raised toward her face, his eyes still fixed on the document in his hand. A full minute passed before he dropped the tattered page onto his desk and looked at his visitor.

"And what can I do for you, Ms. Akhmatova?" Joseph Orbeli said, his hoarse voice and tired eyes revealing the burdens weighing on his soul.

Anna paused, contemplating whether the Director's lack of hospitality in not offering her the customary black tea he liked to serve to important museum guests was an intentional slight or a thoughtless oversight of an overwhelmed man. She responded with a hint of annoyance, "Tea would be a good start."

Joseph eyed the poet with fleeting curiosity. "Of course," he said after a moment, realizing his lapse in manners. Rising from his seat, Joseph began to prepare a cup from his family's silver samovar.

As Anna sipped her tea, her eyes fell back upon the shining tea urn, "I have been told that our two families have much in common. That samovar resembles the one that graced my childhood home. An antique from a distant aristocratic relative, perhaps?"

The faintest of smiles flashed across Joseph's bearded face as he added a sugar cube to his tea. Since the revolution, owning land or being of noble blood was a severe liability, often ending in being stood up against a wall and shot. Anna's inquiry was more than just an innocent question. It was an acknowledgment of his precarious existence. Joseph cleared his throat and responded to the poet's keen observation. "You have a good eye. However, I assume you have not come to see me about my samovar? I am sure you are quite busy Ms. Akhmatova, so let us dispense with pleasantries and get to the purpose of your visit."

Now it was Anna's turn to smile. "I have come to offer my assistance in helping the Hermitage save its art from the barbarians advancing on our city. I was present when you addressed our city's Intelligentsia, appealing for support. I am here to answer your call to action."

Joseph observed the once-celebrated poet with caution, considering the best way to respond. He remembered seeing her at the surreptitious gathering of the Intelligentsia and knew the value of having her as an ally. "What kind of help can you offer?" he said, doubting that she possessed the brute strength or physical stamina required to pack and transport artworks in the museum's galleries.

"Despite the Bolsheviks' best efforts to muzzle me, I still have a multitude of supporters who will do as I ask," she said. "Judging by the activity in your galleries, it seems you need diligent workers. I can provide capable individuals to assist you."

Joseph raised an eyebrow, aware that there must be a catch. "And you offer this out of pure generosity?"

"Yes and no," she said, extending her empty teacup toward him for a refill. "In return, I do require a small favor."

"Ms. Akhmatova..."

"Call me Anna," she interrupted. "There is no need for formality. We are contemporaries and I desire that we should become friends."

Leaning back into his chair, Joseph rubbed his tired face. His bloodshot eyes turned toward a window overlooking the immense Palace Square below. Catching sight of the towering Alexander Column in its center, Joseph thought about how few friends he had left. The revolution had consumed them like a firestorm through a copse of trees. They were kindling for a blaze that was raging out of control. "Both of us have lost family and loved ones to the Great Purge. Chairman Stalin orders arrests and killings without rhyme or reason and the pain I have endured at those losses has been unbearable. I do not need more friends to bury Ms. Akhmatova, I need more workers."

"Without friends, who will mourn you, Joseph, when your time comes to be taken?"

He let out a heavy breath. "I have not slept in two days, and I have an overwhelming number of tasks to complete before the invading barbarians descend upon our city. So tell me, why have you come to see me?"

Anna stirred her teacup with the daintiest of silver spoons considering her next words. "You and I both know that barbarians have long been present in St. Petersburg. We share a deep resentment towards the Bolsheviks, their actions, and the threats they pose to us. I am your ally and I am eager to defy them in any way possible."

"And what small favor have you come to ask of me?"

Anna stared down into her tea for a long moment. "How much do you know about me?"

Joseph sighed realizing that this would not be the short visit he had envisioned. Therefore, he decided to be direct. "I am an academic who appreciates various forms of art, but I must admit that when it comes to poetry, I am not a patron. A bard's heart does not impress me nor the ignoble lack of courage demonstrated by the poets I have had the unfortunate opportunity of meeting."

A boisterous laugh erupted from Anna. "Oh, how I have longed to meet an honest man like you. Truth be told, I have a weakness for artists—a weakness, or perhaps a more fitting description would be they are my downfall. They fall in love with me far too often. Sometimes, I return their affections, sometimes I break their hearts. So, let me be honest with you if I may."

Joseph placed his teacup down and lit a well-worn pipe, craving the relief the tobacco would offer him. Wondering where this bizarre conversation was headed, he leaned forward and shared his match, igniting Anna's cigarette as the flame singed his manicured fingertips.

"I have been married twice and fallen in love more times than I can count," Anna began. "For my second marriage, I spent my honeymoon in Paris. Nikolay, my husband, was also a poet—many years younger than me. His passion and pursuit left me no choice but to marry him. It was blissful for a week or two, and then Nikolay grew bored. It was the chase that excited him, the dream and not the reality of what my aging body was. He lost interest, and as luck would have it, I met my next great love in Paris—Amedeo Modigliani."

"The Italian painter???"

"Ah, you have heard of him. Amedeo was not only a painter but also a talented sculptor. Nevertheless, his style of portraiture aligned perfectly with my own average looks," Anna said with an unabashed smile.

"He primarily painted nudes."

Anna nodded, undeterred. "Of course, why do you think I fell in love with him in the first place?"

Joseph shook his head, trying to grasp the connection he had to the poet's visit. Their conversation was going in circles and he was wasting time better spent packing up the art in his museum. "For God's sake woman, what does this have to do with me?"

"When Amedeo died, he bequeathed to me all the portraits he painted of me."

"And how many of them are nudes?" he found himself asking.

"Thirty," she said with a mischievous wink.

Joseph sank back in his chair again, puffing heavily on his pipe, as a bead of sweat formed on his forehead. The pieces were starting to come together, and the frightening implications were becoming clear to him. When the Bolsheviks realized they were running out of money and that their lack of capital threatened the success of the revolution, they began nationalizing private art collections. Priceless treasures and immense wealth were confiscated. Much of the art was shipped to the State Hermitage Museum and cataloged by him and his staff. However, Joseph did not recall ever seeing any portraits by Amedeo Modigliani in the collection.

"If that were indeed true Ms. Akhmatova, why have I not seen any of these portraits among the confiscated artworks shipped to my museum?"

Anna eyed him coyly. "That is because I never surrendered them to the Bolsheviks. I still possess them."

"This is insanity," Joseph huffed. "If you are caught with those paintings, you will be arrested, convicted of crimes against the state, and likely shot, all within the same hour. Why did you not turn them in?"

Anna's eyes pierced Joseph's as she exhaled a cloud of smoke. "And what do you think the Bolsheviks would do to me if they saw my nude form sprawled across so many canvases?"

"Hmm," Joseph grunted, his mind racing to comprehend the magnitude of the situation. "I see the gravity of your dilemma. So, if I understand correctly, you want me to..."

"I want you to assume responsibility for my portraits and ensure their safety until a more favorable political climate emerges in St. Petersburg."

Joseph pondered the proposition, weighing the potential risks and rewards. "So, in exchange for assuming your risk, you offer me a workforce of how many men?"

"Five hundred men will be at your door tomorrow, ready to provide the labor force necessary to safeguard the remaining artworks in this esteemed museum's collection."

Joseph was stunned, the weight of their agreement sinking in. After a full minute of consideration, he extended his hand and accepted the deal. "To your portraits, may they solve all of our problems," he toasted with his teacup.

The intricate nuances of their unconventional accord took shape within the next fifteen minutes. Once their conversation was concluded, Joseph escorted Anna out of his office and bid her a courteous farewell.

Now alone with his ruminations, Joseph gravitated back to his desk. For the fourth time that day, he revisited the faded, tattered edges of a yellowed page, tracing the last lines delicately with a finger. He could hear the echoes of the tragic tale etched on its surface. The gut-wrenching sobs of a father mourning the loss of his younger brother, and the devastating end of the Romanov family at the hands of the Bolsheviks, were stories he understood all too well. The memory of his own father's love and sacrifice still brought tears to Joseph's eyes. These were painful memories that he wanted to be locked away. Yet, Joseph was aware that these stories needed to be remembered and told, no matter how painful.

A familiar voice echoed through Joseph's office doorway, breaking his concentration. Glancing up, he spotted his eldest brother puffing warm breath onto the tarnished brass nameplate adorning his wooden door, polishing it with a handkerchief. "The Director of the State Hermitage Museum," he said with pride as he read the nameplate aloud. "And yet, here you are, burning the midnight oil on a Sunday."

"It's summer," Joseph explained, placing the paper down on the desk again. "The sun lingers over our city during this season, and my never-ending stacks of paperwork seem to echo its persistence. And have you caught wind of the news? The fascists are flooding through the western borders. There is much to do."

"I have heard," Reuben Orbeli growled, "Regardless, you're still a committed administrator. I do not know how you tolerate it. Archaeology suits me better. I need to be in the field, delving into the earth, communicating with the ghosts of the past."

Joseph cast a sharp glance at his eldest brother. Reuben had always been independent, almost to a fault. Now at sixty years of age, he seemed more like a specter, something dangerous and to be avoided. "Speaking of the past, I would like your opinion on something," he said, handing Reuben the yellowed sheet of paper.

Reuben scanned the tale of the Romanov family's death with intense curiosity. "Where did you get this?"

"It was waiting for me on my desk when I arrived earlier this morning. The better question is: who left it and why?"

Reuben scrutinized the paper once more before replying, "What you have here is what we in the field of archaeology refer to as a Homeric artifact."

"And what exactly is that?"

"Something so rare, so singular, that it is dismissed as fantasy or myth," Reuben explained. "Do you know why historians know so little about the lost city of Troy?"

Joseph shrugged not answering his brother as he started to brew some more black tea. He knew when Reuben made an appearance his life would soon grow more complicated.

Reuben answered for him. "It is because the only mention of the ancient city of Troy and its conflict with the invading Greeks—the only clue to its existence—comes from a Greek poet named Homer."

"The blind poet?" Joseph said, offering his brother tea. "The author of the Iliad and Odyssey?"

"Come now, Joseph," his brother retorted, "I expected you to know more about Homer than that. The name Homer was rather unusual for his time. It is thought to mean 'blind' or more precisely, 'captive'. Therefore, one can assume he was on the losing side of the battle. Yet, his narrative and his chronicle of events, an epic poem, survived for future generations to read. This is quite uncommon since history is typically penned by the victors, and rarely is it accurate. The conquered lose not just their land, freedom, and sometimes their lives, but most devastatingly, they lose their voice. Without Homer, there is no Troy."

Joseph's head suddenly ached. "Isn't it possible it is just fiction written for pure enjoyment?"

"The city of Troy was rediscovered after 3,000 years because a German businessman turned self-taught archaeologist chose to read Homer's tale not as fiction, but as fact."

Joseph pointed to the yellowed sheet of paper. "And this entry here?"

Reuben glanced down at the artifact with reverence once more. "It is an eyewitness account of the Romanov family's execution, written by Alexei Nikolaevich, Nicholas II's only son, the last Tsesarevich, and the heir apparent to the throne of the Russian Empire."

"So why was it delivered to me? Why not just turn it over to the State Library?"

"Libraries can be burned," Reuben reminded him. "Do you know how much ancient wisdom and technological knowledge was lost when the Library of Alexandria was set aflame? If it had survived, we would for example know the true age and purpose of the pyramids. I suspect they predate the pharaohs."

"Alexandria's library was accidentally burned by Caesar during his civil war," Joseph countered.

"There are no accidents, everything happens for a reason. Remember that, brother. Your role will become clear when the time is right."

Joseph pondered this for a moment before deciding to change the subject. "When will you depart in search of the lost city Atil?"

"Prior to dawn, and before the fascists manage to sever the southern train lines. In truth, I worry more about the Bolsheviks. Regardless of who wins this senseless war, the truth will be the ultimate casualty. If I find the lost city of Atil, I fear the Bolsheviks will obliterate any record of it. Stalin, our Red Tsar, would not want evidence of a connection between the Jewish and Russian peoples."

"Perhaps you should write an epic poem to document your ground-shaking discoveries," Joseph suggested with a smile. "That way no one would believe it was real."

"Perhaps," Reuben smiled back as he savored the final drops of the black caravan tea. Preparing to leave, Reuben paused, turned, and addressed his younger brother one last time, offering some advice. "It would be in your best interest to document the impending tragedy that I fear will befall our fair city. Chronicle it, hide it and preserve the truth at all costs. As the philosopher Rousseau said, 'The falsification of history has done more to impede human development than any one thing known to mankind.' He who controls the archives controls the story of our people."

Joseph picked up the age-stained document, scrutinizing it one final time. How was it possible for the rightful successor to the Russian throne to chronicle his mortality along with the downfall of his family? He found himself lost in thought. The widely accepted narrative suggested their collective demise, their remains never to be uncovered, akin to the lost city of Troy. Perhaps he would indulge in his own personalized form of archeology - unearthing the obscure remnants of the Bolshevik's hastily concealed past.

3

THE PROTÉGÉ

Leningrad - June 1941

Anna Akhmatova and Olga Bergholz walked side by side, their arms intertwined, along the tranquil banks of the Fontanka River. Silence enveloped them but their thoughts were absorbed by Director's Orbeli's impassioned call to action. His words had stirred something within them, igniting a flicker of hope. Yet, lingering in their hearts were the haunting memories of their profound suffering under the relentless grip of the Bolshevik regime. Unspoken fears surged through their minds as they traversed the peaceful sanctuary that the river provided.

Anna gazed upward, her eyes catching sight of her former residence, Sheremetev Palace, now known as Fountain House. The opulence and grandeur of the imperial structure mirrored the heights of Anna's illustrious career. Its reflection shimmered on the glassy surface of the river, evoking a wistful sigh from Anna followed by a tender smile. "If only those walls could speak," she said, sharing her thoughts with Olga. "Some of my fondest memories were made within those very walls," she added, her gesture encompassing the facade of the building.

Despite the considerable age difference between them, Olga, twenty-one years Anna's junior, grasped the profound impact of the revolution on St. Petersburg and Anna's life. The city's transformation had been seismic. Once basking in the radiant glow of the Silver Age of Russian poetry, Anna was now perceived as subversive. The Bolshevik leadership loathed her, chided her, and condemned her to a life of nothingness. Gone were the parties, the accolades, and worst of all, the ability to practice her art unencumbered.

"Do you have any regrets?" Olga asked, brushing a wind-blown strand of blonde hair behind her ear.

"Enough to fill two lifetimes!" Anna said, breaking into laughter. "I have loved and lost numerous men," she confessed. "They are either imprisoned or dead. I seem to be a harbinger of bad luck."

Olga frowned, squeezing Anna's hand. "And yet, I would trade places with you in a heartbeat to have witnessed what you have. My own poetry is like that of a toddler compared to yours. I fear my words will never inspire. The world has changed. The future appears rather hopeless."

"You have endured suffering in ways even I cannot fathom," Anna acknowledged, pulling Olga closer to her. "We cannot change the past nor become paralyzed by an unknown future. We only have today. That is the one certainty the Bolsheviks will allow us."

The pair continued their walk alongside the banks of the river. After some silence, Olga announced, "I have committed the poem you gave me to memory. How many others have you entrusted with this same task?"

"All my dearest friends hold fragments of my poems in their minds," Anna said. "You all serve as my living memory. Given the dangers of the current regime, it is too risky to put thoughts onto paper. The Bolsheviks have forced us back into a pre-Gutenberg era. To survive this nightmare, we must avoid printing anything."

"Speaking of survival, what shall we do about Director Orbeli's call for help? Do we align ourselves with him and risk facing further abuse and turmoil from the NKVD if we are discovered?"

Anna contemplated Olga's question as the fading light of a midnight summer sunset cast soft shadows upon the riverbank. "Sometimes, we need to gaze into reflective waters to see the truth. Orbeli is a kindred spirit, a ray of light like us. Despite my fears that he may betray me, I have already pledged my support to him," she said, "but you will have to make your own decision."

"Free will is not something I am accustomed to," Olga admitted. "Nevertheless, I have considered the risks and I, too, will support the

Director and his endeavors. What more can the authorities do to me that they have not already?"

"The consequence of deceiving the Party leadership, if we are discovered, will be death," Anna cautioned. "But I have lived much longer than I ever expected, so death does not trouble me. You should know, though, that Director Orbeli can offer me something I need in return for my help so my motivations are not entirely pure. But you, Olga, have decades ahead of you to live and write. Your poetry has the chance to reach unimaginable heights. Do not feel obligated to make the same choice I have out of loyalty to me or our friendship."

Olga nodded her understanding. "All that I have cared for has already been lost. Helping Director Orbeli save our city's art and cultural treasures from all our enemies is a noble cause, and I am willing to sacrifice my life for it."

"Then let us hope that Director Orbeli has a plan that will prevent such an outcome," Anna said, thinking of her portraits and her deal with Joseph Orbeli.

4

THE GERMAN

JANUARY 1929 - TWELVE YEARS EARLIER

Franz Krüger raised a starched handkerchief and dabbed at his forehead, the sweat droplets were like gnats, an annoying presence that threatened to smudge the inked entries in his notebook. Accuracy was paramount; he could not afford any mistakes.

At only thirty-one years old, the blond-haired, blue-eyed Krüger and his Berlin art gallery had earned a reputation among the continental elite for discretion. His gallery catered to the wealthiest patrons in Europe and America, both old money and the nouveau riche. Krüger had learned that among his clients, new money spoke while old wealth whispered. His current project demanded the utmost secrecy. "Do nothing to draw undue attention to yourself," the museum liaison had cautioned at the beginning of his covert assignment.

Krüger made his way down the Grand Salon of the State Hermitage Museum, his footsteps echoing into the vast darkness. He had already identified ninety-three of the one hundred paintings to be forbidden, slated to be withheld from the upcoming surreptitious auction. These most valuable masterpieces would be spared from immediate liquidation. The weight of responsibility pressed upon Krüger, evident in his cold sweats and uncontrollable shakes, threatening to blur his sharp vision and handwriting. He understood the tragic paradox of his task. The items sold abroad offered the sole avenue of salvation for the priceless relics and paintings detested by the Bolsheviks. Without these sales, many of these treasures would languish or face destruction. "The Hundred," as Krüger referred to them, would be held hostage in a state of purgatory.

Among the immense collection in the Hermitage, there were invaluable paintings that Krüger knew his Western clients would covet, promising him substantial profits. At the same time, Krüger was certain that Leon Trotsky or one of his Leningrad cronies would crosscheck his list with their experts at the People's Commissariat of Enlightenment. Any attempt at deception would, without question, lead to his unfortunate demise before he could return home to Germany. Being a slave to two masters was madness, Krüger pondered.

The list of "never to be sold" items was a remarkable trove of the art world, as was the list of "non-museum quality" pieces destined for auction. While works by Leonardo da Vinci were off-limits, Krüger believed that significant pieces by Monet, Matisse, Renoir, and Picasso had to be sold to save them from certain destruction. The sterile Bolshevik autocrats despised Impressionism, Surrealism, and Cubism. Masterpieces by Raphael and Titian might be auctioned if they did not make Krüger's master list. It was like choosing which of his children were to be eaten for dinner and which were to be adopted by Tartar barbarians—both were despicable acts in Krüger's eyes.

Krüger had also grown to loathe his nightly meetings with the unscrupulous and ancient Director of the State Hermitage, Boris Legran. At the end of each day, they convened to review the updated list of auction-eligible items. Legran believed that antique furniture, magnificent jewelry, and paintings with religious subjects held "little interest to the Soviet-Russian people" and should be "sold to raise additional funds for the ongoing industrialization of their new Union." Legran's ultimate dream was to transform the remaining Hermitage treasures into a grand exhibition imbued with the ideology of the Soviet state. Krüger detested the idea. Offering a glimmer of hope, the Hermitage's much younger Assistant Director, Joseph Orbeli, shared Krüger's sensibilities. Perhaps together they could save everything, maybe even turn a profit, Krüger thought. The sound of approaching footsteps interrupted his musings.

"Krüger!" bellowed the portly Boris Legran, his voice echoing through the room. "Where the devil are you? Show yourself before I die of exertion."

A smile tugged at the corners of Krüger's lips as he contemplated hiding in the shadows a while longer, relishing the thought. However, he quickly changed his mind. Desperate to rid himself of this parasitic presence as soon as possible, he revealed himself. Stepping into the streaming moonlight that bathed the center of the room, he yelled, "I am over here, Director."

"You are late," Legran grumbled. "We were scheduled to meet an hour ago. I have been searching everywhere for you. Scurrying around in this drafty darkness is detrimental to my health."

"My apologies, Director," Krüger lied, his voice tinged with false regret. "I was engrossed in making the final additions to my list and lost track of time. Would you like to see the list now?"

"I would have liked to have seen it an hour ago," Legran snapped. "I do not have time to review it now, as I'm heading to an important committee meeting. Instead, you will report immediately to Assistant Director Orbeli. I have left explicit instructions with him on how to proceed in my absence."

Krüger managed to conceal the relief surging within him, his face impassive. Joseph Orbeli, a hospitable and sensible man, instantly came to mind. Krüger could already savor the exquisite black caravan tea Orbeli customarily served his non-Soviet guests. "I will go to him right away,

Director," he said, his words dissipating into the empty moonlit room as Legran's footsteps faded.

What an insufferable man, Krüger thought as he embarked on the long walk to Orbeli's office in the opposite wing of Winter Palace. In the five months since he arrived in Leningrad, he had met the Assistant Director of the Hermitage only a handful of times. However, after each encounter, Krüger grew more convinced that Joseph Orbeli was not just an efficient administrator and dedicated researcher of Persian arts but a man who despised the Soviet establishment as much as he did. The possibilities that might arise from this intuition were intriguing.

As Krüger drew nearer to Orbeli's office, a faint smell of burning coal wafted through the air, indicating his proximity. It was a less pleasant scent than a wood fire, he mused, slightly dirtier, akin to a Latvian cigar. With each heavy step, anticipation surged within him. Having been awake for nearly eighteen hours, toiling in solitude amidst the paintings in the expansive display galleries of the Hermitage, Krüger looked forward to sitting down and engaging in discussions about art with a man he considered his contemporary. By contrast, his nightly encounters with Legran resembled police interrogations, enduring terse questions while standing upright in the Director's monastic office for over an hour. No food, no beverage, no hospitality. He felt no better than a Russian serf indentured to his master.

"Ah, Franz, my long-lost art aficionado, please come in and have a seat," Joseph Orbeli said with a welcoming smile, rising from his desk and ushering Krüger towards a plush chair. "I am eager to hear about your latest epiphanies regarding our art collection."

Krüger's gaze fixated on the steaming tea service and silver trays of cakes, his stomach protesting with an audible rumble. "It has been a long day, Assistant Director. Please accept my apologies if I appear lethargic this evening. I have just finished compiling the final list, and I have stumbled upon some rather peculiar discoveries..."

"Of course," Joseph Orbeli interrupted. "You must be exhausted. Where are my manners? Would you care for some tea?"

"That would be very kind, Assistant Director."

"Please, Franz, call me Joseph. Tonight, we are alone, and there is no need for pretentious formalities. I do not seek mindless adorations like some others."

"You and the Director are," Krüger paused, searching for the right word, "very different, Joseph."

"Yes, indeed," Joseph smiled again, pouring two cups of black tea from the gleaming silver samovar and settling into a chair opposite the German. "To begin with, I was born in the Republic of Georgia, just outside Tbilisi, near the Armenian border. I am not a true Russian, nor a member of the Bolshevik Party, for that matter. My brothers and I are descendants of Armenian aristocrats who battled fierce Mongols in the 13th century, hence my deep-rooted interest in the Far Eastern arts. I have a keen interest in Persian art and culture. Director Legran, on the other hand, shall we say, had a different upbringing."

Krüger savored the hot liquid as he took a sip, relishing the warmth cascading down his throat and into his belly. "Furthermore, the Director is condescending toward my work, treating me as if I were an inferior schoolboy. It is quite insulting; considering the large fee I am being paid for my expertise. To be honest, I have contemplated resigning on more than one occasion, including tonight."

"Then why have you stayed?"

Krüger exhaled a deep breath, considering how best to answer. Should he be honest? Could he trust a man he had only met a few times with his true motivations? "I have stayed solely for the art; I cannot bear to witness men like Legran who treat it as a mere commodity. Selling irreplaceable masterpieces for fleets of farm equipment is sacrilegious, and there must be consequences."

Joseph Orbeli raised an eyebrow, his gaze fixed on his German guest. Krüger's response was unusually candid and held an air of danger. "Are you not, in essence, a purveyor of art, driven by the pursuit of profit and selling to the highest bidder?"

Krüger's voice conveyed indignation as he swiftly responded, "I am neither a scavenger nor a propagandist. My role is to facilitate the transfer of art to discerning connoisseurs who genuinely appreciate its essence—an embodiment of divinity manifested through the hands of mortals. Art unveils the very nature of God."

Joseph's eyes grew large. "The very nature of God you claim? God's... true... nature."

"Assistant Director," Krüger began, panic creeping into his voice, "I did not mean to offend—"

"Can you keep a secret?"

The question catching him off-guard, Krüger stammered his response. "I represent some of the wealthiest families in the world—the Rothschild's, Habsburgs, and numerous members of the English landed gentry. Each family harbors an intricate web of secrets upon secrets. Rest assured I am not one to divulge such information."

Joseph leveled a penetrating stare at the German seated across from him. "In the midst of uncertainty, the glimmer of joy, or what my father so eloquently called God's grace, emerges." Joseph's expression held a mix of intrigue and contemplation. "Would you like to see God's grace Herr Krüger?"

"Watch your step," Orbeli's voice echoed through the damp, voluminous tunnel, cautioning Krüger as they ventured further into the unknown.

Krüger was at first hesitant, finding himself taken aback by the blindfold offered by the Assistant Director. However, the tantalizing prospect of confirming Orbeli's extraordinary claims compelled him to consent. He yearned to uncover the truth, to witness firsthand the veracity of the Assistant Director's astounding statements.

Sixty feet below the museum's surface, they twisted and turned through endless tunnels. Fine particles of dust permeated the air, clinging to their sweat-drenched faces. Oppressive silence pressed down on them, the weight of secrecy a thick barrier between them and the world above.

"I apologize for the necessity of these precautions," Joseph said, his voice tinged with regret, as he removed Krüger's mask upon reaching a nondescript door. "But I cannot afford to risk your knowledge of the location of the Tsar's Vault. The secret police possess a mastery of persuasion, and I fear they would extract every detail from you if they were to apprehend you," he cautioned, the gravity of the situation looming ominously.

Blinking his eyes, Krüger struggled to adjust to the blackness engulfing him. The rusty creak of a door swinging open pierced the silence, sending an involuntary shiver down his spine. "As if I could ever hope to stumble upon this place on my own."

Crossing the threshold, Joseph ignited a series of torches that adorned the walls, their flickering flames casting a mesmerizing glow upon the chamber before them. The sight was not what Krüger was expecting. Instead of seeing the unimaginable treasures of the Tsar's Vault, only wooded tables crowded with solvents, glass jars, brushes, and white powders sat in the chamber while worn canvases were stacked on one side of the room. "A workshop?"

"Since you are a renowned art expert Franz, I value your professional opinion. What is your assessment of the prevalence of forgeries among the art hanging in galleries, private salons, and in the overall market today?"

"It is a formidable challenge to deceive experienced art authenticators," Krüger said. "While some counterfeit artworks are good enough to slip through the cracks, the majority are sniffed out. I would estimate, at most, only one percent of forgeries possess the caliber of skills to deceive experts like myself."

Joseph brushed a layer of silt off the table centered between them. "So, roughly one out of every hundred paintings. Now, tell me, during your cataloging work at my museum, how many forgeries did you come across?"

"Assistant Director, that question borders on the absurd. The Hermitage houses one of Europe's most magnificent collections."

"And yet, during our earlier conversation in my office, you alluded to having made some rather peculiar discoveries," Joseph pressed. "What did you mean by that?"

Krüger's mind raced, grappling with the unexpected revelation that the Assistant Director had actually heard his words. Fear tightened its grip on his heart, fueling unsettling thoughts of a sinister fate awaiting him in this foreboding place—his body destined to remain forever concealed. "I merely intended to express my inquiries and uncertainties," he stammered, struggling to find the right words. "I had some questions that arose... I speculated the possibility..."

"Of a forged painting hanging within the esteemed State Hermitage," Joseph interjected.

"Please forgive any misunderstanding. Given the extent of my exhaustive work and the strain on my eyes, I may have erred in my observations," Krüger babbled, desperately seeking the correct response amidst the mounting tension.

Joseph enjoyed watching the German expert squirm. "Now, what if I were to disclose that an astounding forty percent of all art sold to collectors worldwide is, in fact, fake? And that twenty percent of the portraits adorning the galleries above us are cunningly executed forgeries?"

"More like, twenty-three out of a hundred," Krüger corrected, determined to assert his expertise amidst these unsettling revelations.

Joseph Orbeli broke out into raucous laughter. "You have exceeded my initial expectations and that is why I find myself in dire need of your invaluable assistance."

"What kind of help do you require?"

Joseph handed a sheet of paper to the German. "These are the names of the one hundred paintings I want you to present to the committee. You will affirm the authenticity of each piece of artwork and emphasize that they must never be sold, regardless of the offer."

Krüger examined the Assistant Director's list with a sense of unease. The works of art listed comprised a combination of priceless masterpieces and lesser-valued paintings. Comparing this selection to his original mental inventory, he was puzzled by the criteria employed to compile the assortment.

"Pardon me, Assistant Director. If the aim of this list is to safeguard the most precious artworks and prevent their sale, I fail to comprehend the rationale behind including many of these particular choices."

"You still believe the Committee intends to withhold the most valuable artworks from the liquidation? The true motive behind your appointment, Herr Krüger, was to identify which pieces within the Hermitage would be most coveted by Western collectors. The Soviet Union is bankrupt and requires capital to fuel its industrialization, and the Bolsheviks view the State Hermitage's art as a means of currency. Your final list will serve as nothing more than an advertisement for a future sale."

The realization that Boris Legran and the other Party bosses had manipulated him ignited a furious rage within Krüger. How could I have been so blind? he asked himself. "The list of one hundred paintings is meant for sale, not preservation?" Krüger's legs weakened as he collapsed onto the floor. All the abuse and all the late nights, a ruse as fake as the counterfeit portraits that were produced in this very room. And then he comprehended the Assistant Director's scheme. "You intend to sell the forgeries!"

"I intend to do only what must be done," Joseph whispered to his newest co-conspirator. "Come, we have much to discuss."

5

THE AUCTION

LONDON - 1930

Franz Krüger was not surprised when he learned a few months after his fateful meeting with Assistant Director Orbeli that many of the one hundred paintings he had identified as too valuable to be sold at any cost had ended up on the auction block in Paris. Joseph Orbeli had been right all along, and the immense dread that washed over Krüger upon seeing the names of the artworks sold only fueled his anger. However, what surprised him even more was the identity of the buyers.

Calouste Gulbenkian, the Iraq Petroleum Company founder, acquired many of these priceless artworks through a deal that seemed like a theft. By trading oil reserves to Stalin and the Bolsheviks instead of using hard currency, Gulbenkian had outwitted the "blockheads," as Krüger called them. The oil magnate was a cunning businessman who, in Krüger's opinion, cared more about the negotiations than the art itself. Every aspect of this initial sale disgusted Krüger.

Gulbenkian's greed was so insatiable that he even attempted to hire Krüger's Berlin art gallery to represent him at future auctions, hoping that Krüger's relationship with the Bolsheviks would give him an advantage in acquiring future priceless items at rock-bottom prices. However, Krüger wanted no part in dealing with the millionaire. Utilizing his influence and reputation, he instead partnered with London's esteemed art purveyors, Colnaghi & Co.

Colnaghi possessed an extensive network of British and American collectors that Krüger believed would be better suited to owning these paintings. At the very least, they would have to pay in cold hard cash, ensuring a more appropriate price for the artwork. Several potential buyers had already been identified.

The fact that many of these paintings were forgeries crafted in the subterranean tunnels of the Winter Palace seemed to matter little to Krüger. He was a man who lived and breathed art, and his passion was for fellow admirers to possess these paintings, regardless of their authenticity. If Joseph Orbeli's claim was valid—that more than forty percent of the art adorning galleries and private collections worldwide were cunning counterfeits—what difference would it make if the buyers were deceived? The belief was that owning a masterpiece was worth the price of acquisition. For this reason, he chose to help the Assistant Director in authenticating the forgeries. The genuine works of art needed protection in this tumultuous era.

"Mr. Mellon, what I am proposing is to grant you the exclusive right of first refusal on any future sales from the esteemed Hermitage collection. What this means is that you will have the privilege of handpicking and buying any desired pieces before they go to public auction, thus eliminating the risk of another buyer swooping in and outbidding you."

"And at what cost, Mr. Krüger, would I have the pleasure of this privilege?" inquired the skeptical former U.S. Secretary of the Treasury, now an avid art collector. Paul Mellon had long cherished the dream of establishing a national art gallery in Washington, D.C. His art appreciation had blossomed during his formative years at Yale, where he would spend countless hours engrossed in the university's extensive art gallery, marveling at its riches. Later, as Treasury Secretary, he had the opportunity to visit Europe's finest museums—the Louvre in Paris and London's National Gallery—which left an indelible impression on him. Following an extended visit to the National Gallery in London, Mellon became obsessed with his desire to create a comparable institution in his homeland.

"I must confess that the paintings you have expressed interest in are not only exquisite but also carry a hefty price tag, commanding the attention of many discerning art connoisseurs," responded Krüger, laying a skillful trap. "In fact, Calouste Gulbenkian has been pressuring me to strike a deal with him, similar to the one I am now proposing to you." Krüger spied a flicker of concern cross over Paul Mellon's face. "Of course, if you are not interested, I can pursue other potential buyers."

"I did not say I was not interested," Mellon insisted. "I merely inquired about the cost. I will not pay an exorbitant sum for a single painting, since we are both aware that the Soviet government is eager to sell."

"A price will be negotiated for each individual piece. Rest assured, the more artworks you acquire, the more favorable the discounts will become," Krüger said with matter-of-fact poise.

Mellon's gaze met Krüger's, his eyes searching for signs of trustworthiness. After a moment of hesitation, Mellon reached into his pocket and produced a typewritten list of the desired paintings, each accompanied by a handwritten price. "I trust that what I am offering constitutes a more than generous deal in your eyes."

Krüger examined the former Treasury Secretary's list, attempting to conceal his growing excitement. The prices were more than fair, but his ego compelled him to push for even more money. "Your price for Raphael's *The Alba Madonna* is far too low."

"I am offering six million dollars for the twenty-one paintings on my list. Each painting's value has already been appraised by Sotheby's," Mellon said firmly. "I will not pay a penny more."

"But Calouste Gulbenkian will," Krüger reminded him. "For six million dollars you can have 20 of the 21 paintings on your list, but not *The Alba Madonna*. Consider yourself fortunate that I do not demand a much higher price for Titian's *Venus with a Mirror* or Van Eyck's *Annunciation*."

Mellon contemplated walking away from Krüger, a man he perceived to be a snake oil salesman, but the grand vision of an American gallery filled his mind, clouding his judgment. Snatching his list from Krüger's surprised hand, Mellon testily crossed out his original number and wrote a new one before handing it back. "That is my final offer."

Krüger's smile betrayed his satisfaction upon seeing the figure on the paper. Extending his hand, the two men sealed the deal. The art, a mixture of genuine and counterfeit, would serve their respective purposes and grant Joseph Orbeli more time.

The news of Paul Mellon's magnificent art acquisition would remain in secrecy for over two years until the *New York Times* sniffed it out and reported it. However, Joseph Orbeli was privy to the sale's details within a month. His partner in crime had accomplished this feat not once but twice. The moment had arrived for Joseph to implement the second phase of his intricate plan.

Joseph Orbeli paced his spacious office, his mind consumed with the weight of the letter he had just dictated. It was a missive of utmost importance, requiring a delicate balance of words. As his secretary read the letter back to him, he listened, ensuring each nuance was captured and conveyed the urgency necessary to spur action.

"In conclusion, I adamantly oppose the deplorable practice of liquidating the precious artifacts and materials housed within the esteemed State Hermitage. The ongoing sale of these invaluable treasures at ludicrously low prices sends an unequivocal message to the Western nations: that the Soviet Union is financially destitute, casting doubt upon the very foundations of our revolutionary ideals. Europe looks upon us with scorn, and I cannot idly stand by, allowing this ill-conceived endeavor to persist. Whoever is responsible for this misguided notion should tremble at the thought of Comrade Stalin's wrath, for they have brought shame upon our union, making us appear desperate for mere hard currency. There exist far superior ways to utilize the treasures enshrined within the Hermitage, ways that align with the objectives of our great state and pay homage to the toil of our diligent citizens. I would be honored to present these ideas to esteemed party officials and stand ready to take decisive action to rectify the grievous harm inflicted upon our proud nation."

As the words hung in the air, Joseph knew he had captured the urgency and resolve required to address the dire situation. The fate of the State Hermitage and its invaluable treasures now rested upon the power of his pen.

"Well Nadia, what are your thoughts?" Joseph inquired of his childhood friend and now secretary, a hint of anticipation in his voice.

Nadia's reply came with a blend of deadpan wit and cautionary realism. "You have either set yourself up for great rewards by sounding the alarm, or you have unwittingly penned your own death warrant," she said, her tone devoid of any lightness.

Joseph could not help but offer a half-joking inquiry, seeking her opinion on the mention of the Red Tsar. "Do you think I went too far with invoking Stalin?"

Her response, laced with pragmatism and a focus on self-preservation, left little room for doubt. "Self-preservation is an instinct that rules us all. If Marshal Zhdanov values his own life, he will swiftly find a scapegoat for his own policy decisions, all the while patting himself on the back for having the wisdom to uncover the supposed imbecile responsible," she said, her words a stark reminder of the delicate political landscape they navigated.

Joseph contemplated Nadia's words, recognizing the gravity of the situation and the potential consequences of his bold stance. His path was treacherous, but the cause was noble, and the urgency of preserving the nation's art weighed on him. He could only hope that his words would resonate with those in power and that their collective vision would align with his: the need to preserve Russia's pre-revolutionary cultural heritage at all costs.

The speed of Marshal Zhdanov's response to the letter astounded even Joseph himself. As he entered his office the following day, a chilling sight greeted him—four soldiers stood with an air of menace. The lead soldier addressed him, "Director Orbeli?"

Joseph's throat went dry, beads of perspiration forming on his forehead. Had he overstepped his bounds? Did he misjudge the reaction of the party leadership to his correspondence? Fear and dread consumed him as he imagined these soldiers escorting him outside for an unceremonious execution. In a hoarse voice, he said, "I am the Assistant Director."

Another soldier thrust an official-looking document in front of him. Joseph reached out, his trembling hands taking hold of what he believed to be his signed death warrant. Unable to focus his eyes, he handed it back to the soldier, requesting, "Can you please read it to me? I seem to have misplaced my glasses."

With a dispassionate tone, the soldier cleared his throat and began to read, "By order of the party leadership of Leningrad, Joseph Abgari Orbeli is as of this date promoted to the position of Director of the State

Hermitage of Leningrad. Congratulations, Comrade," he said with little enthusiasm.

The soldiers turned in unison and departed. Their heavy boots echoed down the corridor as they went to Joseph's now-former supervisor's office. Though the exact words were muffled, the sounds of outrage and disbelief permeated the air, followed again by the somber trudging of boots as they led Boris Legran away to an uncertain fate.

Joseph was unaccustomed to employing underhanded tactics, yet any guilt he initially felt was swiftly replaced by an overwhelming sense of relief. He had accomplished it—he was now the Director of the State Hermitage Museum. All would not be lost, not if he had anything to say about it.

Later that day, Joseph Orbeli sat in quiet contemplation in the Dionysus Room of the Winter Palace, absorbing the weight of his recent appointment as the museum's Director. This room had always held a special place in his heart. Its copper-colored walls evoked the warmth of a sunrise, contrasting against the green-gray marbled wainscoting that encircled the space. Greek statues, pristine and white, stood sentinel along the room's periphery. Was this room a rising sun symbol, or did it foreshadow the fiery sunset of a bygone era?

His gaze drifted upward, fixating on the white crisscross of wooden beams adorned with delicate blue snowflakes of Delft pottery where the beams intersected. The sight brought solace to his weary body and mind. How many hours had he spent in this very room, sketching the Greek Muses with a charcoal pencil? He believed Thalia, Terpsichore, and Polyhymnia engaged in a silent dialogue on the loftier realms of art. Joseph observed a young girl working in her sketchpad.

"I thought I might find you here," a voice interrupted, pulling him back to the present.

"I was reminiscing about the countless hours of my youth I spent in this room, striving to master the form and composition of the Greek statues, much like that girl does now. Do you remember when we were her age?"

A tender laugh escaped Sophia's mouth, "I recall you stealing a kiss from me in this very room when I was fifteen and you were only twelve."

"That was a long time ago. I must have been under the spell of the Soranzo Eros," he said, gesturing toward the white marble statue of the God of Love as a coy smile played on his lips.

"Yes, blame it on the gods," she laughed again. "You do know that statue is a replica of an earlier classical Greek style? And now, that girl over there on the cusp of womanhood continues the tradition by creating a copy of a copy. Through the hand of God, she becomes a mirror, crafting something new and not so new for you."

"Perhaps you're right. That young artist may create new life for us, new guardians of the art once we are gone."

"Maybe even sooner, the stakes have never been higher or more perilous. What we are undertaking could lead to our deaths if we are discovered," Sophia cautioned, her thoughts on more than just the forgeries they were producing.

"Now that I have been appointed Director, my foremost responsibility is to protect the art. It will be my sole focus. I will ensure that our secret remains hidden."

"So far, things have exceeded our expectations," Sophia reminded him. "We have only lost four original paintings to the auctions."

"Five," he corrected her. "The inflated offer from the American to purchase twenty-one paintings forced us to include one piece that we had not finished replicating yet."

"That is unfortunate, but maybe the Party's claim that 'once the revolution takes hold in America,' we will retrieve the paintings for free?" Sophia said, her voice tinged with sarcasm.

Joseph let out a cynical laugh. "If the Party believes that, they are even more foolish than I thought. The revolution is bankrupt. It stands no chance of taking hold in America."

"Then we accept our losses and proceed with the rest of the plan. We do not know when or where our next opportunity will arise, but we must be ready when it does, Joseph."

"We will stay committed, but we will need more help. You and your small team of forgers have done remarkable work, Sophia, but we cannot generate an entirely new collection of paintings without more help. We require additional skilled labor."

"I agree, but each person we approach and recruit into our circle increases our risk. We must be cautious about whom we bring into the fold."

Joseph's fixated on a chiseled white marble panther anchored in the center of the room. The beast was watching him, waiting for the moment he let his guard down. He was certain It would pounce without hesitation, given the chance. "I will remain vigilant at all times. I will find the right individuals who share our beliefs and cause. Those willing to deceive the Bolsheviks.

"So shall I," Sophia said as her eyes turned back to the girl with the sketchbook. "Your words remind me of some incendiary newspaper editorials published before the revolution. Conservative editors relished the opportunity to snub the Tsar in the years leading up to his removal. They liked to hide behind Leo Tolstoy's words as a shield."

Joseph nodded, his thoughts drifting back to those tumultuous days. "I remember you telling me that Tolstoy was a family friend."

"After one audacious editorial," Sophia continued, "Tolstoy deemed it prudent for his children to adopt his wife's surname for their safety. From then on, they ceased to be Tolstoy's. This was an eye-opening event for me. I never forgot how easy it was to change one's identity, to morph into someone else, when the need arose."

"What was in the editorial?"

"It was an astute observation of the political climate at the time." Sophia's mood became somber as her gaze drifted towards the statue of Melpomene, the muse of tragedy. "It read, 'There are two Tsars in Russia, Nicholas II and Leo Tolstoy. Which is more powerful? Nicholas can do nothing about Tolstoy; he cannot shake his throne. But Tolstoy, undoubtedly, is shaking his.'"

"And now we'll shake Stalin's throne."

"Before we do that Joseph, would you allow me the privilege of painting your portrait?"

"Why would you want to immortalize my dog ugly face?"

"Because I predict that you will do extraordinary things in the years to come. Things that you do not even know you are capable of doing. Your portrait should hang within the walls of this venerable museum to chronicle your achievements and celebrate your deeds."

"You put far too much faith in me. I am just a common administrator and an even worse forger. But if you want to waste paint on my visage then go-ahead, I will sit for you."

"You are much more than that to me, Joseph. At some point, you will realize the truth about yourself and me. Now let us go find the perfect place for your portrait to hang."

6

THE DEPARTMENT HEADS

Bright and early, the morning after his speech to the Intelligentsia, Joseph was back in his office, flanked by the department heads from across the Hermitage. Their collective mood was far from pleasant, having been summoned to work on their usual day off – a Monday when the museum was customarily closed.

Stealing a glance at his desk calendar, Joseph began, "As you are all aware, over the weekend, the fascists breached our western border. Their offensive was launched at the dawn of the summer solstice, the longest day of the year, and 129 years after Napoleon first stepped foot on our land. I fear they will move with a speed akin to lightning, reaching our city's gates before we have the chance to fully comprehend the situation. Therefore, effective immediately, all future days off are canceled. Our complete focus will shift towards preparing for the evacuation of the Hermitage's artistic and cultural treasures."

The groans that ensued were as predictable as the inevitable flurry of questions. "Excuse me, Director, have we received any instructions from Moscow regarding evacuation?"

"I attempted to secure evacuation instructions from the State Committee on Arts in Moscow yesterday. Despite my best efforts, I was unable to make contact."

"So, you are making this decision unilaterally?" another department head asked.

"I am choosing to do what effective administrators do in times of crisis - I am choosing to lead. Rest assured, any repercussions from this decision will be my burden to bear. It is my neck on the line, not yours."

With visible relief, a chorus of voices asked in unison, "Where do we begin?"

Joseph Orbeli spent the next two hours outlining the tasks ahead. Every department within the Hermitage—Western European, Russian, Antiquity, Prehistoric, Art and Peoples of the East, Numismatic—would be responsible for evaluating and prioritizing the removal of their cultural treasures from the museum's walls and rooms. These pieces would then be transported to the expansive vaults beneath the Hermitage, where they would be cataloged and packed away using the supplies Joseph had been systematically gathering over the past year. When the order for evacuation arrived, they would be ready.

Less than twenty-four hours after the fascist guns had swiveled towards the Soviet Union, the Hermitage museum's staff had already begun packing their prized works of art. Meanwhile, the Red Army's leaders engaged in a futile game of blame-shifting, petrified of making a move without Stalin's endorsement. Through it all, Moscow remained ominously silent.

Vladimir Levinson-Lessing lingered after the other department heads had dispersed, orders in hand. As the Assistant Director of the Hermitage, the wise and frenetic Vladimir often conferred in private with Joseph, offering sagacious advice and reporting on staff morale.

"What is on your mind, Vlad?"

"Why was I not informed about your accumulation of packing materials in the museum's vaults?" Vladimir asked, a hint of apprehension creeping into his voice. "And that you suspected we might need them?"

"I just did," Joseph answered as he shoved papers into his briefcase.

"No, what you have just done is disclose to everyone here that you have been disregarding Chairman Stalin's explicit orders for years," Vladimir said, panic tingeing his voice. "He ordered us not to stockpile packing materials or make any war preparations. You knew Moscow would perceive such actions as defeatist and disloyal to the Soviet regime, yet you proceeded."

Joseph's eyes drifted back to the paperwork sprawled across his desk. "Sometimes it is easier to seek forgiveness than permission. Have courage. It will all work out in the end."

"I have always been a coward," Vladimir admitted. "Even when we were children, you were always pushing me to take risks."

"And look at you now, Vlad. You are the Assistant Director of the prestigious State Hermitage Museum."

"I sometimes regret accepting this position," Vladimir confessed picking lint off his fine-tailored suit. "I still do not understand why you believe in my abilities."

Joseph paused, studying his visibly distressed childhood friend. "I offered you the position because I needed someone who would tell me the truth. Despite your claims of cowardice, you have never been afraid to speak the truth to me."

Vladimir sank into the plush leather chair beside Joseph's desk. "May I have some tea?"

"No," Joseph flatly refused.

"Why do you offer tea to everyone who visits your office, except me?"

"Tea makes you nervous. I cannot afford to have you more on edge than you already are. I need you to be my eyes and ears with the staff."

Vladimir pondered this while reflecting on the day's events. "The Hermitage has over 2.5 million exhibits, including 15,000 paintings, 12,000 sculptures, and 60,000 drawings. We also house more than 600,000 archaeological relics and over a million coins and medals."

"Get to the point, Vlad."

"We are all under significant pressure. You need to know when to be firm and when to be lenient. Would it have hurt to give the staff one last day off with their families before springing this gargantuan task on them?"

Look at you! Speaking truth to power. I knew I made the right decision to bring you on board. Now, I am leaving you in charge for a few hours."

"What? Why? Where are you going?" Vlad stammered, anxiety returning to his voice. "What could be more important than overseeing the packing of the Hermitage?"

"I need to ensure that our State Library, along with Voltaire's Library and the Pushkin Archives, do not 'accidentally' get burned during this civil unrest," he explained. "Then I will visit the drama theater, opera, ballet, and the Zoological Gardens. They need to be making their own evacuation plans. If they wait for a directive from Moscow, I fear it will be too late."

7

THE CARETAKER

PETERHOF PALACE – JUNE 1941

J oseph Orbeli strode across the rolling manicured grounds of Peterhof Palace, his keen eyes dissecting the topography with a mind attuned to its defense. Labored breaths escaped his chest, and he paused, wiping the beads of perspiration from his brow. Amidst the descending twilight, a symphony of cascading water filled the air, echoing against the backdrop of a sun-kissed sea in the distance. Elongated shadows cast by the opulent golden fountains painted a peaceful tableau, enveloping the landscape in an otherworldly allure.

Joseph's thoughts drifted back to his youth, recalling the countless visits to this Russian Versailles with his grandfather, where peace and introspection always found solace. The mere notion of such grandeur falling victim to ruin and desolation churned his stomach. His gaze shifted to a row of freshly planted apple trees standing beside a rectangular reflecting pool. Turning to his companion, Joseph said, "Those apple trees appear out of place, don't you think?"

"Perhaps," said the aged caretaker after some contemplation, his voice carrying the weight of accumulated wisdom. "But you know what they say: the best time to plant an apple tree is yesterday. Our own Peter the Great understood the value of such fruit for his burgeoning capital and planted hundreds."

"I was unaware," Joseph confessed. "It is a shame that in a few months, it will be the fascists who reap the harvest."

The caretaker plucked a small, verdant apple from the tree and sliced it in half with his knife. As he did, a wistful sigh escaped his lips. "Even if I knew that tomorrow the world would crumble into pieces, I would still plant an apple tree."

Joseph responded with a hint of skepticism. "Your words are as enigmatic as a passing rain shower."

A gentle smile danced upon the caretaker's weathered face. "Do not feign ignorance with me, Director. With your aristocratic upbringing, you are familiar with the words of Martin Luther. Like him, you question the dogmas imposed by those in power. It was Luther's audacity that sparked the Reformation in the 1500s. These trees, too, will outlast the fascists, shriveling away like rotten fruit. Remember that."

Joseph's gaze turned eastward toward St. Petersburg. "I only hope our unfortunate city can endure the same fate. Unlike apple trees, its people have no respite from the chilling grip of our Russian winters. I fear that many will succumb to the impending storm brought by the fascists."

A reassuring tone laced the caretaker's voice as he spoke. "Those who survive will have the rejuvenating nectar of my Antonovka apples, ripening to a golden hue. They shall provide sustenance and nourishment in the darkest of times."

"I hope your optimism proves true, my dear friend," Joseph said, diverting his gaze back to the resplendent golden fountains. "Is it possible to relocate them?"

The caretaker, hobbled and weathered, contemplated in silence for a moment before answering. "I can deactivate some of the fountains and move a few, but it would undoubtedly result in some damage."

"My brother has informed me that the army's defensive perimeter might extend far enough to safeguard the palace. What do you think, Pasha?"

With a knowing look, the caretaker began to speak. "Over the years, I have witnessed countless German tourists on their Grand Tour visiting Peterhof. They are as mesmerized by its grandeur as you and I. Should we leave it unprotected, the fascists will occupy it and pilfer anything of value remaining in it, but they will not destroy it. In my humble opinion, it is the Bolsheviks who will burn it to the ground. They are the bigger problem."

Joseph issued a playful warning. "Take care, my friend. As my brother Levon has reminded me time and again, 'A spoken word is not a sparrow. Once it takes flight, you cannot retrieve it.' Remember, the wretched Cheka and their lowly informants are everywhere."

"Ha! What can they do to an old man like me? I am the sole keeper of the fountains. They would not dare lay a finger on me."

Joseph erupted into hearty laughter. "I could not agree more. It is the Bolsheviks who pose a greater threat. They will go to any lengths to dismantle our westward-looking, Russian culture, even resorting to shelling Peterhof if the fascists occupy it."

The caretaker's uttered curses. "I do not trust them either, and I sure as hell will not lend them any assistance. Why do you comply with their demands?"

"I do not. My brothers and I are survivors. We merely undertake what is necessary to safeguard our people's art and culture."

"You mean the Eurocentric art and culture of Petersburg? The Muscovites hold a vastly different perspective. They yearn for a return to village life, to reconnect with the land. They perceive a moral purity in that way of living."

Joseph gently reminded his old friend of a fundamental belief. "True Russians have dual loyalties—Russia and Europe. Had the previous uprising a century ago succeeded, we would not find ourselves in this precarious situation today."

"Did I ever share with you the story of my youth, when speaking Russian was strictly forbidden? It was beaten out of me, suppressed like the devil himself. My tutors were always French and German, and my dear mother conversed solely in the language of Hugo and Musset. To learn Russian, I resorted to breaking into my father's locked library under the veil of darkness. Pushkin, Gogol, and Fonvizin became my teachers. I discovered the duality of being Russian, the temperament that shapes our lives. 'Have a heart, have a soul, and you will always be a man. Everything else is mere fashion.'"

Joseph frowned. "The Bolsheviks possess neither heart nor soul."

A grave expression settled upon the caretaker's face. "Then you are aware, Joseph, that they will dispose of you once they have exploited your worth. Even your brother Levon, the charming general, cannot shield you indefinitely."

"They will not harm me. They need me just as much as they need the art. It is their sole currency and I am their banker. The Bolsheviks do not hesitate to sell a Dawes or a da Vinci painting, only to use the blood money to purchase industrial tractors."

"And once the Hermitage has been fully evacuated by you, the Bolsheviks will no longer require a director or a local banker. They will have their precious art safely relocated elsewhere."

Joseph remained silent, a subtle smile playing on his lips as he gazed at the dark waters of the Gulf of Finland in the distance.

Observing his friend's expression, the caretaker's voice trembled, "My God! All the art will not make it out of St. Petersburg will it?"

"Some of the art will indeed find its way to Sverdlovsk, but it is best if you do not know the complete truth, Pasha. Rest assured, the art will be shielded from all perils, even the insatiable greed of the Bolsheviks."

The caretaker's eyes widened. "You are deliberately deceiving them?"

"A deception that elevates us is dearer than a host of low truths," Joseph said quoting Pushkin.

The caretaker shot back. "And moral maxims prove remarkably useful when we struggle to find alternative justifications for our actions. See, you are not the only one capable of quoting our beloved Pushkin."

Joseph locked eyes with his old friend. "If you only knew the fervent flames that rage within me, flames I try to suppress with reason. Everything I do is for the preservation of art. Trust me, Pasha, the outcome will vindicate the means employed."

In a fleeting moment, the caretaker glimpsed a fiery wrath flicker across his friend's face. "Why do you endanger so much for something that appears insignificant when compared to a human life?"

Joseph inhaled the crisp, pine-scented air and closed his eyes, seeking composure. "Man was molded in the likeness of God," he whispered. "When we create art, we emulate the divine. It is our loftier purpose, the essence of our humanity. The revolution extinguished all that is sacred, claiming the lives of my father and grandfather. We are now compelled to exist within a secular Soviet society, where churches have been transformed into propaganda-laden museums. Art is all that remains of our spiritual essence, and the Bolsheviks cannot part with it swiftly enough. The Hermitage stands as a sanctuary, housing art that embodies our humanity and offers comfort. This is why I jeopardize everything I possess to safeguard it. It is the final refuge of God Himself in Russia."

The caretaker nodded in agreement. "Then we must hasten and relocate as much of Peterhof's art and imperial adornments to the Hermitage. There, they shall find greater protection against both the fascists and the Bolsheviks."

"I will mobilize the labor force and coordinate the trucks," Joseph said. "As for you, commence your work on the fountains. After, the evacuation of Peterhof Palace is complete. You will stay on at the Hermitage as my head caretaker."

"I shall do whatever is necessary to safeguard them and you, Joseph."

"You are a man of exceptional character, Pasha. I entrust you with my very life."

"Come now, Director. Let us embark on a closer inspection of those resplendent fountains. I have had my fill of discussions on Pushkin and religion for today."

Joseph cast a final, fleeting glance at the foreboding expanse of the distant sea. "If only you knew, Pasha. Our most revered poet may once again rise as Russia's lone savior."

8

THE ASSISTANT DIRECTOR

"Vladimir, why is this room still not packed?" Joseph Orbeli's voice reverberated through the Hermitage's galleries like a thunderous deity.

"Good morning, Director," Vladimir Levinson-Lessing said meekly. "As you are aware, our teams have been toiling day and night for the past week, packing and cataloging each precious artwork. The process demands utmost care and precision."

"Your teams are working with undue caution. The packing must progress at an accelerated pace," Joseph bellowed, his voice reaching across the room to grab the workers' attention. "Train them to work faster. We cannot afford any delays. Have you not been following the radio reports?"

"State radio has been broadcasting glowing accounts of our Red Army's unwavering resilience against the fascist invaders," Vladimir countered. "Why, then, do you harbor such concerns?"

"The more optimistic the reports, Vladimir, the graver our predicament becomes. Stalin's ego blinds him to the truth. His lies could be framed and showcased alongside the esteemed masters in this very gallery. The fascists will be upon us within weeks, not months. We must hasten our efforts."

The Joseph's blunt retort wiped the smile from his assistant director's face. "Our art historians and workers inform me that pushing any faster would risk irreversible damage to these priceless exhibits."

Joseph's gaze fixed on a team handling Rembrandt's *Return of the Prodigal Son* on the opposite end of the gallery. Their movements were methodical but too slow. "The first pancake is always lumpy," Joseph said, reminding his friend of the age-old Russian adage. "Instruct your teams to cut the portraits from their stretchers and roll them up. This will expedite the process."

"Director, I simply cannot!" Vladimir gasped. "It would be akin to asking them to carve out each other's hearts. They would never consent."

"They will have no choice, Vlad, unless they want the fascists to gleefully tear out their hearts before setting fire to the Winter Palace."

"Is the situation truly that dire?"

"More dire than any of us could have imagined. My brother Levon keeps me informed about the latest troop movements. The fascists' Northern Army has just captured Minsk, and their Panzers are advancing with alarming speed. Time is running out."

"We will find a way to expedite our work," Vladimir reassured him, determined to rise to the challenge. "But we need more help."

"Help is on the way. However, there is one more favor I must ask of you," Joseph said, his voice lowered as he motioned Vladimir toward a secluded side room housing remarkable works by Italian masters.

Vladimir instructed the museum laborers, who continued their diligent packing on the other side of the gallery, before following his mentor into the isolated space. The walls painted a deep crimson, were adorned with golden-framed watercolors and oil paintings.

"Do you know what has always troubled me about this particular room?" Joseph said.

With weary eyes, Vladimir scanned the portraits lining the walls finding nothing amiss, and shook his head.

"There is a painting in this room by a non-Italian artist."

Vladimir surveyed the room, studying the portraits. His expertise leaned toward neoclassical art, but with effort, he located the misplaced piece. "This one... it is by Edward Hau."

"Excellent, Vlad! Edward Petrovich Hau was an exceptional Russian artist, renowned for his detailed renditions of the rooms in the Winter

Palace. Through his art, we gain a glimpse of the palace as it stood over a century ago."

"Hau's work is stunning," Vladimir admitted, captivated by the painter's skill. "It almost resembles a photograph."

"Yes, but why, throughout the years, has this solitary painting remained in the Italian room? Previous directors of the Hermitage could have moved it. Why not exhibit it in the Russian School Room alongside the other great works?"

"Perhaps because it is titled *The Cabinet of Italian Schools* and depicts this very room," Vladimir suggested.

"That would seem logical on the surface, but I believe there may be another reason. Take a closer look at the painting. Tell me, what do you see?"

Vladimir sighed, growing weary of his childhood friend's intellectual exercises. He should be overseeing the packing of the art, not engaging in these trivial pursuits. Nevertheless, the assistant director complied with his director's request. "The painting portrays this room, looking out into the main Italian room," he observed, shifting his gaze between the painting and the actual space. "The artworks currently on display differ from those depicted in Hau's work. Given the vastness of our collection, we cannot exhibit everything at once, so we rotate the pieces semi-annually."

"Now, focus your attention on the two portraits flanking the doorway in Hau's painting," Joseph directed.

Vladimir scrutinized the painting once more, and his face drained of color. "They are identical," he uttered in astonishment, glancing back at Joseph.

"Exactly. Two versions of Titian's *Venus with a Mirror* hung on this very wall in 1856."

"What happened to them?" Vladimir asked. "I've never seen this particular piece in the Hermitage."

"The short-sighted Bolsheviks sold one of them in 1931 to an avid art collector named Andrew Mellon, a former United States Treasury Secretary."

"They sold one of our masterpieces?" Vladimir gasped.

"The Bolsheviks have indeed sold numerous priceless treasures to finance their revolution. Stalin depleted the Tsar's known gold bullion reserves in a mere three years. When money ran dry, our fearless leader resorted to selling our cultural treasures and replacing them with tractors, oil, and grain imports."

"We cannot allow this, Director... it's... it is intolerable!" Vladimir stammered his outrage palpable.

"I am glad you share my sentiments, Vlad. The Russian Intelligentsia and prudent members of the Tsar's court have been taking measures for well over a century to safeguard our art and culture. Hau's painting stands as a testament to that, and this is why I need your assistance."

"What would you have me do?" Vladimir said, ready to take action.

"I believe it is best if I show you," Joseph said, his smile taking on a mischievous quality as he pressed a hidden panel above Hau's masterpiece. Vladimir's mouth gaped as a secret door materialized within the wall.

Motioning for his friend to follow, Joseph beckoned Vladimir into the clandestine passageways that snaked beneath the museum. "Come, it is high time you witnessed the true *Venus with a Mirror*."

As Vladimir stepped into the wall, the door closed behind him. Stale air enveloped him in the blackest of spaces. There was no turning back.

Sixty feet beneath the Winter Palace, a maze of steam pipes and open aquifers snaked through the murky subterranean depths of St. Petersburg. These shadowy passages had provided generations of Romanovs with a clandestine network, allowing them to move like ethereal phantoms throughout the city beyond the prying eyes of their enemies. Secret meetings were held within these covert corridors, and roughly hewn chambers, and forbidden pleasures were indulged, shielded from judgment. Yet, these hidden recesses served an even greater purpose—they acted as a repository, concealing the vast wealth of the Romanovs and safeguarding three centuries of their most intimate secrets.

"Why have you brought me down into the bowels of our city?" Vladimir said, pressing a handkerchief to his nose to ward off the unpleasant odor.

"You have been far too sheltered, Vlad. Did you never play in the dirt as a child?"

"My mother despised soiled hands. Only peasants got dirty."

"Even the Tsars occasionally dirtied their hands," Joseph said with a menacing undertone. "You might be surprised to learn how much of the Romanovs' wealth lies underground. Like an iceberg, outsiders saw only a fraction of their imperial fortune."

"The Bolsheviks exposed their nauseating opulence when they raided the palace," Vladimir said. "They took everything."

"The Bolsheviks has no idea how much they overlooked," Joseph said, as they arrived at a sturdy oak door.

"Where are we?" Vladimir asked, feeling a sudden chill in the air.

"We are beneath the Neva River. When Peter the Great built our magnificent city, he drained the swamps. These passages were likely constructed during that time."

"Why go through all the trouble?" Vladimir wondered.

Joseph pushed open the colossal door. "Little thieves are caught, but the truly great ones always find a way to escape."

The flickering light from their resinous torches unveiled fleeting glimpses of the treasures within. Reflective glimmers of alabaster and gold assaulted their eyes while a pungent scent invaded their nostrils. Joseph lowered a torch and ignited a cauldron standing sentinel beside the entrance. A cascade of light flooded the room, stealing breath from the assistant director's lungs.

Vladimir lifted his fogged glasses and inched closer to a nearby painting. "This piece is extraordinary. It is as if God himself wrapped his spectral hand around Titian's, guiding each magnificent brushstroke."

"Portraits are not the only things being hidden or replicated here," Joseph gestured toward a splintered wooden table overflowing with parchment and blotting paper. He picked up an official-looking document, "Did you know that Stalin signs all his official records with a red crayon?"

"As if we needed further evidence of his childlike intellect," Vladimir scoffed.

"Let us not forget his temperament Vlad, which rivals that of a child. If Stalin discovers this chamber, he will decimate all of St. Petersburg. It will become our tomb."

"Why have you brought me down here, Joseph?"

"I need you to comprehend the gravity of what I must do and the consequences you will face if you choose to assist me. I cannot demand your loyalty."

Vladimir let out a heavy breath. "The only loyalty I owe is to those who never made me question theirs. I have known you my entire life. You saved me from the Red Terror."

"Yes," Joseph whispered from the room's shadows. "The Great Purge claimed both of our fathers. What I propose will not bring them back but safeguard what they cherished most."

"My loyalty and my life are yours," Vladimir declared. "Ask, and I will undertake whatever you require, even if it means the possibility of sacrificing my own life in the process."

Vladimir's words hung in the still room, reinforcing Joseph's apprehension. The thought of losing another friend was unbearable, but to allow the Bolsheviks to triumph would be nothing short of criminal. "Failure is not an option. I need you to become the new Director of the Eastern Branch of the Hermitage."

9

THE GENERAL

STATE HERMITAGE - JULY 1941

Vladimir Levinson-Lessing hurried through the twisting hallways and odd-shaped galleries of the Winter Palace, searching for his boss. Beads of sweat trickled down his nose as he struggled to regulate his breathing, desperate to avoid succumbing to full-blown hyperventilation. Thirteen long minutes had elapsed since the unannounced arrival of General Markian Popov, the Commander of the Northern Front. The General had demanded to see "the person in charge of this abomination of a museum dedicated to European culture." Vladimir had attempted to explain that the Director of the State Hermitage was currently indisposed, but his words were abruptly cut off. "Find your director now before I decide to set fire to the Grand Salon myself."

Navigating past the imposing black pillars of the Twelve-Column Hall, Vladimir caught sight of Joseph ascending the Imperial Staircase just as a wave of panic washed over him.

"Director," Vladimir panted, struggling to catch his breath. "I'm ... I am relieved I found you. General Popov is waiting to speak with you in the..."

"Did he specify his purpose?" Joseph cut in, unfazed by his assistant director's obvious stress.

"I tried to inquire, believe me, but the General's disposition is highly irritable. He threatened to burn down the Hermitage if I did not present you to him within the quarter of the hour."

Joseph checked his pocket watch before retrieving a sterling silver case from his tailored jacket pocket. "Care for a cigarette?"

"Joseph! We do not have time for socializing. This general means business."

"All generals mean business, Vlad. Just ask my brother. From the sound of it, this Popov harbors no affection for our museum. He is probably a Muscovite. Show him our collection of icons and inform him that I will join him when I am free to do so."

Vladimir stared at his friend with a look of horror etched across his face, incoherent sounds struggled to escape his mouth. "Uh... I... I..."

Joseph burst into laughter. "Well, since you put it that way, let us go meet this General Popov now."

Nervously dabbing his forehead with a handkerchief, Vladimir led Joseph back to the General, akin to a desperate fox doubling back towards a pursuing hound. They reached the expanse of the Grand Salon, spotting General Popov and his aide-de-camp, engrossed in two paintings adorning the far wall.

"General Popov, may I present Director Joseph Orbeli, the esteemed administrator of the State Hermitage," Vladimir said, clicking his heels and bowing with respect towards the Commander of the Northern Front.

The tall, athletically built general disregarded Vladimir's introduction, continuing his scrutiny of the artworks. Pointing to one of the pieces, he remarked, "If not for the label or the artist's name etched upon the canvas, I would not have guessed this composition to be the work of a Russian painter originating from our homeland. It is nothing but an imitation of the European Salon style, serving no purpose for the people."

"The purpose of all art is to inspire thought in people," Joseph replied. "I am certain the adjacent painting will align more with your taste."

"Ah! Yes, this other piece is remarkable! I greatly admire paintings depicting the everyday lives of ordinary people."

"It is Repin's *Barge Haulers on the Volga*. It stands as the most renowned painting of the Itinerant movement, revered for its unflinching portrayal of backbreaking labor," Joseph added. "We have other works by Repin that you might find intriguing, General."

"Perhaps another time," General Popov said with a weary sigh. "I am here solely to inform you that the Kremlin has ordered that you make plans to evacuate the art. I must urge you to act with haste. The fascist forces are advancing with relentless speed, like hellhounds. There is no doubt they will attempt to sever the rail lines to the south as they push northward toward Leningrad. We must get the art out of the city before that happens."

"How much time do we have?" Joseph asked, although he already knew the answer.

"Not enough... two, maybe three weeks at most. You must remove as much of the art from the city as possible. Two trains are ready and waiting for your cargo. Chairman Stalin himself has ordered me to ensure there are no delays in evacuating the art eastward. Should you require any assistance, notify me immediately."

"Of course. And how may I reach you if any issues arise?"

General Popov turned to his companion. "This is Major Bitsky, my aide-de-camp. He will be conducting rounds throughout the city while checking in with various committees over the next few weeks. You can relay a message to me through him. Director, you have no time to waste, nor any time for sleep. I expect the first train to be in motion by the end of this week. Do you understand?"

"As you command, General."

"I am grateful I never joined the army," Vladimir remarked, ensuring the General was out of earshot. "It seems everyone in a uniform is perpetually in a foul mood."

"In such men, to smile is to show weakness," Joseph explained.

"Then I am glad that I am not such a man."

Although Joseph had anticipated this worse-case scenario, even he realized not all the art could be evacuated in time. He drove his museum's work crews harder, pushing them to their physical limits while outside the walls of the Winter Palace the Red Army prepared to repel the coming storm.

❧ ❧

The Winter Palace in St. Petersburg is a colossal edifice. Commanding in its presence, this green and white structure serves as a stunning testament to Baroque architecture. One side, stretching over 700 feet, abuts the equally grand Palace Square, which hosts the red granite guardian, the Alexander Column, at its center. The Bolsheviks, in their typical fashion, rechristened the square as Uritsky Square in memory of the city's assassinated secret police chief. While a cadet claimed the life of the Cheka leader, it was widely believed that the untimely demise of this political rival had Stalin's fingerprints all over it.

Regardless of its name, the square could accommodate crowds of 120,000 people. Its vast, open expanse at the city's heart also presented an alluring landing zone for fascist paratroopers or so thought the Red Army tasked with the city's defense. Therefore, the Leningrad defense force had stationed machine gun nests on the rooftops surrounding the square. Their objective? To create a deadly web of crossfire that would mow down enemies descending from the sky. However, this strategy would without a doubt inflict monumental collateral damage to the architectural gems of the Winter Palace and the Hermitage found within it. For this reason, Joseph Orbeli, ignoring the chain of command, marched across the vast square, through the double arch of the General Staff building, and directly into General Popov's office to voice his dissent.

"It is unfathomable to me, General, that you would fulfill the fascists' aims by positioning these machine guns throughout the square," Joseph argued. "You are, whether you realize it or not, transforming us all into military targets."

"It is a sound military strategy, Director. I refuse to be taken by surprise by an airborne assault."

"Or perhaps what you mean to say is that you will not be held accountable by Chairman Stalin, who has left your army woefully under prepared and put you in the unenviable position of having to achieve the impossible."

General Popov rose, walked across the room, and closed his office door. As he paced behind Joseph, he began to speak with an unusual frankness. "My father was a public servant, not dissimilar to your own, except my father had no faith. Instead, he was a man of wisdom who shared your passion for painting. Like any son, I idolized him and later defied him by joining the army at eighteen and the Bolshevik Party a year later. He fell victim to the purges, along with all others associated with the Tsar's Court. I survived because I rejected him at a young age. I am now thirty-nine years old, and as you have pointed out, I am tasked with achieving the impossible. You would be around my father's age had he lived, so tell me, Director, what would you do if you were in my position?"

Joseph's anger subsided as he faced another daunting task of making sense of an impossible situation. With no good choices in sight, Joseph did what he had always done: he told the truth. "It must be evident even to you, General, that the square is not a viable target for the fascists' paratroopers. Unlike most of the Red Army's current leadership, you understand tactics. The purges not only claimed the lives of our most experienced generals in addition to your father and mine, but they also arose because Comrade Stalin viewed anyone with an ounce of intelligence or a backbone as a threat to his tyrannical rule. If you remove the guns from the Winter Palace and the surrounding buildings, you would spare us from future bombardment and suffering. Furthermore, you could reposition your men to more strategic locations throughout the city to repel the fascists at our borders. In return, I can have my staff keep a lookout from the rooftops and relay any threats to your command."

"I will consider it," Popov said after a disconcerting moment of silence, during which Joseph was confident the General was contemplating having him executed for numerous state transgressions.

As Joseph rose, readying to leave, he halted and said in a somber voice, "Your father would be proud of you, Markian."

The General gave a nod, acknowledging the sentiment. "I would be grateful for a chance to view Repin's works, given the opportunity. They were my father's favorites. And please inform your timorous assistant director that I am capable of a smile. It has just been a long while since I have found a reason to do so," he said, a hint of a grin beginning to shape his features. "Take care, Director. You would have made an impressive general," he paused, reevaluating his words, "in another country's army."

As Joseph ambled back towards the Winter Palace, navigating a meandering path around the vast square, his thoughts veered towards his youth and discord with his father during his coming-of-age. Although he had forged a connection with General Markian Popov today, Joseph was wise enough to avoid considering him an ally. Their relationship was akin to respected rivals, each striving to accomplish their objectives, sometimes at the cost of the other's needs. Finding mutual ground would prove crucial in the times to come if he were to safeguard the lives of his staff and his own.

Therefore, Joseph was taken aback the following morning when he discovered that the guns previously aimed at the square had been removed under the cover of darkness. He assumed this was done to keep enemy eyes from noting the number and caliber of guns relocated and their new positions within the city's defensive perimeter. Sometimes, speaking truth to power could work miracles—provided it did not martyr you first.

However, a message also arrived that morning from General Popov, which could only be viewed as quid pro quo. Joseph read the letter in despair.

'Mobilize seventy-five physically capable men from your staff for defense work. Each should be provided with shovels, picks, crowbars, saws, and axes. They must each carry a five-day food supply, a cup, spoon and pot, a change of underwear, warm clothing, and money. Inform those mobilized that their assignment will last no less than two weeks.'

"Two weeks!" Joseph railed at his department heads. "The General expects me to complete the packing and loading of the art onto the trains within these same two weeks, and then deprives me of the critical workforce I need if I stand any chance of accomplishing this impossible task!"

"Well, one must anticipate the fate of Sisyphus when one speaks truth and cheats death," Vladimir quipped after the department heads had scurried away to select the required laborers.

"Did I mention that you will be giving General Popov a personal tour of Repin's work when he finds time to visit us again?" Joseph said, metaphorically rolling his boulder down the hill to crush his assistant director flat.

"So, how do we accomplish the impossible?" Vladimir said after his fear subsided. "If we are feeling frustrated and losing hope, how do we prevent the staff from feeling the same way?"

"We establish a new routine, a new reality, Vlad. We keep people busy, give them a purpose, work both their bodies and minds, delegate responsibility, prepare for every contingency, and most importantly, we make plans for the future. A future that may not even come to pass."

"You have forgotten one crucial element, Joseph. When circumstances become unfavorable, we should not hesitate to adjust our sails against the wind and alter our approach. Adherence to a failed course has wrecked larger ships than our own."

10

THE TRAIN

AUGUST 1941

The first reconnaissance patrols of the invading German North-ern Panzer Division reached the city's outer defense perimeter earlier than anyone had thought possible. The ensuing panic prompted the railroad crewmen and local representatives of the State Committee on Arts to secure the second to last train's half-filled boxcars and push up plans to depart for a location known only to a select few. Despite the train's abrupt impending departure, Joseph Orbeli was able to communicate last-minute instructions to his childhood friend and soon-to-be Director of the Eastern Branch of the State Hermitage Museum, hidden away in the Urals.

"Listen to me, Vlad. Including the last cargo deliveries loaded early this morning, a total of 1583 shipping crates are bound for the Urals. When this conflict ends, you are to return to St. Petersburg with exactly 1582 shipping crates. Do you understand what I am saying?"

The Assistant Director nodded indicating he understood his role in the intricate task of cat and mouse. "I wish you could come with me," Vladimir said, fear visible in his eyes.

"I bet you do, my friend, do not worry. I will manage just fine. If the Bolsheviks have not killed me yet, I doubt the fascists will fare any better."

"Do not underestimate the resourcefulness of the Germans," Vladimir cautioned, "They are a crafty bunch, sometimes capable of achieving the impossible."

Joseph's thoughts turned to the unsinkable Franz Krüger and the critical role his old associate would continue to play in the months ahead. "Safe travels," he said. Vladimir's hand waved goodbye before vanishing into a curtain of steam as the locomotive inched out of the station.

It wasn't long before the steady rhythm of the train's wheels on the steel track, coupled with the gentle swaying of the passenger car, lulled Vladimir into a deep sleep. The relentless pace of the past few weeks had deprived him of any restful moments since the war began. Fear and anxiety had plagued his waking hours, but now, with nothing to do but sit and reflect, Vladimir surrendered to slumber. In his dreams, he received the Order of Lenin for saving priceless art and escorting it to the Urals, and he was greeted with a hero's welcome upon his return to Leningrad station.

A sharp jab to his ribs abruptly wrenched Vladimir back to reality. "Wake up," barked a soldier assigned to guard the train and its precious cargo. "We're approaching Station Chudovo."

"So what," Vladimir groaned, rubbing his side. "Why does that matter?"

"You might die in the next ten minutes," came the soldier's chilling response.

"What? I thought this was an armored train," Vladimir's voice trembled with apprehension.

The soldier's face broke into a grin. "Our train is formidable with three heavily armored Zaamuret cars each equipped with two fully traversable 57-millimeter turrets and dozens of machine guns. Few can match our firepower."

"Then why did you wake me?"

"Chudovo is a crucial supply hub on the main line between Moscow and Leningrad. The fascists will be desperate to capture it to cut off all resupply routes to Leningrad. They'll throw everything they have at us. We'll be passing through at high speed, hoping to catch their artillery spotters off guard and avoid their guns and bombers."

"And if we don't catch them by surprise?"

"Then you can sleep forever, comrade!" the man laughed heartily before slapping Vladimir on the back.

A deep hum, faint at first but growing steadily louder, silenced the man's laughter. Squinting out the open passenger car's window at the low-hanging sun, the soldier cupped his hand to his ear. The sound intensified menacingly, like the approach of a swarm of bees.

"What is it? What's happening?" Vladimir's voice trembled with rising panic.

"Stukas," the soldier replied tersely, before shouting orders to the other men lounging at the far end of the car. "The Luftwaffe's most fearsome bombers," he added a moment later.

"How can you tell?"

"The Stuka's scream is unforgettable," the soldier said, his face grim. "It terrorizes the soul and haunts your dreams. You never forget the sound or the fear that follows."

"What should I do?" Vladimir asked desperately.

"Pray," the soldier said, before darting out the door.

There was barely time to kneel, let alone pray, before the piercing shrieks of two dive-bombing Junkers Ju 87 Stukas filled Vladimir's ears. The shockwave of an explosion shattered the train car's windows and knocked him off his feet. Moments later, the Zaamuret's devastating 57mm guns roared to life, spewing hot metal and smoke into the sky.

Vladimir was overwhelmed—unable to breathe, hear, or see clearly. His senses were assaulted from all sides. Terrified, he soiled himself, groping along the floor until he found refuge under a bench. The attack lasted less than a minute, but to Vladimir, it felt like an eternity and the fear he felt would haunt him in nightmares for the rest of his life.

War had come, and whether he liked it or not, Vladimir would have to get his hands dirty, if he hoped to reach the Urals or return triumphantly to Leningrad. The fascists would show no mercy. The train rolled on and five days later after a grueling journey that included evading relentless German artillery barrages and repeated strafing runs from the Luftwaffe, the last train out of Leningrad finally reached the fortified settlement of Sverdlovsk in the Ural Mountains.

11

THE COMPOSER

LENINGRAD – SEPTEMBER 1941

Dmitri Shostakovich, an ungracefully thin and tall man of thirty-five years old, gazed out of the window of his upper-level apartment, eyeing the swift-flowing Neva River carrying a boat towards the open and frigid waters of the Baltic. In the distance, invisible lights of a faraway coast called out to him. The totality of events that had caused one of Russia's greatest composers to fall so hastily out of favor with the Soviet state tumbled in his head. The deafening applause of the adoring crowds still rang in his ears, the clanging of crystal champagne flutes making his heart race. But now, a nothingness of false patriotism and a never-ending fear of the secret police had replaced his former life. The trepidation was so overwhelming that he had developed a habit of sleeping on his apartment's landing to avoid waking his wife and children when the NKVD came to take him away.

Dmitri had spent five long years trying to regain Stalin's favor but stopped all his efforts and began living again today. "Resistance will be my parting gift to the people of Leningrad," he thought to himself.

"Dmitri," a soft voice called from behind him. "What are you looking at? What could you possibly see at this hour?"

"Nothing Nina," Dmitri whispered. "I have seen nothing, I am nothing, and I will die with nothing."

"What did you say?" Nina Shostakovich said as she turned to face her husband.

"Nothing," Dmitri answered his wife in a firm voice.

"Did you go and see the Commissar today as I suggested?"

"Yes, dear. They do not need a nearly blind composer in the Red Army. They asked me how my sense of smell was and then told me to join the fire brigades."

"Fighting fires is important," Nina said, trying to sound sincere.

"Killing fascists is important," Dmitri reminded her. "Regaining my reputation is important, but sitting on a rooftop like a simple-minded pigeon looking for smoke is meaningless. An old nanny can do that."

Nina next proposed Dmitri enlist with the Citizen Defense Brigades, yet he had already entertained the idea. Instead, he shocked his wife by confessing that he had stealthily attended a meeting at the State Hermitage two months prior. The staff was in need of assistance, packaging the myriad of paintings and artifacts in a frantic attempt to evacuate as much of the museum's collections as possible before the imminent arrival of fascist hoards. Now cut off, Dmitri reconsidered their plea for help as the museum staff shifted their efforts to securing the remaining art and converting the Winter Palace into an impregnable fortress.

"The museum's director, Orbeli, is quite inspirational. I met him once before at a reception after one of my concerts. He almost made me feel like I was back in the old St. Petersburg, a land of culture before this terror-filled nightmare descended upon us all."

"Dmitri!" Nina hushed him. "The walls have ears you must not talk like that."

"I have ears, and I have a brain too. I will talk any damn way I please. I am tired of living in perpetual fear. I want to compose great things again without worrying about how the 'Great Leader' will react to my music. Can you understand that?"

Nina looked at her husband with the saddest of eyes. "Yes," she said in a whisper. "I know you yearn to be celebrated again. It is not fair what they have done to you."

"No," Dmitri corrected her, "I yearn to be alive again. Since that criminal Stalin and his entourage walked out on my opera five years ago, my life has been a shell of itself. He denounces me through the pages of that wretched rag, Pravda, spewing his venomous accusations of anti-Bolshevik sentiment that have turned my life into a nightmare. The words of a single man have cast me into the shadows and stripped me of my voice and livelihood. My friends, once my most ardent supporters, have been silenced or sent to labor camps for daring to praise my earlier work. The fear of retribution has left me sleepwalking through the past five years, but no more. I will be damned if I continue to live the life of a coward."

Nina's voice cut through the gloom like a ray of sunlight. "Can you learn to live two lives then? A fairy tale can have many different interpretations, Dmitri. Why not write a new symphony with dual meanings? One that inspires the defense of our city and another that voices your rage toward Stalin. He has taken so much from you."

Dmitri rubbed his temples, struggling to control the emotions that threatened to overwhelm him. "Do you think I am capable of such a creation?"

"If you are not careful, it might be the last thing you ever do," Nina warned. "But yes, I have faith in you, Dmitri. Pour every frustration and passion you just expressed into its creation. Purge your soul of all the darkness and fear that have paralyzed you for far too long. Breathe life into it, and let it breathe life back into you."

Dmitri pondered the challenge of writing another symphony. The majority of his symphonies were tombstones. His 5th symphony had been deemed too transparent, too blatantly counter-revolutionary by the Composer's Union. It had nearly cost him his life. The 6th symphony had been more subtle, using coded notes and musical quotations to express his protest while evoking an emotional response in an audience that had suffered immense pain during the Great Purge. But a 7th symphony...that might give him the opportunity he sought. "I shall dedicate this next symphony to the city of Leningrad," he declared. "It will be my magnum opus."

"Then you must get to work at once," Nina urged. "For those who have ears to hear, will hear what you intend to say."

Two fluted stone pinnacles, adorned with intricate masonry flowers, stood upright like majestic sentinels guarding the roofline of the Winter Palace. Unbeknownst to most, concealed within the heart of each eastward-facing stone blossom lay a hidden doorway—an enigmatic entryway into the enchanting realm of the hives. From the first blush of dawn to the final golden rays of sunset, the industrious bees worked their exquisite magic, transforming the nectar of acacia trees into ambrosial honey.

Dmitri Shostakovich first discovered these mesmerizing creatures during his daily fire watches atop the Hermitage's section of the sprawling palace building. The long hours of his mind-numbing shifts had thus far been a tedious affair, but the presence of the bees breathed new life into his monotonous routine. Dmitri became an avid spectator of their complex orchestrated movements, studying the geometric patterns of both hive and flight of the bees. Nature, as ever, had a way of imparting invaluable lessons and endless wonders to him.

So work the honeybees,

Creatures that, by rule in nature, teach

The art of order and God's endless reach.

Pulling out his worn notebook, Dmitri sketched his next musical idea. "It shall commence with the march of an invading army, but from which direction shall it emerge? From the east? Or from the west? It matters not; the adversary remains the same—the despoilers of our cherished city on the banks of the Neva River. Note by note and bar by bar, the formidable march will grow louder and more pronounced until the blaring trumpets and resounding brass herald the arrival of the ruthless hordes at the gates, stirring frantic alarm."

The Great Dmitri Shostakovich would immerse himself in this creative process for hours until his shift ended. Returning to his cramped apartment, he would resume his work on the musical score. Writing fervently, Dmitri was focused on transposing his ideas into melodic notes. Often, his concentration would be disrupted by a new annoyance: air raid sirens, signaling impending danger. Marking his place on the sheet music, Dmitri would gather his wife and children, seeking refuge in the basement shelter of his apartment building until the all-clear sounded.

It was an absurd existence shaped by the capricious whims of a tumultuous city. Yet, amidst the chaos and madness, Dmitri had discovered a new purpose that allowed him to persevere and thrive.

"Now that inspiration has returned to you, Dmitri, why must you persist in your rooftop vigil at the Hermitage?" Nina asked. "Would it not be wiser to channel all your energy into the creation of your new symphony?"

"Without my rooftop duty, we would all face starvation. Holding a Party-sanctioned position means we receive a worker's ration card, coal, and if luck favors us, a few meager lumps of sugar."

"Then why not seek a job with shorter hours or even a night shift, allowing you more time at home with the children and me?"

"Not all jobs offer the same advantages. Working for the museum comes with certain privileges, but I will ask Director Orbeli for consideration if a night position becomes available."

"You are a brilliant composer; all this seems beneath your talents."

"Nina, even Russia's most eminent living poet, Anna Akhmatova, stands guard outside the Sheremetev Palace. Am I superior to her?"

"Marshal Zhdanov denounces her Dmitri, labeling her 'half-nun, half-whore.' I cannot trust her intentions or methods."

"May I remind you Zhdanov also denounces me." Dmitri drew his wife in closer, enveloping her in his wiry frame. "Akhmatova possesses influential connections. In the harsh reality we find ourselves in, survival often demands such associations.

"And with whom do you associate with, Dmitri? I am filled with fear. Fear for you, fear for our children, and fear for our city. Why can't we escape now, before the fascists truly seal off all the exit routes?"

"The era of free will has ended my love. The Party alone determines who can depart and who must remain. We are stranded here until we are ordered otherwise."

Nina let out a weary sigh, acknowledging the validity of her husband's words. However, she could not shake off the overwhelming fear that consumed her. Despite being the one who had encouraged Dmitri to seek employment when he was at his lowest point, Nina now longed to have her husband all to herself. She had shown strength during Dmitri's darkest days, but now she needed someone to be strong for her. She yearned for Dmitri's fame to pave the way for them to leave Russia behind and live as celebrated exiles in the safety of America or anywhere far away. Remaining in Leningrad seemed like sheer madness, a path that would lead to the demise of her entire family. "Let us pray to God for deliverance then."

They did not have to wait long for divine intervention. It would soon arrive in the form of a dead man and a bomb.

12

THE LOVER

STATE HERMITAGE – AUTUMN 1941

The sudden departure of Vladimir by train with the art had unanticipated repercussions for Joseph Orbeli. Bereft of his assistant director's buffering presence, Joseph was saddled with increased daily responsibilities and more pressing issues than he could tackle amidst this crisis. His expertise was in strategic, long-term planning. Presented with such a problem, Joseph could sit and think his way out of any conundrum. However, the eruption of numerous daily mini-crises within the Hermitage and the necessity for swift, decisive action left his head spinning. Therefore, Joseph embarked on the urgent task of appointing a new assistant director. His choice, a woman, stirred some initial discontent among the all-male department heads - that is until they encountered the formidable force known as Tatiana Tolstaya.

Tatiana was born at the Hermitage. Her mother, a master painter, had been recruited into Sophia's secret guild of forgers, years prior after Tatiana's father had abandoned them both. Tatiana's childhood had been spent running through the museum's galleries, hallways, and Raphael-inspired Vatican loggias connecting the Hermitage's various buildings. She was always watching, learning, and waiting for her opportunity to join either her mother, working in the Tsar's Vault, or as part of the Hermitage's Antiquities department.

Tatiana was an accomplished sketch artist and painter like her mother. She inherited a dogged stubbornness from her father along with his innate cleverness to accomplish any task no matter how insurmountable it may appear. Her skills had caught the eye of Sophia, who had taken it upon herself to find her a position on the museum's staff. Now at age twenty-six, having served three years as Joseph Orbeli's secretary, Tatiana knew more about his day-to-day responsibilities than he did. She was a bold but ideal choice to become the new assistant director with one minor complication - Tatiana was in love with the Director of the State Hermitage Museum.

Joseph had not encouraged her affections; on the contrary, he had averted them with all the strength he could muster. Their age difference was significant, and she was undoubtedly yearning for a life he could not provide. Joseph was nearing the twilight of his life, while she was a radiant star ascending amidst the gloom and desolation of an unwanted war. However, it seemed the gods of love and war had different plans.

During the early months of the fascist siege, their relationship remained strictly platonic. However, under intense stress, boundaries and societal divisions can become blurred. After all, Joseph was only human. Decades had passed since the tragic loss of his wife during childbirth. In the aftermath, he had immersed himself in his work, navigating through bureaucratic webs that often ensnared less skillful administrators. Tatiana managed to rekindle a passion in him he thought had long been extinguished, but this came accompanied by an unprecedented sense of guilt. His usual way of handling this overwhelming emotion was to bury himself even further into his work.

In his urgency to coordinate the packing of thousands of paintings, sketches, and sculptures housed within the Hermitage for evacuation and the growing distraction of newfound love, Joseph overlooked some oversized items that fell outside his usual purview. The imperial carriages were precisely such items, and they would soon become some of the earliest casualties of the siege. Their destruction would be one of Joseph's most profound regrets.

Even if Joseph had prioritized the carriages, their sheer size and weight made them impractical for transportation to the safety of the Urals in the east. The railroad's loadmaster had informed him that they could transport, at most, a single carriage if he wanted to evacuate the majority of the Hermitage's vast art collection. With this knowledge in mind, Joseph selected the royal carriage of Catherine the Great to be transported away from danger.

Joseph's decision was agonizing; it felt akin to choosing which family member to save from drowning. Ultimately, Catherine's golden coach seemed the most fitting choice for reasons Joseph would later forget. As empress, Catherine ushered Russia into the arena of Western civilization, integrating the country fully into Europe's political and cultural life. She was also an ardent champion of the arts. In contrast, Stalin despised the arts, viewing them only as tools to disseminate his fabrications. Could there be a starker difference, he wondered.

Joseph also reasoned that the remaining carriages could be disassembled and stored in the Hermitage's underground vaults alongside the other art pieces that were not evacuated. That, at least, was his plan. However, as Joseph later reminded himself, 'the best-laid plans of mice and men often go awry.' The fascists arrived earlier than he had anticipated, and their shelling of the Winter Palace, which housed the Hermitage, was an act of terror that contravened all norms of 'civilized warfare.'

The first train, bearing some of the Hermitage's treasures, set off for the Urals less than a month before Leningrad was encircled and isolated. A second train, laden with additional artifacts and Vladimir Levinson-Lessing onboard, barely escaped a week later. However, a third train became ensnared, trapped just like the other unfortunate inhabitants of the ill-fated city when the remaining roads and railways out of the city were severed.

The third train was unloaded, and its invaluable cargo returned to the museum for storage. This left scant space in the vaults for the carriages, especially considering the need to accommodate over two thousand museum staff members with makeshift beds. These individuals had chosen to remain behind in the face of looming danger and needed shelter from the impending fascist storm.

Therefore, when the news reached Joseph that a shell had obliterated the Carriage House and all within, he felt as if he had been mortally wounded. He never forgave himself for the loss of the remaining carriages. He had failed to protect what he knew needed safeguarding. How could he trust himself to keep two thousand souls safe?

"We require more secure space," Joseph announced through gritted teeth.

"The military engineers have determined that the walls and arches of the Hermitage's lower floors can endure both artillery bombardment and aerial attack," Tatiana relayed, delivering the welcomed news. "Why not relocate the remaining crated artwork to these floors and potentially clear some additional living quarters in the underground vaults?"

"We should have conducted this evaluation earlier, Tatiana."

"We were managing a thousand other tasks, Joseph. We barely had enough time to evacuate any of the art, let alone formulate a plan for an impending siege."

Joseph grunted his understanding, "If the lower floors are indeed safe, then let us liberate some space in the vaults and expand the staff quarters. I wish to designate some provisional workspaces for artisans to carry on their craft."

Tatiana scribbled instructions into a notebook. "The scientists are also voicing the need for more laboratory space. What should I convey to them?"

"Continued scientific research by Hermitage staff will be restricted to work that directly contributes to the war effort. All other research is to be suspended now. We have to conserve our resources and maintain the energy of every soul in our care. No one will be exempted from work assignments. If they do not contribute, they will not eat."

Food scarcity was escalating into a serious worry, not just for Joseph but also for the city's besieged residents. The relentless assault by the fascists' artillery and the intensifying air raids of the Luftwaffe necessitated a tightening of belts across the population. Desperation reached new heights when the warehouses containing most of the city's food reserves succumbed to fire in the second month of the siege. Joseph mulled over the disheartening possibility of the fascists' strategy to starve them into surrender being successful. His concerns, tormenting his sleep and plaguing his waking hours, impelled him to seek comfort in the embrace of a love he had once spurned.

Joseph emerged beneath the layers of furs and blankets adorning the imperial bed, his weary feet touching the cool, gray marble floor. The chilling sensation pricked his skin while his bleary eyes gradually regained focus. A fleeting thought of seeking refuge in the bed's warmth alongside the woman still there crossed his mind. However, duty beckoned. There was always work to be done.

"Are you attempting to slip away before I awaken?" Tatiana said as Joseph rose and stretched his tired limbs.

"No, I merely wish to avoid any prying eyes and potential gossip. There are watchful eyes everywhere."

"Why not marry me then? No one would dare gossip about a husband sharing a bed with his wife."

"In this opulent palace once adorned with priceless art, my gaze is solely fixed upon you, Tatiana. However, I am too old for marriage. You deserve a husband younger than I."

"I did not hear you complaining about your age last night when you slipped into my bed," Tatiana teased.

The truth of her words pierced Joseph's heart. He had sought solace in the passion of the previous evening, but now he grappled with the weight of guilt, knowing that his desire to return to work overshadowed the intimacy they had shared. The burdens on his shoulders were suffocating, threatening to consume all of him.

"These are desperate times. Each day, mothers and fathers wake up to the grim reality that it could be their last. They agonize over how to feed their children and provide them warmth. I apologize, my love, but marriage is a luxury we cannot afford amidst such circumstances."

"I prefer you when you are not burdened by such seriousness," Tatiana said, sitting up and encircling her arms around Joseph's neck. "Stay a while longer. The birds have yet to awaken."

"We have consumed all the birds in the city," Joseph reminded her. "Their joyous melodies will not return until this wretched war comes to an end."

Sensing the weight of his foul mood, Tatiana decided to change the subject. Joseph's dark temperament at times frightened her. "Tell me, what urgent tasks await your attention today?"

"My brother attended a meeting with Marshal Zhdanov yesterday. He disclosed that the city's food reserves have reached critical levels: only seven days of flour, eight days of cereal, fourteen days of fats, twenty-two days of sugars, and no meats left. Even the military is reducing their rations.

Our museum's provisions are also dwindling. We will need to cut staff rations. We can no longer count on any resupply. We are now deemed non-essential. We are left to fend for ourselves."

Tatiana's eyes widened in disbelief, "But how is that possible? Just months ago, Zhdanov assured the public that the city's warehouses were fully stocked."

"Zhdanov is a liar and a coward. He made those claims to conceal his lack of preparation from Stalin. The supply trains from Moscow have been diverted elsewhere, and now, when we need food the most, we are left isolated."

A sense of desperation crept over Tatiana as she grappled with the harsh reality. "What can we do?"

Joseph exhaled a heavy breath of frustration. "I must find a way to secure new provisions for the staff. Soon I will not be able to feed everyone. We are down to our last 'five loaves and two fish.' We are in dire need of a miracle."

Tatiana's mind raced, and an inevitable answer formed in her thoughts. With hesitation, she whispered, "My father might be able to help us."

"What are you saying? You told me your father passed away years ago during the October Revolution. How can a deceased man aid us now?"

Tatiana's gaze shifted away, burdened with the weight of her revelation. "My father is dead to me, but his physical body still exists. He aligned himself with the Bolsheviks in the early days, and it changed him. He is no longer the man I once admired as a child. I disowned him long ago."

Struggling to process this information, Joseph pulled on his trousers while mixed emotions swirled within him. "How can this ghost of a man offer any assistance?"

"My father is Sergi Agron."

The name struck Joseph like an artillery shell, leaving him speechless, his eyes filled with betrayal. "That cannot be possible."

"Please, Joseph, do not look at me like that. I despise everything he represents and all that he has done. I would just as soon pull the trigger myself from a thousand yards away and end his life. He is the embodiment of evil. But I fear he may be our only hope."

Joseph's anger surged, his voice rising with indignation. "You expect me to beg Sergi Agron for help? You believe the leader of the Haymarket Underground will extend assistance out of the goodness of his heart? This is beyond belief."

"Do not be angry. I understand what drives him. You will not have to lower yourself to beg like an animal."

Joseph scoffed, "So I should simply stroll up to the notorious crime lord of St. Petersburg and ask him for enough food to sustain two thousand people, and he will hand it over without hesitation? Your naivety knows no bounds."

"Listen here, Comrade Director. I have had my fill of your condescension. Yes, you may be older and more knowledgeable about the ways of the bourgeoisie, but I have witnessed firsthand the workings of the underworld. Remember, I have watched my father put bullets into his enemies. I am telling you he will provide the food if you give him what he desires."

"He has no wants or needs, Tatiana. I possess nothing of value to offer him."

"There is one thing he desires above all else, and it is something you alone can provide."

Joseph's gaunt hands rubbed his tired, deep-set eyes. "And what would that be?"

"Offer him Titian's original painting of *Venus with a Mirror*."

Silence enveloped them as Joseph stood motionless, his eyes confirming what Tatiana already knew. He possessed the painting. While his motives for the deception were noble, a haunting question lingered. Was he indeed any different from Sergi Agron?

"How do you know I have this?" Joseph said, breaking the silence.

"My mother once confided in me that she saw the painting in the tunnels beneath the Winter Palace. She said it was hidden within the Vault of the Tsars."

"Such a chamber is nothing but a myth. It does not exist," Joseph said, not willing to share this secret with her.

Tatiana's tone turned defensive. "Are you implying that my mother is a liar? She has worked side by side with Sophia for years, creating numerous forgeries for you."

"I apologize if my words came across that way. I meant to say that your mother might be mistaken. The harsh realities of the fascist blockade can cloud even the sharpest minds."

Tatiana was undeterred. "Then let us go and visit my mother immediately. You can tell her directly that she is losing her faculties. I am sure she would be grateful to know what you think of her now."

"Tatiana, please, let go of this madness. Even if I possessed Titian's original masterpiece, why would your father desire it? What value does it hold for him? It will neither feed nor sustain him amidst the chaos of this fascist-infested hornet's nest. Art has lost its worth among the starving citizens of St. Petersburg."

"Although my father fought for the revolution, deep down he is an opportunist. He thrives on advancing his status in society, but he is also a romantic at heart. The painting fulfills his deepest desires."

"Then why wouldn't he accept any classical painting as payment for food? We have a wealth of desirable artworks in the Hermitage. He could choose from a da Vinci, a Rembrandt, or even a Raphael. The painting, *Venus with a Mirror* was sold by the Bolsheviks to a wealthy American long ago. It is simply not an option."

"Do not lie to me again, Joseph. *Venus with a Mirror* was Titian's most beloved composition. As you are aware, there are at least fifteen known copies or variations that were created by Titian or one of his numerous assistants. However, only one of these copies remained in Titian's studio until his death. That particular painting is his original masterpiece. Sergi Agron would give anything to possess it."

"I am only trying to protect you, Tatiana, but I struggle to comprehend your father's infatuation with this painting."

Tatiana's voice trembled. "My father has everything in the world except love. To have the enduring gaze of Venus, the goddess of love, bestowed upon him for the rest of his days would be irresistible to him."

Standing half naked in the Tsar's bedroom, Joseph caught sight of Tatiana; her tear-streaked reflection mirrored in the gilded imperial wall. The words of the renowned Italian poet Serafino dell'Aquila reverberated in his mind. *'Oh, mirror, I envy you only because of her... Alas! I would gladly trade my place with yours.'* At that moment, Joseph Orbeli felt a profound realization of what he must do for Tatiana, the museum staff, and himself. "Very well, let us go and find the insufferable Sergi Agron."

13

THE CRIMINAL

LENINGRAD - AUTUMN 1941

The pangs of a broken heart pale compared to the roar of an empty stomach. Joseph Orbeli had experienced hunger before, but never to this extent. It was clouding his ability to think, pushing him towards desperation. And in desperation, even the most virtuous can resort to unsavory acts. He had no choice but to strike a deal with the devil.

"Yuri, are my eyes deceiving me? Who is approaching us?" Sergi Agron asked, his gaze fixed on the lean figure drawing near them.

"It is the Museum Director," replied a stocky man, looking up from his newspaper and puffing on a pipe.

"I cannot believe it, the elusive Hermit of the Hermitage - the once great Joseph Orbeli standing before me? You must be lost, Director. Be cautious where you wander in our famine-stricken city. Thieves lurk at every corner," Sergi said, his voice dripping with false concern.

"And they all work for you," Joseph replied, his eyes scanning the opulent surroundings while his stomach rumbled. "Your ex-wife informed me that I would find you here,"

"Ah, she is an angel with the heart of a serpent and the mind of an ass. I secretly pray for the fascists to overrun our city and relieve me of the memory of her incessant nagging."

"Despite her many flaws, Sergi, she did give you a daughter, Tatiana, who has proven to be an invaluable asset to the Hermitage. She is leading our efforts to protect the art."

"Why have you come, Director? What do you want from me?" Sergi yawned, growing disinterested in their exchange.

"You misunderstand comrade. The question is not what you can do for me, but rather what I can do for you."

"Me? I have everything I need, except for one of my arms," the leader of the Haymarket Underground laughed, taking a bite of an apple. "What could you possibly offer me that I do not already possess?"

Joseph felt a surge of frustration at Sergi's dismissive attitude. "Before I reveal what I can offer you, I must emphasize the urgency of the situation. The museum staff is working day and night, battling the flames and scanning the skies for fascist paratroopers. The preservation of our cherished art continues, but I can no longer provide sustenance for my workers. I require your assistance."

With a casual gesture, the crime boss tossed his half-eaten apple over his shoulder. "If you have the means to pay for it, I can offer you jars of Badaev dirt. It is an acquired taste, but it beats starving."

Joseph felt a surge of revulsion at the mention of Badaev dirt. The stories of the city's desperate inhabitants consuming the burned warehouses' ashes were well known. The inferno had turned tons of stored sugar into molten rivers, saturating the remains of the buildings and the earth below. Desperate citizens had traded their valuables for the opportunity to consume the contaminated dirt—an unimaginable act of desperation.

"A glass from the first meter of soil will cost you one hundred Rubles. Deeper layers are only fifty," Sergi continued, his smile oozing with contempt.

Joseph's stomach churned at the inhumanity of it all. He refused to let his people suffer such degradation. "Sergi, I cannot accept such a proposition. Our people deserve better than to be reduced to eating dirt. We are fighting for the preservation of our culture and humanity itself. I implore you to help us provide real sustenance for the museum staff and the starving masses in our city. Together, we can make a difference."

Sergi and his rotund crony erupted into boisterous laughter. "We cannot always get what we want, Director. For instance, I have an insatiable desire to sleep with Princess Julianna of the Netherlands. However, depending on what you have to offer, I might be inclined to provide you with just enough bread to keep the scent lingering in your nostrils."

Joseph observed the repugnant figure before him. Having lost an arm in the early days of the Bolshevik revolution, Sergi had proven to be an astute entrepreneur. He amassed a fortune by selling high-quality cigarettes from the Kremlin to the affluent citizens of Leningrad. However, it was the harsh reality of the fascist blockade that propelled him to legendary status. Sergi had become renowned as the man who could acquire anything one desired if the price was met. His clientele included Red Army officers and city officials, ensuring his protection and influence.

"Look at this," Joseph said, reaching into his pocket and producing a weathered photograph. He handed it to the black marketeer, his eyes gleaming with anticipation.

Sergi scrutinized the photograph, his expression one of disbelief. "What is this?" he asked, his tone tinged with confusion.

"It is something your daughter informs me holds great value to you," Joseph said, a hint of satisfaction gracing his features. "Behold, Titian's original *Venus with a Mirror*."

Sergi's disbelief turned into a mixture of astonishment and intrigue. "Impossible! You no longer possess such a treasure. I know it was sold long ago."

"Ask your daughter. She has seen it with her own eyes."

Silence enveloped the room as Sergi assessed the truth of Joseph's words. Breaking the silence Joseph listed his demands. "I expect the first delivery in two days: fresh eggs, vegetables, fruits, hearty black bread, cured meats, and fine cheeses. And let me be clear, I have no tolerance for the repugnant trade of human flesh you peddle." Joseph then envisioned the additional advantages of knowing a man like Sergi Agron. "Furthermore, I have several other discrete tasks that must be fulfilled before the painting becomes yours." He then proceeded to outline the tasks and the inherent risks that came with them.

Sergi tilted his head as his eyes returned to the photograph. "I am many things, Director, but I am not a savage cannibal. I do not deal in human flesh. I shall personally oversee the delivery and the completion of your other tasks, but let this be clear: do not dare to deceive me in this matter. Though I may possess only one arm, the pain I can inflict with it is beyond measure."

"Rest assured, if the provisions are delivered as agreed upon and the tasks completed with discretion, both of us shall find contentment," Joseph said, reaching for an apple from the bowl beside Sergi. Taking a bite, he relished its tartness and the aromatic explosion of flavors. At that moment, his thoughts drifted to his old friend, Pasha. While a sense of regret lingered within him for stooping to this level, the juice of the apple, dripping from his mouth, silenced his staunch morality. He had made his choice.

"You shall have all that you need," Sergi said, his voice filled with determination and intrigue. "And so shall I."

※ ※

Two days later, a thick ice fog enveloped the slumbering city of Leningrad, casting an eerie atmosphere as a silent procession of men traversed the Lion's Bridge. Their movements were swift and purposeful, their shadows elongated and distorted against the stone alleyways. The muted echoes of their footfalls punctuated the pre-dawn night, shrouded in secrecy. Stealth was their greatest ally.

Each man bore a cargo more valuable than gold in the desolate city. Crates brimming with root vegetables, oranges, and apples rested upon their broad shoulders, while carts laden with canned herring and live chickens were deftly maneuvered through the narrow alleyways. Their journey led them to the Winter Palace, undetected and unseen. They were guided through a rusted metal door that beckoned them into the depths of the sprawling building. Museum workers greeted their arrival with silent embraces and muted exclamations of joy. Sergi Agron, the black market's most ill-revered figure, arrived to a hero's welcome.

"We are fifteen minutes ahead of schedule, Director," Sergi declared with satisfaction.

"I am certain you have been called many things over the years, Sergi, but 'late' was never one of them."

The master of the black market roared with laughter, extending an invoice listing the delivered provisions to Joseph as the two men entered an empty gallery room. It was there that Sergi posed the question Joseph had anticipated. "When do I have the pleasure of beholding the painting?"

Joseph responded with a coy smile, teasing him as he asked, "Do you doubt my possession of it?"

"I trust no one, not even my daughter. That is why I thrive while others perish."

"I presume you will be making further deliveries as the need arises?" Joseph asked, "And the other tasks too?"

"Yes, as per our agreement, every two weeks or even sooner, if necessary. I am working out the details for your other delicate tasks as well."

"Excellent! You have exceeded my expectations."

"And the painting?" Sergi prodded once more.

"If you do not mind me asking, what is your fascination with this particular artwork?"

"I am sure my astute daughter has already enlightened you with her theories on why I desire it, has she not?"

"Tatiana indeed has many theories... perhaps too many. However, I would prefer to hear it directly from you."

Sergi bellowed, "Is that why you have evaded her marriage proposals? Do you fear you will never find a moment's peace if you do say yes? I, too, have made promises of being an honorable husband many times. I yearn for deep love, but I also seek a partner who like the moon will not appear in my sky every night."

"Tatiana deserves better than me."

"She deserves happiness. If she finds it with you, then do the honorable thing, Director, and marry her."

"What do you know about honor? You are just a petty thief," Joseph snapped.

Sergi's eyes flashed with anger before he regained his composure and forced a smile. "I understand that you disapprove of what I may seem to be, but when one does not have a real life, one must live in mirages. Never make the mistake of questioning my honor again, Director, or it will be the last thing you do."

"Tell me, then, why does a 'honorable' man like you want the painting *Venus with a Mirror*?"

Sergi pulled a hand-wrapped cigar from his coat pocket and brought it close to his nose.

"There is no smoking in here."

Striking a match, Sergi ignited his cigar. "I might be dead in five minutes. I will smoke whenever the mood strikes me." He extinguished the flame, allowing wisps of smoke to encircle his head. "The Dutch make the finest cigars."

Suppressing the urge to lecture the man on the inherent danger fire posed to the Winter Palace, Joseph repeated his question instead. "Why do you desire *Venus with a Mirror*?"

"I am just a wretch," Sergi said, exhaling a delicate smoke ring. "True love has eluded me throughout my forty-eight years of existence. I have shared intimate moments with countless women, but they have never returned my love. People enter my life solely to exploit what I can offer them. Take this Wilhelm II cigar, for instance. It is one of the best in the world. A factory worker in Valkenswaard smuggled these out of a storeroom to repay his debt to me."

"You are evading the question, Sergi. Give me a straightforward answer."

"I already have. Beauty has always been beyond my reach. *Venus with a Mirror,* the goddess of love, her reflection illuminating my existence, is all the affection I desire or deserve."

"It's just a painting," Joseph lied, "It can never replace the warmth and intimacy of another human being."

"Yes, but unlike a woman, it will not betray me either," Sergi winked.

"That is a bleak perspective on life."

"I am Russian, what do you expect? I dare say it is also the safest outlook to have. Are you so naive that you believe that every member of your staff is one hundred percent loyal to you, Director?"

"If I can provide for them, then yes."

The crime boss's laughter returned, reverberating through the ghost of a hall like the determined voice of a woman hell-bent on having the final say. "Do you know how many times I have pledged my loyalty to someone or something? A thousand times...perhaps ten thousand," Sergi said, shrugging his shoulders. "In the end, I have betrayed every single one of them."

Joseph shook his head, not understanding this 'honorable' man before him. "In the spirit of Chekhov, let me respond with his words: 'Love, friendship, and respect do not bind people together as much as a shared hatred for something.' Women are not your enemy, the Germans are. There is a first time for everything, Sergi. You might keep a pledge after all."

With a fresh bout of laughter, Sergi retrieved a silver flask from his coat. "I will drink to that," he declared, taking a swig before passing it to his newfound ally. "Now, let us discuss your other tasks."

Joseph's mind was occupied with thoughts about who among his staff would be the first to betray him. He took a generous nip of vodka from the flask. Then, he began to unveil his plans for Anna's paintings and one crate stashed away in the Urals.

⁂

The unexpected knock at the door startled Anna Akhmatova, and then a wave of terror washed over her. She had received no visitors to her meager apartment for nearly a year. Only a select few knew her current address after the Bolsheviks evicted her from the Fountain House decades earlier. The late hour of this visit added to her disquiet. With trepidation, Anna answered the door after a second round of forceful knocks shook the walls. Standing before her was a relatively short man, she noted, dressed in an old soldier's coat.

"Anna Akhmatova?" the man said in an authoritative tone.

"Yes," she said, her throat dry. "I am Anna."

The man extended his left hand politely as if to shake hers. Then, Anna noticed his missing arm, the long empty right coat sleeve flapping in the breeze. "I was sent by Joseph Orbeli to collect some items from you."

Still shocked by the realization that this man was not here to arrest her, Anna welcomed him inside her home. She stood in the kitchen, speechless and unsure of what to do. Thus, she felt relief when the man broke the silence.

"I assume the items are not here?" the man said looking around. "It would be foolish to keep them in this place, as the authorities could barge in at any moment and conduct a thorough search."

Anna regained her composure and asked the man to identify himself. "How do you know Joseph Orbeli?"

"It is best that you do not know too much about me. Let us just say that Director Orbeli and I have a beneficial business relationship."

Anna could not help but think that this man was neither an artist nor someone who moved within the upper-crust social circles she and Joseph frequented. Nevertheless, he seemed precisely the type of person Joseph would send to clean up her mess. "What has he told you about my 'items'?"

"You possess thirty paintings that are now illegal, according to the Soviet state, to own. I am here to take them off your hands."

Anna snorted. "So, he sends a one-armed business associate to carry them off to God knows where?"

"I have a work crew standing by, ready to descend upon the location where your paintings are stored," he explained, ignoring Anna's provocative remark. "I am not a mere laborer. I am a man who cleans up messes and greases the wheels when things need to get done. Time is of the essence Ms. Akhmatova, so please," he gestured toward the door, "can you lead me to your paintings?"

14

THE SAGE

Joseph Orbeli developed a routine of taking early morning walks through the now-empty galleries of the Hermitage Museum. He found comfort in the serene silence that enveloped the space just before the first rays of sunlight pierced through the skylights. To him, the packed-away paintings still seemed to have a voice, whispering messages from their creators across the centuries. Joseph saw this as his preferred method of problem-solving. By wandering through the museum's hallowed halls, he believed the answers he sought would reveal themselves in time. On this particular morning, bathed in the predawn glow, Joseph strolled while listening to the ghosts of the departed art.

"What weighs on your mind, my friend?" the walls seemed to ask, sending a shiver down Joseph's spine. Astonished by the unexpected question, Joseph glanced around, questioning his sanity. Had the stress of shouldering numerous responsibilities finally taken its toll?

"Hello?" Joseph managed to stammer in response to the darkness surrounding him.

"You pace these halls like an expectant father," the voice persisted.

Stepping into a beam of an early ray of sunlight, Joseph caught sight of his old friend from Peterhof Palace, now the museum's head caretaker. "You startled me," he said with relief. "I thought the Renaissance masters were speaking to me through the ghosts of their paintings."

"Well, I am old enough to be considered a Renaissance master, so you were not entirely mistaken."

"Tell me Pasha, what brings you here at such an early hour?"

"I am visiting an old friend—a painting that provides me comfort."

"But there are no paintings left in this gallery. They have all been packed up and stored away. Only their empty frames remain. How can you visit them?"

Pasha chuckled at Joseph's confusion and pointed to his forehead. "I visit them in here. If you study a painting with enough intensity, it leaves an indelible mark on both your heart and mind. I see every detail, every brush stroke."

"Tell me more about this painting that stirs you so much you feel compelled to visit its specter at such an early hour."

"It used to hang over there, in the corner, a massive canvas by Van Dyck titled *The Madonna with Partridges*.

"Ah yes," Joseph said, trying to visualize the painting. "One of his greatest works, and if I am not mistaken, the first work by Van Dyck to grace the Hermitage."

"You are correct. Catherine the Great purchased it, and it hung in her Empress gallery, which she visited daily to absorb its radiance and grace—God's grace," Pasha added after a moment's thought.

Joseph nodded, questioning in his mind if God's grace remained in these troubled times.

"Alexander Pushkin was so enamored with it that he visited it every day as well. He even referenced it in his classic work, 'Eugene Onegin.'"

"You have taught me something I did not know," Joseph admitted.

Pasha cast Joseph a judgmental glance. "Have you not read this definitive work of Pushkin's?"

Joseph gave an uncomfortable laugh, feeling as if he were back in school and the headmaster was scolding him for failing to complete his work. "I was born with a paintbrush in my hand. Poetry is an art form that still mystifies me, and Pushkin?" Joseph gestured to indicate that the master poet's intricate writing was challenging.

Pasha sighed in exasperation, "One is never too old to learn. Allow me to enlighten you, dear Director. In 'Eugene Onegin,' Eugene meets a woman named Olga and describes her features to his friend Lensky. 'Olga's features have no life / Exactly like Van Dyck's Madonna. / She is round, red-faced, like this stupid moon / In this stupid sky.'"

"She sounds quite appealing, Pasha."

"Hush! Lensky later becomes engaged to Olga, much to Eugene's surprise, as he is smitten with her bookish sister, Tatiana—much like you with your own Tatiana."

"I must make an effort to give Pushkin another chance," Joseph said, sidestepping Pasha's barb. "What else do you remember about Van Dyck's painting?"

"Hmmm," Pasha pondered, closing his eyes. "The Madonna and child are tranquil, seated under a shady apple tree—a tree of knowledge, heavy with forbidden fruit. They have triumphed over the original sin. At Madonna's feet lies a ripe pomegranate—a symbol of resurrection, its engorged red seeds spilling the stinging nectar of eternal life as cherubic angels dance at her feet. A parrot perched in the tree on her right and a solitary sunflower on her left allude to her divine essence as the Virgin Mary. Two partridges take flight in the upper right, symbolizing the banishment of sin. Its image, etched into my mind, is quite spectacular and comforting in these dark times."

"It has been too long since we last had an earnest conversation," Joseph said, his voice tinged with melancholy. "Your decision to relocate

Peterhof's isolated art and imperial treasures to the Hermitage proved wise. Just as you foresaw, the Bolsheviks put up a meager defense at the outer perimeter. The invaders overran the palace without much resistance."

"I have been lurking in the shadows for the past few months, observing you from a distance. I understand that you have been burdened with weightier matters, unaware of my presence. Nevertheless, I have witnessed your remarkable efforts amidst these crippling circumstances," Pasha acknowledged, his voice filled with admiration. "If your father were here, he would be filled with pride."

Joseph contemplated the old man's words, grateful for the dim light that concealed the tears in his eyes. "I wish he were here to offer me his wise counsel."

Pasha inched closer, his movements betraying the strain it took on his frail body. Despite the increased rations provided to the museum staff, he appeared thinner than ever. "Did I ever tell you that your father once spent a stormy night at Peterhof, and we stayed up late, drinking and reminiscing about the glory days of the empire?"

Joseph shook his head, indicating his ignorance of this particular story. "I wish I had been a fly on the wall."

Pasha settled on a dusty, red-cushioned bench that had once been opulent furniture. He patted the seat beside him, and Joseph obediently joined him. "I recall, your father made a rare confession to me about Tsar

Peter the Great," Pasha began, his laughter tinged with irony at the peculiar role reversal between the head priest of St. Petersburg and a poor caretaker. "He believed that despite his bouts of tyrannical insanity, Peter was, in fact, the best leader Russia ever had."

"Didn't Peter deceive his son into returning to Russia after he had fled, fearing for his life, only to subject him to fatal torture?"

"We all possess our shortcomings," Pasha said, dismissing the comment.

"Peter did acquire, some would say 'borrowed', much of the Western art that once adorned the walls of the Hermitage," Joseph interjected. "I guess that is one sign of greatness."

"But what mattered even more," Pasha continued, "was Peter's profound religious devotion in his youth. Peter was a member of the Orthodox Church. However, he grew distrustful of the Church's leadership, observing how their faith in God had become eclipsed by their worship of wealth and opulence."

"And the Bolsheviks took that mistrust to the most extreme conclusion. They executed all the priests, including my father, for they understood that their loyalty did not lie with the revolution."

"They were aware that men like your father could see through the facade of the revolution's dogma. It was never truly about granting control of industry to the workers or empowering the people. It was always about the leaders' power and greed. And now, look at what we have—a Red Tsar who surpasses all the previous dictators in his tyranny."

"And now we bear the weight of that blame, Pasha."

The old caretaker patted Joseph's knee, "I once confided in you that as a young boy, I was forbidden to speak Russian. I resorted to breaking into my father's library in the middle of the night to learn the language of our Motherland. Those books became my teachers. But there was one volume written in English, and its lessons have remained with me, proving to be quite relevant in the present times. That book warned us of the perils of revolution. Let me see if I can remember the exact words."

> *'Every civilization carries the seeds of its own destruction, and the same cycle shows in them all. The republic is born, flourishes, decays into plutocracy, and is captured by the Shoemaker whom the mercenaries and millionaires make into a king. The people invent their oppressors, and the oppressors serve the function for which they are invented.'*

Joseph's eyebrows furrowed in curiosity. "And who was the wise sage behind those words?"

"An American by the name of Mark Twain. Satire was his weapon, and yet his admonitions seem to have fallen on deaf ears."

"At times, protecting the art—Russia's heritage, Russia's humanity—feels like a futile endeavor as well, knowing that Marshal Zhdanov and Stalin himself view it merely as a commodity. They, too, only value me, because I guard it like a treasure. In the end, I fear that my efforts may be in vain."

"Hogwash," Pasha said. "Do not fret over what you cannot control. Focus on the good you can accomplish and are accomplishing for the two thousand souls sheltered within these walls. They believe in you and will stand by your side no matter the path you tread. And if you grow weary, any one of them would gladly step in to give you respite, allowing you to revive your spirit and rejuvenate your body. Myself included."

Joseph laughed at the idea of a man twice his age taking his place. "Then I better return to my duties before I find myself replaced by something even more counterfeit than what used to hang on these walls."

"Genuine or not, the wisdom they convey is timeless. Through the hands of the artist, God's voice resonates. It is not the finished picture that holds significance, but rather the act of creation itself, which unveils the true nature of God. Be a vessel, allowing the creator to flow through you. Only then, Joseph, will the path become clear." Pasha yawned before succumbing to a predawn slumber.

"But what if I no longer believe in God?" Joseph whispered to himself, his thoughts drifting to the Van Dyck painting stashed away in the darkness—its existence now a memory held only by the few devout souls still left alive.

15

THE ADVICE

Joseph Orbeli's office exuded a comforting ambiance reminiscent of a crackling campfire, intermingled with the elegant scent of acacia. The source of this delightful aroma was the silver samovar, fueled by the wood, from which he still served his cherished Russian Caravan tea. Anna found herself transported back to the warm memories of her childhood as she observed a female staff member pouring the tea with care. Upon this woman's departure the office, Anna could not help but notice her distinct tenderness towards Joseph. Boldly, Anna posed a question lingering in her mind: "Why have you not yet married that young woman?"

"Must you always speak your mind? Do poets have no tact?"

"I can recognize the look of love in a woman's eyes when I see it. Are you too blind to notice?

"She is much too young for me. She should direct her affections towards someone closer to her age," Joseph dismissed, hoping to hide his feelings and divert the conversation.

141

"I once loved a man thirty-two years older than me, and I was never happier."

"If I recall, the last time we met you also told me that you married a man, decades younger than you, and he lost interest as soon as he possessed you. Something about the thrill of the chase is more exciting than the catch. I don't think you are the best person to be advising me about matters of the heart.

"It is different for women," Anna explained. "We are more sensible when it comes to matters of the heart. Physical attraction is just one desirable trait, but what matters more is the soul of a man. A kindhearted soulmate who sees you as an equal is worth ten Adonises."

"I would never want to burden her in my old age," Joseph admitted, not understanding why he was revealing his thoughts to his guest.

"Having loved and lost a man old enough to be my father, was one of the most precious experiences of my life. It was a privilege to love him in the twilight of his years, never a burden. I have no regrets."

"Poets live in a heightened state of awareness. They are live wires crackling and humming until they burn out. Painters are a different breed," Joseph said. "They live for color, form, and composition. My life is a dull gray. I will not allow her to settle for me, a still life, when she deserves a vibrant landscape."

"Joseph Orbeli," Anna teased, "your words are more poetic than even mine. Perhaps deep down inside, you are a frustrated poet? Embrace the love that stands before you. In these dark times, a long life is not guaranteed. Seize each day to the fullest while you can. Marry the girl."

Joseph raised his teacup to his lips, savoring the rich, hot liquid as it warmed his body while contemplating the wisdom in Anna's words. "Now that you have analyzed my personal life, perhaps we should focus on more pressing matters?"

With a slight tip of her teacup, Anna consented. "Very well, it has been months since my portraits have been taken away. I would like to know what you have done with them?"

"As with most things, it is best that you remain unaware."

"As with most things," Anna echoed Joseph's words, "it is prudent for a woman to decide what is best for herself, without a man offering dismissive answers under the guise of protection. I am more than capable of taking care of myself."

"Why is it, madam, that after every conversation with you, I feel exhausted? You truly know how to drain a person."

"Tell me, then, who was that man who appeared at my door unannounced? He seemed audaciously crass in both appearance and demeanor, hardly someone I would expect you to associate with given your position."

Joseph considered brushing off the question but decided against it. "He happens to be the father of the young woman you so ardently suggest I marry," he said, surprising himself with his uncharacteristic transparency.

Anna choked on her tea, recovering after the initial shock had passed. "My God, no wonder you are reluctant to marry the girl."

"That girl, Tatiana, led me to believe her father was deceased. I only just discovered she not mean it in a literal sense."

Anna peered at Joseph, her gaze penetrating. "Does he know about your affair?"

Joseph feigned outrage, attempting to divert the conversation yet again. "You are utterly reprehensible, no wonder the Bolsheviks despise you."

Anna laughed, relishing the verbal sparring with a man she liked and respected more with each passing encounter. "I have reached a point in my life where I no longer give a damn about people's opinions or expectations. I live life on my own terms now."

Joseph's demeanor turned somber as he acknowledged the stark contrast in their situations. "I do not have the same luxury, Anna. I bear the responsibility of overseeing more than two thousand staff members and safeguarding millions of priceless artifacts. I fear the situation will only worsen as the fascist forces tighten their grip on our city. The Red Army, once formidable, now seems like a mere paper tiger."

"Then I need to know the whereabouts of my paintings. If anything were to happen to you or those who hold your confidences, I must be able to retrieve my portraits at some point."

"They are in the possession of a man named Franz Krüger in London," Joseph revealed. "In our city, nothing is safe anymore, regardless of who claims to possess it. Barbarism has taken hold."

Anna, surprised by the revelation that her cherished portraits were no longer in Russia, felt a tinge of panic. "And how will I locate this Franz Krüger when the time comes for me to be reunited with my paintings?"

"He is a partner at the Colnaghi gallery in London. However, I must caution you. Your portraits will likely endure a life akin to exile, forever separated from Russia. You may need to embark on a journey if want to ever see them again, and the sooner you do so, the better. You are not safe here, Anna. My brother informs me that there is growing support to arrest what remains of the Intelligentsia."

"There is only one remaining escape route out of the city, which leads eastward, not west. How do you suggest I make my way to London?"

"We both know of a man who possesses the uncanny ability to get things done. If you choose to leave now, he will find a way to get you out of the city and to London."

Anna drained the remainder of her tea pondering her next move. "Contact your one-armed man. I want to go to London."

16

THE PROPOSAL

Alongside his early morning walks through the Hermitage, Joseph Orbeli also treasured the evenings when he and Tatiana would choose to sneak out of the museum and wander through the darkened city. They would stroll along the expansive boulevards and beside the narrow canals, recounting the time of remarkable freedom under Tsarist rule. Joseph conceded to himself that only some things had been malevolent under Nicholas II. Indeed, life had deteriorated under the Bolshevik regime in almost every aspect. He found himself questioning how the citizenry of his esteemed nation could have allowed such a transition. 'We grow accustomed to the dark when light is put away,' he recalled a quote from a book in his father's library that he had read his youth. What had happened to that child's innocence and faith?

Joseph observed Tatiana's graceful silhouette cut through the night as they navigated the city's shadowed streets and arched bridges. Under the soft luminescence of an ascending moon, her raven-black hair moved with the gentle breeze, akin to dainty snowflakes. Despite her undeniable beauty, Joseph's heart was suffused with sorrow. He should have treated her as a priceless work of art, ensuring her safety in the East, along with the other masterpieces by da Vinci, Dawes, and Titian. Instead, Joseph had exposed her to the escalating nightmare of what promised to be an endless siege. Much like the imperial carriages reduced to ash by an enemy shell, he feared his inability to protect her.

When the Hermitage's evacuation plans were first formulated, Joseph tried to persuade Tatiana that staying was too dangerous, but she rejected all his arguments. Tatiana refused to renounce her duty. They both understood that she was the natural choice to co-lead those who remained behind in the Hermitage after Vladimir left with the art. But as their relationship had changed, their love intensified from a mere spark into a roaring flame. The thought of losing her was unbearable. Yet, the thought of marrying her stirred an equal measure of trepidation. He found himself trapped in the torment of these twin unendurable possibilities.

Joseph averted his gaze from Tatiana's eyes. Looking at her would only deepen his despair. Instead, his eyes fixated on the surrounding buildings, their boarded-up doorways and blackened windows serving as somber witnesses to his silent conversation with himself. Amidst the utilitarian decay, the ornate Church of Our Savior On Spilled Blood stood.

"Come with me," Tatiana said, as the distant murmurs of a roving patrol echoed from a nearby alley, seeking those who dared to defy the city's evening curfew. With a gentle grip, she led Joseph into the sanctuary of the former house of worship. The once-sacred church had somehow managed to survive the relentless assault on religion by the Bolsheviks, but it had remained closed for decades. "Sometimes, when I feel lost, I sneak in here. It is like my window to heaven," Tatiana confessed, her voice filled with reverence and longing.

It had been years since Joseph set foot in a holy place. Stepping into one now invited suspicion from party officials and their numerous spies. His eyes ascended, beholding the vaulted ceilings with rich murals adorning the church. A haloed saint, arms raised to heaven, stared down at him. If the unknown artists who labored in this space intended to evoke a sense of insignificance in the presence of the divine, they had succeeded, Joseph thought.

"Pray with me, Joseph," Tatiana whispered, kneeling on the mosaic floor and producing a wooden icon from her pocket.

Joseph joined her, unable to control his trembling legs. "I fear I have forgotten how to pray," he confessed. "It has been too long."

"Fear not, for the creator of the universe understands. Simply express what you feel in your heart," Tatiana reassured him.

"I am afraid, God," Joseph began after a moment of reflection upon the icon.

"As am I," Tatiana echoed.

"I have tried to remain strong, but I feel weakened and exhausted," Joseph continued. "I have endeavored to protect those who cannot protect themselves, but death looms over us all. Why do you persist in punishing our city? Why do you punish me?"

After a quiet minute without a response from the Almighty, Tatiana broke the silence. "To suffer and endure hardship is the curse of the Russian people."

"Then, for the first time in my life, I wish not to be Russian."

"Do not say that, Joseph. I know your family has endured more than their fair share of heartache, but you and your brothers have been beacons of light to so many in this time of darkness. You are our city's rock."

"Even a rock will sink when thrown into the deepest well of despair," Joseph sighed.

"Why did you and your brothers choose to stay after the overthrow of the Tsar?" Tatiana asked, knowing he dared not lie in this sacred place. "You could have gone anywhere. Your family's talents are immeasurable. Nations would have surely fought over you and your brothers. You could have led a rich and fulfilling life as exiles."

Joseph placed his hands on his head, exhaling as he tried to recall the decision-making process. "I remember there was a heated debate between Levon, Reuben, and myself after our father was killed during the purge. Once our anger had subsided, we decided to employ our vast individual talents to influence the revolution from within, as internal exiles. We believed we could help stabilize the turbulent forces tearing our homeland apart. How arrogant and foolish it all seems now."

"It is not arrogance, it is noble thinking, Joseph."

"The era of the Russian gentry and noble thinking has passed. We should be focused on our survival. Instead, I dare to curse you, leaving you in harm's way to save what amounts to nothing more than meaningless canvas and paint. I suppose I still value art more than life itself," Joseph confessed, his voice filled with self-doubt.

"You value what is right, And I choose to stay of my own free will."

"You only do it because I requested it as your employer."

"That's nonsense. I am not some kind of serf bound to the museum. I have no obligation to listen to anyone. You hold no dominion over my life." Tatiana gazed upwards at the Christ figure. "However, if I were your wife..."

"As my wife, you would be obligated to follow my wishes," Joseph reminded her of the traditional expectations.

"I will do whatever you ask of me, except abandon you or the art. I have loved you my entire life, Joseph, and I believe you love me too. If that is true, then marry me now, in this house of God."

"I do love you, but I am not worthy of you. Even if I desired to marry you tonight, the Bolsheviks have taken the lives of all the priests,"

"We do not need a priest, Joseph. We have each other in this sanctuary of the Holy Father. What more do we need, my love? Take me as your wife,"

Joseph's eyes wandered around the sanctuary, searching for divine guidance. He longed for a message from God to show him the way, but the only words he found were those of Alexander Pushkin, etched into the opposing wall. Joseph read the dead poet's words aloud:

'*But whom to love?*

To trust and treasure?

Who won't betray us in the end?

And who'll be kind enough to measure

Our words and deeds as we intend?'

"The answer is me, my love," Tatiana said her lips gently brushing against his beneath the heavenly windows. "I am your wife, and you are my husband, now and forever."

Joseph caressed Tatiana's flowing black hair. "You are like a daughter of the Ganges," he whispered into her ear. "Dark and exotic, with curves that any man would yearn to get lost in. I do love you with every fiber of my being, but I cannot marry you if you choose to stay behind in this city of the dying."

"But why?" she said, tears filling her eyes.

"You are young," he said, his voice heavy with resignation. "It's natural for you to think about marriage and, eventually, children. I lost my wife and our unborn daughter to unforeseen complications. I cannot face that kind of loss again."

"I am not your first wife, Joseph. That fate will not befall us."

"That outcome is beyond our control," Joseph said, raising his voice and pointing at the depiction of God's only son emblazoned on the dome overhead. "I will be damned if I leave it to His discretion."

Tatiana placed her hand over Joseph's pounding heart. She sensed the pain and guilt gnawing at his soul. "God resides in each of us, Joseph. To be at war with God is to be at war with yourself. If you can learn to love yourself and find a way to forgive yourself, you will begin to heal. As much as I wish I could, I cannot do it for you."

17

THE ROMANOV

JULY 1918 - TWENTY-THREE YEARS EARLIER

Alexei Nikolaevich, the last Tsesarevich and heir apparent to the throne of the Russian Empire, hobbled across his cramped and barren chamber, contemplating his fate. At only fourteen years of age, he was the youngest of the Tsar's children. Stricken with hemophilia, Alexei was also the least likely to live a long life. And yet, he was the sole survivor of his imperial family's slaughter.

Under Lenin's orders, the firing squad was initially meant to execute only his father, the Tsar. However, the local Bolshevik commanders feared the advancing White Army might liberate the remaining Romanovs and reinstate Tsarist rule. Therefore, the Captain of the guard made the impulsive decision to not only kill the Tsar, but also his wife and five children.

'Peace, Land, and Bread' was the Bolshevik mantra, but the revolution's aims had gone awry. Only a last-second moment of clarity had spared Alexei. However, the Bolsheviks were now at a loss about what to do with him—an eyewitness to the cold-blooded murder. In the end, they decided to hide him in the last place the White Army would think to look for him—the Winter Palace in Leningrad.

Alexei had been imprisoned in his bedroom chamber for the past month while the Bolshevik leaders pondered his fate. Encouraged by the woman who served him his meals, Alexei began documenting what had happened on the disastrous morning and since his return to Leningrad. Each entry was smuggled out by the same woman and preserved in the Chronicle for future generations to read. The truth had to be preserved at all costs while he was still alive.

'I heard my father crying behind the weighted doors of his private bedroom chamber. It had become a weekly ritual for me. He was once again mourning the loss of his younger brother. George was not supposed to die at such a young age, but the tuberculosis that festered in his lungs did him in. The grief was unspeakable. My father could not even utter George's name. He would only refer to him as my weeping willow.

As expected, the guttural sobs of the man I admired most turned to quiet laughter. The last Tsar of Russia was reading the ancient jokes again. "Your uncle was quite the buffoon," my father would tell me. He adored his brother's humor, writing down all of George's jokes on tiny scraps of paper when they were young. He would stash them out of sight in an ornate ebony box emblazoned with the majestic double-headed eagle seal —twenty-plus years of jokes laid to rest in their own coffin.

While I did not know it then, my Uncle George would spend more years walking the Earth than my four sisters or I. Our deaths would be so much more painful and less dignified. I remember hearing my father call out his brother's name one last time just before they shot him dead. The guards woke us up before dawn and told us we were being evacuated for our protection; the White Army was approaching. We were to wait in the basement for the trucks to arrive. My father tenderly carried me into the darkened room. I was far too weak with illness to walk on my own. Setting me down on a rickety wooden chair, he listened without emotion as a Bolshevik officer read the decree condemning us to death. The firing squad marched into the room, took aim, and shot my father in the chest a moment later. He turned to face us as he fell, his eyes conveying his deep love for each of us. It was the last thing he ever saw.

My sisters would not die so swiftly. They survived the initial volley of bullets. Gems and coins sewn into their clothing and hidden had initially shielded them from the onslaught. The soldiers hacked them to pieces with bayonets instead. During the chaos, I fell to the floor unharmed. Unable to walk or crawl due to the ill effects of my hemophilia, I lay there face-to-face with my sister Maria. She was still alive, but not for long. I remember the sound of screaming. Deafening shouts as the realization of what the soldiers *had just done began. Three centuries of Romanov rule ended in that cold basement. Despite the Bolshevik's exhaustive efforts to erase history, the truth survives in this chronicle. I pray someone will read it. - July 17, 1918'*

18

THE BOMB

STATE HERMITAGE - FIRST WINTER OF THE SIEGE

A low-frequency thump reverberated through the bunker sometime past midnight. Dim lights flickered, casting eerie shadows in the cavernous space while a fine-grained shower of silt descended from the arched, bricked-lined ceiling. It was another onslaught from the Luftwaffe, bombing the sleeping city. The night raids offered no respite for the already weary museum staff, their nerves frayed and exhausted.

Joseph Orbeli, his wiry beard coated in dust, gently rose from his cot and reached for his glasses, careful not to disturb the sleeping figures around him. His aging body, once robust and round, now bore the signs of his long-lived life, his protruding ribs a testament to the hardships endured. Despite longing for rest, Joseph knew he had to assess the damage caused by the raid and check in with the night watch. The threat of fire loomed as his greatest fear. Holes in the structure could be repaired, but a fire left unchecked would reduce the Winter Palace and the museum within it to smoldering ash within minutes.

As Joseph navigated the twisting black depths of the museum's subterranean levels, a lone rat scurried along an elevated steam pipe. Little Ivan and the other museum cats had vanished weeks ago, leaving the rat to roam without fear. Joseph missed his feline companions, but the scarcity of food had made cats a luxury the museum could ill afford. For now, they had to contend with disease-infested rodents, though Joseph feared that the city's citizens might resort to even more desperate measures as the blockade continued through the first winter of the siege.

Acrid smoke stung Joseph's nostrils as he entered the museum's Twenty Column Hall. The night watch was already in action, throwing sand on a smoldering carpet ignited by the bomb blast. Gold-plated windows lay blown out, and shrapnel peppered the opposite walls. Another near miss, Joseph thought to himself. Seizing the opportunity, he grabbed the nearest worker rushing past and inquired about the extent of the damage.

"Director, two bombs fell within the perimeter. One in the courtyard, just outside, and the second penetrated the roof above the hall," the worker reported, pointing to a gaping hole in the ceiling. "We are lucky the second bomb did not detonate."

Joseph gazed up at the pierced ceiling, imagining the catastrophe they had avoided. "We will need to remove the unexploded bomb as soon as possible once the fires are extinguished. Can you handle that?" he asked the worker.

The man looked up at the ceiling; dread etched on his face. Unexploded ordnance tended not to stay unexploded for long. Joseph understood the risks involved. He was also sure this worker would prefer this safer duty on the Hermitage's fire watch brigade rather than face the onslaught of the entire German 4th Panzer Group. "As you wish, Director."

Noticing the worker's emaciated appearance and evident fatigue, Joseph asked, "When was the last time you ate something?"

"Two...maybe three days ago," the man responded devoid of emotion.

Reaching into his coat pocket, Joseph retrieved a day's ration of bread and handed it to the worker. The hardened black bread was nearly inedible, its ingredients consisting of sawdust and putrid admixtures, but the worker welcomed anything that could fill his empty stomach. The meager daily ration of bread kept them alive, but barely so. The fascists' genocidal plan to starve the city's inhabitants was proving to be effective.

Joseph studied the worker's face in the darkened hall. "You look familiar. Do I know you?"

"I met you once before Director, under much different circumstances. We were drinking champagne and toasting the success of my opera."

"My God...it is you...the composer," Joseph said, his eyes widening with recognition. "I never thought the party officials would let you stay in Leningrad."

"I am not very popular anymore," Dmitri Shostakovich admitted, his smile forced and weary. "I believe only our fascist invaders are below me on the list of enemies of the state."

Joseph remembered the rumors about Stalin's disapproval of the composer's *Lady Macbeth* opera. "I heard stories that Stalin hated your composition, but he is no theater critic. That opera was wildly popular throughout Europe. What happened?"

"I believe my early work was too radical for the new Soviet state," Dmitri said with a touch of resignation. "It did not reinforce the Bolsheviks' propaganda. I keep waiting for them to come and take me away. I sleep on the landing of my apartment. I do not want to wake my wife and children when the time comes."

"Staying in Leningrad might as well be a death sentence anyway. I feel it is much worse than being sent to Siberia," Joseph said, attempting to lighten his somber mood. "Are you still writing?"

Dmitri nodded, his expression filled with both determination and weariness. "Can you keep a secret? I started writing a more state-friendly symphony. It has bought me a little more time. I believe what I am composing will be my greatest achievement yet. It is called 'Leningrad', and it personifies the spirit of the city while faintly hiding my disgust at the absurdity of the Soviet cause."

"Is it complete? I would love to hear it."

"Not quite, but it's close to being done if this bomb does not kill me first."

Returning to the punctured ceiling, Joseph watched in amazement as a stray sheet of paper floated delicately downward from the jagged hole above, resembling the first stray snowflake of an advancing storm. He picked it up, studying the yellowed page. Though tired and sleep-deprived, Joseph immediately recognized what he held in his hands - another Homeric artifact. Excitement coursed through his veins as he contemplated his next steps.

"On second thought," Joseph said. "Let us leave the fascists' bomb where it lies. I will have a munitions expert from the Kirov Works come by in the morning and remove it."

Dmitri breathed a sigh of relief. "My wife and children will thank you."

"Finish the Leningrad Symphony so we can all hear it, including the fascists. They need to know we are still here and are not going anywhere," Joseph urged. "And I am reassigning you to a teaching role at the Hermitage. It aligns better with your skill set, is far less dangerous, and it may aid your musical productivity. Now, go home to your family."

Dmitri shook Joseph's hand with more excitement and vigor than he been able to muster in weeks before dashing into the still-dark streets. Meanwhile, Joseph folded the timeworn page with care and nestled it into his coat pocket, his mind grappling with doubt. Could the tales be authentic? Did these chronicles – these Homeric artifacts as Reuben had dubbed them, verses conveying the true history of the Russian people – really exist? Could they be ensconced within the Winter Palace's walls, undetected under the oblivious gazes of the now-deceased Romanovs? Joseph considered the magnitude of such a discovery, trying to temper his rising anticipation. He felt sure the answers he craved lay somewhere beyond the breach in the ceiling. The remaining question was whether his destiny would draw him upward or pull him downward into the chasm.

⚘⚘⚘ ⚘⚘⚘

The next day, Dmitri Shostakovich returned to the Hermitage, his wife at his side and their arms laden with as many instruments as they could bear. No detailed plan, timetable, or even a designated teaching space was available, yet Joseph admired the composer's unfettered enthusiasm.

"I would prefer a hundred Dmitri Shostakovich's over a single Leo Tolstoy," Joseph said to his long-time confidante, Sophia. "Enthusiasm has been a scarce commodity around here."

"Did you express that sentiment in front of the department heads? With Tatiana present?" Sophia asked. "You do remember that Leo Tolstoy was Tatiana's grandfather, do you not?" This information explained Tatiana's recent cold demeanor toward him, Joseph thought.

Dmitri was a globally recognized composer and an exceptional music teacher—a rare combination of talents. What astonished Joseph even more was hearing Nina Shostakovich's angelic voice for the first time; she had been a world-class soprano during the zenith of the couple's fame. In recognition of their remarkable contributions, Joseph gave them two additional daily ration cards. This relieved some of Nina's concerns about her family's survival, though it merely postponed what she feared would be their inevitable downfall—succumbing to illness or starvation.

19

THE VERSEMAKER

In the depths of the first winter of the German blockade, the citizens of Leningrad began to freeze. Daily temperatures that hovered around -4 degrees Fahrenheit plummeted cruelly at night to 40 below. The unrelenting Arctic blast caused the city's electricity and water systems to fail, along with its vital transportation network. People burned anything they could find in a desperate attempt to stay warm. Thousands succumbed to the elements during this grim season of darkness, yet a glimmer of hope persisted in the form of a chronicle stashed away within the Hermitage.

Sophia's eyes narrowed in the flickering candlelight as she wrapped herself in another quilt. "Tell me again, Joseph, how did you come across such intriguing information?"

"As you know, for well over three hundred years, an esteemed scribe has held a distinguished position in the Tsar's Court, entrusted with the solemn task of documenting the decrees, laws, and treaties that shaped the reign of the Tsars," Joseph said with growing excitement. "Concurrently, an enduring rumor has permeated the dark corridors—a whispered legend of an elusive chronicler, a shadowy figure who without detection observed and chronicled the Tsar's unofficial engagements, interactions, indiscretions, and fleeting moments of madness. These covert entries were recorded in secret and submitted to an enigmatic chronicle. Until this moment, the existence of this fabled record and the true identities of its Versemakers have remained shrouded in mystery."

"Continue," Sophia said as she closed her eyes.

"Just two weeks ago, as the fascist bombers unleashed their instruments of terror near the Winter Palace. One of the bombs breached the palace roof, penetrating the ancient structure and revealing the sealed off attic spaces that once housed the palace servants and staff. Yet, by some miraculous twist of fate, the bomb failed to detonate, leaving behind a gaping hole in the ceiling of the Twenty-Column Hall."

Sophia coughed, releasing a puff of steaming breath that lingered above her head. "Are you suggesting that you alone stumbled upon tangible evidence within the palace's sprawling attic spaces, substantiating the existence of this secretive chronicle?"

Joseph paused, aware of the doubt in Sophia's voice. "In truth, the initial discovery of the hole and the unexploded bomb was credited to the nightly fire watch, a man who's name we both know well—Dmitri Shostakovich. Destiny seemed to have favored him that fateful night."

Joseph recounted the encounter in the Twenty-Column Hall—the night he stumbled upon the renowned composer moonlighting as the night watchman. He reminisced about his offer to dispose of the bomb, relieving Shostakovich from the perilous hazards that could have ended his life.

Sophia's gaze sharpened as she connected the dots. "So, the aged leaf of yellowed paper that fell through the ceiling's cavity compelled you to believe that the rumors were indeed true. You sent Shostakovich home and then found a way to ascend into the attic space, confirming your suspicions."

A smile flickered on Joseph's face. "You will never guess what I discovered up there," he said, pointing towards the ceiling.

Sophia's voice grew hushed, her words leaving Joseph dumbfounded. "A windowless, amber-paneled study adorned with an imposing wooden-carved desk, bearing the resplendent emblem of Catherine the Great's dynasty—a double-headed eagle."

Joseph stood in stunned silence, his jaw agape. How could Sophia possess such intricate knowledge and speak with such unwavering certainty? A cascade of thoughts swirled in Joseph's mind, contemplating the depths of her hidden secrets that eluded even the Director of the State Hermitage. "That is no mere lucky guess," he managed to say. "Enlighten me, Sophia. What other knowledge do you possess that you have withheld from me?"

"And have you not harbored your share of secrets from me?" Sophia's voice resonated with feigned hurt. "We are both aware that you have undertaken questionable actions to safeguard the art and ensure provisions for your staff. I, too, have been your co-conspirator in some of these endeavors."

Joseph's eyes widened. He recognized the truth in her accusations.

"It is high time you engage in a conversation with the current caretaker of the records to uncover the complete truth behind the Chronicle," Sophia said, breaking the uneasy silence between them. "After all, they work in your very own museum, Director."

Joseph's pulse quickened at the weight of Sophia's declaration. The reality behind the Chronicle— an issue he had sidestepped for far too long—loomed before him. He understood the urgency of facing the situation head on, uprooting the secrets long buried within the museum's walls.

Joseph accepted Sophia's proposition. The enormity of the task dwarfed him, and he found reassurance in her support. Together, they would navigate their way to the custodian of records, prepared to unfurl the concealed truths of the ancient Chronicle.

Sophia's stunning revelation about the Versemaker, a grandchild of Alexander Pushkin, working in the museum hung in the air like a descending firework, igniting a sense of urgency within Joseph. The knowledge that someone on his staff held insights into the enigmatic Chronicle and could shed light on its mysteries propelled him to action. The prospect of uncovering long-awaited answers within the very walls of the museum stirred a potent mix of curiosity and apprehension within him.

The following day, as instructed, Joseph inhaled a deep steadying breath before he stepped into the Malachite Room of the Winter Palace; unsure of what awaited him. The room boasted an extravagant display of decorative gold leaf and majestic green columns, evoking a feeling of grandeur that never failed in the past to captivate visiting European dignitaries. Even Joseph could not help but be awestruck each time he passed through. As he entered, his gaze fell upon a woman standing near the fireplace; her back turned to him. A gilded mirror above the mantle reflected her face.

"You???" Joseph said, a mixture of surprise and realization coloring his words. "A grand-daughter of Pushkin? Impossible, I have known you since childhood. Pushkin's granddaughter was named Sophie of Merenberg. She died years ago. You are two separate people."

"You remain oblivious to your own ignorance," Sophia rebuked him. "How long will you persist in believing the Bolsheviks' narrative of truth and falsehood? The Chronicle exists because the truth must exist. I am Sophie of Merenberg, I am the guardian of the Chronicle, and the 29th Versemaker."

Joseph ruminated on her words, striving to separate fact from fabrication. The hints had been present, but he had stubbornly ignored them. "Is it truly you who has been cataloging and safeguarding these records all these years?"

Sophia answered Joseph's question, detailing her path to becoming a chronicler. "As my grandfather became engrossed in his literary work, my grandmother, Natalia, assumed the role of chronicler, and then others took on the task. Alexander Pushkin's responsibilities as a husband, father, and rising literary star made it increasingly difficult for him to observe the royal court without drawing undue attention. On the other hand, my grandmother and later my mother remained as inconspicuous as ghosts, much like my unnoticed presence now and my actions veiled in secrecy. The mantle passed to me after my mother unveiled her secret before her death in 1913."

"Four years before the revolution," Joseph noted.

Sophia continued, reflecting on her unique position, "Aristocrats, magistrates, and even museum directors engaged in their discussions and deliberations in my presence, unaware of my role as an observer. They indulged in open gossip and even voiced their criticisms of the Tsar and then the Bolsheviks, creating an environment that made it effortless for me to capture the essence of those moments in my journal entries. I simply had to be present in the room, absorbing the conversations like a silent witness."

Joseph interjected, "But as the revolution unfolded, I suppose being a mere impassive observer became more difficult for you. The time came when one had to take a stand, choose a side."

Sophia's voice carried a hint of remorse as she responded. "It was a challenging task to reconcile my deep disdain for the Tsar and his oppressive policies with the tenderness he displayed towards his children. I often wished he had been offered exile in France, England, or Spain, sparing the children from the horrors that awaited them."

"Now, we find ourselves entangled in a shared predicament," Joseph said. "If the fascists seize our city, they will undoubtedly find and exploit the art and the Chronicle as propaganda, before consigning them to the personal collection of Herman Goering or someone even more nefarious. Yet, the stakes become even more dire if the Bolsheviks were to uncover our joint subterfuge."

"And then there's Tatiana," Sophia added. "She holds a special place in both our hearts, and ironically, she is the one person capable of safeguarding both the art and the Chronicle should we both leave St. Petersburg. Yet, we are torn, wanting to keep her out of harm's way."

A look of confusion crossed Joseph's face. "What...why would we even contemplate leaving the city?"

"I am dying, Joseph. I will not live to see the end of this siege. Therefore, securing a successor is now a necessity. You, being one of my most trusted confidantes and a fellow conspirator, are the natural choice. In addition, there are rumors of a plan to evacuate the leaders of Leningrad's cultural centers."

"How could you possibly know this?"

"I am a ghost," she whispered, "I see and hear everything."

"It appears we are caught between the hammer and the anvil, with no easy choice in sight. Which devil shall we choose, Sophia?"

"I know you have already struck a deal with the devil once. It shouldn't be hard a second time."

"I had no other option. As the director, I bear the weight of responsibility for so many souls, including yours. I could not sit back and watch them wither away, succumbing to hunger and death, when there was a means to provide food for them."

"The ends do not always justify the means," Sophia said. "The Bolsheviks serve as testament to that old adage."

Joseph exhaled in frustration. "I have always prioritized the needs of others over my own personal happiness. Whether it is right or wrong, it needed to be done."

"That is why you will make the perfect guardian and keeper of the Chronicle."

"You are asking the impossible, Sophia. I cannot realistically do more than I am already doing. I cannot risk more. I am already sticking my neck out to save the art."

"Then I will ask Tatiana to accept this challenge, along with all the risks it carries."

Joseph shook his head at the proposition. It was another impossible scenario, reminiscent of the challenges his father used to present him with during his childhood. He longed for his brother Levon's wise counsel in such dire times.

Sophia reached out and grasped Joseph's hand; her grip was surprisingly firm for someone so frail. Though old and tired, her eyes still held a fierceness. "I understand that this is an enormous task that I am asking of you but the Chronicle must not be allowed to die with me. It is too important. It is too valuable. It is our legacy. Do you understand that, Joseph?"

Joseph had always known the importance of the Chronicle. It was a book that contained the truth of their people and the stories of their ancestors; knowledge that would help them survive both the current siege taking place outside their walls and the political repression happening within.

"You have a gift, Joseph. You can tell stories and inspire others. You have the courage and the strength to protect the Chronicle, to keep it safe as the Versemaker.

"There must be others more suitable than I," Joseph countered. "I am no wordsmith. Why not consider Akhmatova or her protégé? They possess the requisite skills for the Versemaker. Their words resonate, brimming with more sentiment than I could ever summon."

Sophia's grip around Joseph's hand grew tighter. "But they lack your heart, Joseph. True, they wield passion and vigor, but they are missing the impartiality and crucially, the accessibility required to scrutinize the Bolsheviks. They are considered persona non grata in the eyes of Zhdanov and Stalin. You are the only one I confide in to undertake this task. You alone can carry on our legacy and keep our authentic history alive."

Joseph was rendered speechless. The implications of Sophia's words and the enormity of the responsibility they carried were overwhelming. He had never considered himself a writer or a chronicler of their people's history. He was a connoisseur of art, an efficient administrator, and when needed an ordinary forger. But as he met Sophia's gaze, he recognized that this was his obligation. This was his purpose.

"All right, I will do it. I will safeguard the Chronicle and ensure the truth endures."

Sophia's eyes twinkled with something resembling pride as she squeezed his hand even harder. "I knew you would recognize the magnitude of this mission." Releasing his hand, she eased back into her chair, exhaling a satisfied sigh. "Now, I must rest. I am not as spry as I once was."

Joseph lingered for a moment, a surge of sorrow sweeping over him at the prospect of losing her. Sophia had been a fixture in his life, a source of friendship and wisdom, similar to an older sister. But with the siege grinding their city into capitulation and the future of their people uncertain, he could not afford to indulge his emotions.

Exiting the Malachite Room, Joseph's mind teemed with strategies. He needed to secure the covert location of the Chronicle and begin crafting his entries, ensuring the book would always be recovered and preserved. He now understood the ruthless nature of the Bolsheviks and their relentless pursuit of the one known as the Versemaker. However, Joseph was resolved to preserve the Russian people's history and relay their tales and trials to generations yet unborn. Lost in thought, he navigated the deserted galleries and corridors of the Hermitage. Rounding one endless corner after another until he came face-to-face with his brother Levon. He had been Joseph's confidante, mentor, and dearest ally as children. But with time, their paths had split. Levon had become a Red Army officer, while Joseph adopted more diplomatic roles within the local universities and museums.

As they confronted each other, Joseph experienced a wave of relief. Levon was someone he trusted, and his help would be invaluable in safeguarding the Chronicle. With urgency, he recounted the situation to Levon in hushed tones.

Levon paid careful attention while his expression remained serious. "This is a tremendous responsibility, Joseph, but I stand by you. I will help you safeguard the Chronicle."

Hearing his brother's affirmation, Joseph felt a weight lift off his shoulders. Their paths might have diverged, but they remained family, prepared to always support one another.

"Tell me, did Sophia reveal the Chronicle's current hiding place?"

His brother's question stirred an unfamiliar mix of emotions within Joseph—between fear and paranoia. He trusted his brother, but the sight of Levon donned in his Red Army military uniform gave him pause. For the first time in his life, Joseph deceived his brother. "No, she is not well and requires bed rest. When she is able, she will guide me to the Chronicle."

"And if she does not survive long enough for that? How will you locate it then?"

"As the new Versemaker, I am confident that the Chronicle will somehow find its way to me."

20

THE VOICE OF LENINGRAD

LENINGRAD - FIRST WINTER OF THE SIEGE

Olga Bergholz moved with grace through the cramped hallways of the Leningrad Radio Committee building, her presence akin to a warming sunrise dashing away the chill of a cruel night. Her arrival at 'Radio House' in a city marred by growing hardships was a beacon of light. Despite enduring a litany of heart-wrenching tragedies and battling deteriorating health, Olga emanated a rare and infectious positivity that touched the lives of all she encountered.

At the same time, Olga questioned why she had been chosen for this task. Her friend and mentor, Anna Akhmatova, was undeniably more qualified, talented, and better equipped to uplift the hearts and minds of a dying city. However, Olga understood that Anna's fraught history with the Bolsheviks rendered it impossible for her to assume this role. As a result, the responsibility of conducting the daily broadcasts fell to Olga.

The effects of her declining health were evident as a deathlike pallor related to jaundice settled upon her face. Having endured the painful loss of two husbands to the Purge and the anguish of giving birth to a stillborn child on a cold, unforgiving interrogation room floor, Olga's resilience was nothing short of remarkable.

In the face of immeasurable grief, Olga found unwavering determination to wield the power of her poetry, unafraid of the tightening grip of censorship. She saw it as her duty to use her words to unveil the truth and to fortify her beloved city against the relentless onslaught of the fascist siege.

Amidst a city suffocating under the weight of death, despair hung heavy in the air. Food shortages had morphed into a merciless predator, descending upon the vulnerable populace. The sick and elderly, forsaken by their meager ration cards, were the first to die. With winter's icy grip tightening, thousands more faced a bleak fate unless a lifeline of supplies could breach the relentless blockade.

Stepping into the silent confines of the broadcast studio, Olga's hands trembled as she clutched the notes that would shape her upcoming transmission. The war with Germany had given her a chance to resurrect her poet's voice, albeit within the confines of state-mandated propaganda. Her loyalty to the Soviet regime had long faded, extinguished by the relentless brutality of the secret police. Tonight, Olga stood not for the ideals of Communism but for the besieged city and its resilient citizens who clung to flickering embers of hope.

Olga's gaze fixed upon the clock, its steady rhythm marking the approach of five o'clock. The monotonous click of the metronome, a constant companion across the airwaves for twenty-three hours a day, would soon yield to Olga's voice. She swallowed the staleness of the studio air, and her throat cleared in anticipation. Three, two, one.

"Leningrad, under the cloak of darkness, I stand before you," Olga's voice, weakened but resolute, echoed through the airwaves. "I am Olga Bergholz, and this is The Voice of Leningrad, a testament to the indomitable spirit that courses through our veins. Let it be known tonight, amidst the chaos and the invaders' relentless siege, that I am alive. Our city's heart still beats, defiant in the face of adversity. Life, against all odds, persists within our war-torn streets. We shall never be conquered."

With a deep breath, Olga steadied herself, her voice quivering with determination. "Tonight, I bring forth a poem, born from the depths of my own experiences. Just a week ago, I embarked on a treacherous journey from the heart of our city to the Nevsky Gate, seeking solace at my father's side. Along the way, I bore witness to the harrowing sight of a lone woman, her sled burdened with the frozen body of her mother. In this desolate landscape, such scenes have become all too familiar, a haunting symbol of our city's starvation. It is this encounter that fuels the verses of my poem."

With the weight of those tragic moments upon her shoulders, Olga took a deep breath, ready to unleash the power of her words, piercing the darkness that enveloped their beloved Leningrad.

'I walk to the house of my Father

And do not wipe away the tears.

It was hard to raise my hands.

An icy crust hardened on my swollen face.

Made it difficult to walk between the snowdrifts:

You stumble, barely able to drag yourself along.

You meet a coffin and can't get past it.

You clench your teeth - and step over it.

My friend, I, like you,

have met a hundred souls crawling over the snow.

I, like you, have stepped over coffins

May the memory of such steps live forever.

May the memory live forever in silent glory,

The easy luminous journey

Those who then could step over

A coffin - have a right to life.'

"These words, my dear listeners, reside not within the confines of my journal or the fragments of paper that have long vanished into ashes. The scarce remnants of paper have been sacrificed to fuel the flames of survival, leaving only the indelible inscriptions etched upon the margins of my heart. These eternally imprinted words are a beacon of remembrance, a testament to our resilience. Let them kindle the embers within your souls, igniting flames that shall never be extinguished. We are the people of Leningrad, and our spirit shall not yield to the encroaching darkness of the winter night."

As the echo of Olga's voice dissipated, swallowed by silence, the haunting drone of the metronome reemerged. Its relentless 'tic-tic-tic' reverberated through the city, a steadfast companion to the lonely and the desolate, staunchly guarding against the encroachment of hopelessness until the next day's broadcast.

Olga's trembling hands wrestled with a solitary cigarette, a feeble source of relief in her desolate existence. Her numbed, yellowed fingers struggled to grasp the match, eventually coaxing a flicker of flame that ignited the tip, granting her a momentary respite from the oppressive reality. Though she had already exhausted her daily allowance, she could not deny herself this fleeting pleasure, fearing the day when her one true vice would be no more. In a world plagued by scarcity, Olga's concerns extended far beyond her dwindling supply of cigarettes. *How much longer can we bear this burden?* She asked herself.

Drawing a worn square of fabric from her pocket, Olga embarked on her familiar writing ritual. The words poured forth with an urgency born of desperation, yet her handwriting, a testament to the weariness etched into her very being, proved challenging to decipher. Yet, she persisted, for clarity of script had long ceased to hold significance in her world of enduring hardship.

'Fascists bury deep.

Seeds of rebirth in us all.

Come spring we will Bloom.'

21

THE TOURIST

On the cusp of spring, Anna Akhmatova located the Colnaghi art gallery in London's St James neighborhood with ease. Standing across the street from the unremarkable gallery, its entrance partially boarded up, she attempted to steady her nerves. This should have been the most straightforward step in her challenging journey out of Leningrad via the Gulf of Finland. However, as Anna felt her heart racing, she braced for the long-awaited reunion with her cherished portraits.

The gentle chime of a bell signaled Anna's arrival as she entered the once majestic building. Glancing around, she was taken aback and puzzled by the absence of paintings adorning the shop's walls. Doubts crept into her mind—had she made a mistake? But her uncertainty dissipated when a man, younger than herself, approached her with a welcoming smile. "Ms. Akhmatova?" he asked, his words in German-accented Russian, catching her off-guard.

Hesitant and with caution Anna answered, "Yes, and you are?"

"Franz Krüger," he said in a gentlemanly manner, taking her hand and planting a delicate kiss upon it. "Welcome to my gallery." Anna glanced again at the vacant walls, perplexed by the notion of calling this place a gallery. "Ah, I can see that the state of our shop has left you puzzled. Allow me to explain, due to the ongoing bombings by my misguided former countrymen, we have been compelled to temporarily relocate our collection to the subterranean floors."

"You are German, and the English authorities allow you to operate a shop during a time of global conflict?"

"Half German, to be exact," Krüger corrected her, his voice conveying vulnerability and defiance. "My mother was English, which posed quite a conundrum for me. The current political climate in the Fatherland is far from friendly towards those of mixed bloodlines, making it impractical for me to remain there. I decided to leave shortly after..." He paused, his words lingering in the air, unsure how much he should reveal to his esteemed guest.

"Shortly after you met Joseph Orbeli?" Anna said, her perceptive gaze fixed on Krüger. His smile confirmed that she had indeed hit the mark.

"Something along those lines," he replied coyly, his eyes gleaming with shared understanding. "The vast majority of my clientele comprises English and Americans, so it felt like a natural evolution for me to establish my residency in England. At least here, the politicians offer some form of compensation for their acts of thievery."

"In Russia, they simply lay claim to everything and execute anyone who dares to voice their dissent," Anna said, her tone filled with the weight of bitter experience.

"That is precisely why I assumed your portraits needed a new home," Krüger added, his voice tinged with sympathy and determination. "I have found many deserving and secure homes for the Hermitage strays. Though they may live in exile, they will, at the very least, continue to exist and be cherished."

Anna set her jaw and said with defiance, "My portraits do not require new homes. They simply needed a safe refuge to endure the ravages of war until the day comes when they can be reunited with me."

Krüger's expression turned cautious as he began questioning Anna's sanity. "And...that is the reason for your presence here today? You believe it is now safe to repatriate your paintings?"

A frown deepened on Anna's face as conflicting emotions tugged at her heart. "I am a realist, Mr. Krüger. I have little faith that my paintings will ever find safety on Russian soil again unless the Bolsheviks are toppled from power and the reign of the Red Tsar comes to a permanent end."

Krüger pondered the unlikelihood of that scenario ever happening within their lifetimes. "So, you have come to visit your children," he said gently, acknowledging the deep bond Anna had formed with her artistic creations.

Anna's impatience seeped through as she sought a resolution. "In truth, I have come to bid them farewell. May I see them?"

"Of course," he said, gesturing with his arm as he guided Anna down a winding staircase to the gallery below.

As they traversed the corridor, Anna peered into petite alcoves that lined the hallway. Near the end of the passage, they turned right and entered a spacious showroom that held not only her thirty paintings but more of her Amedeo's creations.

"You have chosen to display my portraits?" Anna said with a curiosity bordering on annoyance. "These hold great personal significance and are private."

"Please accept my apologies, but I find them truly extraordinary," Krüger confessed. "I must express my gratitude to you for introducing me to Amedeo Modigliani. While my expertise and my client's interests primarily lie with the Renaissance masters, I could not help but appreciate these more contemporary works."

Anna's gaze narrowed as she focused on the additional paintings and statues that adorned the gallery that were not her possessions. "It seems you have been quite busy acquiring more of Amedeo's pieces beyond my portraits."

"Yes," he admitted sheepishly, "you would be surprised at how reasonably priced his works are, given that he remains relatively unknown to high-end collectors. I have no doubt they will appreciate considerably once the war has ended."

"And undoubtedly, you will reap a handsome profit as well," Anna said, tracing the contours of an oversized white marble bust belonging to her deceased lover.

"A man must make a living, my dear."

"Ah, ever the capitalist," Anna observed.

"The world will cease long before capitalism does," Krüger lamented. "Marxism has no future, and as you have witnessed firsthand, Ms. Akhmatova, it seeks to obliterate the past." Krüger paused as a new idea began to percolate in his mind. "Why not...remain in London and forge a new life here through your portraits? Pen new poems, ignite a fresh generation of dreamers, and preserve the memories of the past for those who can no longer recall them. The Russia you once knew is deceased, and you cannot revive it."

"Do you believe that I and others like Joseph Orbeli, Dmitri Shostakovich, and my beloved Osip Mandelstam never pondered leaving Russia after the revolution devolved into corruption?" she said, her voice filled with anguish. "We did consider it, and perhaps in the beginning, when we still had a chance, we should have departed. It exacted a great toll from all of us—Orbeli lost his father's life, Mandelstam lost his own."

"But you are alive, Anna," Krüger dared to use her first name, "And you possess the power to reclaim what was taken from you. Why do you maintain blind loyalty to a nation that no longer reciprocates that loyalty? I abandoned my own country when it ceased being German and transformed into a chaotic sea of brown shirts and mindless Sieg Heil salutes. Russia no longer exists," he reminded her.

"Don't you think I am aware of this?" Anna said, her heart heavy with pain. "I lead the life of a vagabond because there are millions who lack the same opportunity to leave, given my fame. I am compelled to chronicle the terror of the Bolsheviks through my poetry because words are older than any state, and my words will serve as a requiem for all those lost. One hundred million voices shout through my tormented mouth, Franz, I don't need anymore."

Her words enraptured Krüger. He longed to possess her like all the precious paintings gracing his gallery walls. Anna was exquisite yet venomous, and Krüger trembled with uncontrollable emotion. Eventually, he managed to say, "Please have dinner with me tonight. There is much we have to discuss."

Anna Akhmatova and Franz Krüger sat ensconced in the warm glow of a corner booth, a crisp white tablecloth before them. It bore the weight of a decadent spread—from a bottle of fine French wine to the evening's exquisite seafood cuisine.

Silverware clinked against fine china, a soft melody faintly perceptible amid the low hum of hushed conversation and muted laughter that filled Wilton's—London's oldest and most exclusive restaurant. A kaleidoscope of light cast from the wall sconces reflected off the mahogany-panels separating the plush, green velour booths, casting an intimate light on the patrons. Outside, the city braced itself for another potential air raid, but within these culinary sanctuary walls, life carried on with a defiance that felt quintessentially British.

"Considering the surroundings," Anna mused, taking in the opulence, "it is almost hard to believe there is a war going on. The sacrifices the English speak of in their radio broadcasts seem to pale in comparison to the realities in St. Petersburg."

"The British RAF has lost thousands of pilots while repelling my former countrymen, Anna," Krüger countered, his tone serious. "Their life expectancy is less than four weeks—roughly the lifespan of a gnat. I would consider that a significant sacrifice."

"Franz," Anna began, her gaze firm and her voice steady, "In this world where nations divide and humanity loses its essence, art and verse are our only refuge. It is the bearer of our shared history and the only testament of a world that once was."

Krüger nodded, recognizing the truth she spoke. He took a sip from his wine glass, the pale, straw-colored liquid shimmering in the candlelight. "And that is why, Anna, we have an immense responsibility to protect it," he said, his tone serious, "And I do not just mean from physical damage or theft. We need to protect it from being forgotten, from being misused."

Among the elegance and sophistication of a London high society, a poet from St. Petersburg and a half-German art dealer discussed the future of art and culture in a world that seemed determined to destroy its past. Heavy with the burden of responsibility, their words echoed in the restaurant, a clandestine vow to safeguard history and humanity's shared legacy.

"Good God, it's Franz!" A voice, clearly steeped in an evening of libations, bellowed across the room.

Turning at the sound, Krüger recognized Olaf Hambro, chairman of Hambros Bank and one of his most ardent collectors. "Nice to see you, Olaf," he said, rising to his feet and grasping the meaty hand extended towards him. "May I introduce..."

"It's her!" Olaf interrupted, his eyes widening in surprise. "The angel immortalized on canvas. It is you, is it not?"

Caught off guard, Anna looked to Krüger, seeking an explanation for the man's cryptic outburst.

"Olaf, please," Krüger appealed half amused. "You must be hallucinating again. If you do not lower your voice, I am afraid you will be shown the door of this venerable establishment."

"I purchased this 'venerable establishment' last week, so I will behave as I damn well please," Olaf said with a laugh.

"Surely you jest," Krüger said, glancing at Anna and indicating with a knowing look that the man had likely imbibed more than was advisable.

"It is the absolute truth," Olaf insisted. "I was enjoying my roast beef last week when Jerry decided to attempt to blow me to oblivion by dropping a bomb on the nearby street. By some stroke of divine luck, I was not killed. I was so thrilled by my good fortune that I asked the waiter to add the entire restaurant to my bill. So, I bought the whole kit and caboodle."

Anna had a hard time fathoming the larger-than-life figure of the rotund man standing before her, but she politely acquiesced to the banker's attempt at gallantry and allowed him to kiss her hand. "It is a pleasure to meet you," she said coolly. "I am Anna Akhmatova."

"Russian?" Olaf acknowledged warmly, winking at Krüger. "Who would have thought a Russian, a German, and an Englishman would dine with such civility during these grim days. Regardless, tonight, your meal is on the house. I apologize for my intrusion," he concluded with gentlemanly grace. "I will call on you next week, Franz, and I will not take 'no' for an answer. I want all of the Modigliani's," Olaf declared, his eyes stealing another glance at Anna as a puzzling expression crossed his face.

"Who was that man, and why was he regarding me as if I were a piece of meat on his plate?" Anna asked once Olaf had wandered off to claim another bottle of champagne.

"He is a client with eclectic tastes. When he last visited the gallery, he saw your portraits and was instantly captivated by your..." Krüger hesitated.

"Nudes?" Anna supplied the word.

"I was going to say 'backside,' but 'nudes' would work too," Krüger laughed, a smile playing on his lips as he contemplated the peculiar situation he found himself in. "He does not know you are Amedeo's muse."

"The devil he doesn't," Anna said. "But it matters little. I will be gone and my portraits will be tucked away somewhere more private before he can make an offer you cannot refuse."

"You and your portraits cannot return to a city under siege," Franz reminded her. "You must take shelter here in London or perhaps even in America for the rest of the war. You can return to your homeland once the Allies triumph."

"There will be no triumph, and nothing will remain of St Petersburg or its people unless the Allies establish a second front," Anna said. "Despite all respect due to the RAF, it is Russian blood that is fueling this war and combating fascists while the Americans and the English hide behind a protective channel and a vast ocean."

"Then, perhaps, you should consider using your fame and your words to influence public opinion," Krüger suggested, grasping her hands and peering deeply into her eyes. "Anna, you possess an extraordinary talent to encapsulate the essence of any situation. Your words have a greater impact than bombs. Use them strategically to convey the urgency of immediate action."

Anna considered Krüger's proposition. Could she, with words alone, be strong enough to open a second front? "As they say in England," Krüger went on, "'the pen is mightier than the sword.'"

"Do you know what is ironic?" Anna said after some additional contemplation. "It is only at this very moment that I truly comprehend the words of my esteemed compatriot and fellow writer, Dostoyevsky, when he said, 'The best way to prevent a prisoner from escaping is to ensure he never realizes he is in prison.' We are all prisoners in the Soviet Union, and Stalin is our jailer."

"So, liberate them with your words, Anna. Illuminate their plight with your poetry. Take to the airwaves on the BBC and banish the demons besieging your city, as well as those already entrenched within," Krüger implored.

"To do that would be tantamount to signing my death warrant, as well as those of my many friends striving for change within Russia. There are exiles both internal and external. I cannot bear the thought of finding safety on the outside, while so many of my compatriots continue to endure hardships within. Doing so would make me a coward."

"No, you are a sane individual who recognizes the truth," countered Krüger. "Remain here in London and battle with your words. Embody the woman I see in Amedeo's portraits - uninhibited and free, with the confidence to bring down the sociopath steering your nation towards destruction. You can vanquish him."

Anna's mind wandered to an Old Russian adage: 'Do not dig a hole for someone else, or you will fall into it yourself.' Raising her wine glass, Anna offered a 'Last Toast.'

'I'm drinking to a ruined home,

And to my life in hell,

To us together, yet alone,

And to you too, as well, —

To lies of lips, betraying love,

That ice-cold deathly stare,

The world, so merciless and rough,

And God, who wasn't there.'

London's Claridge's Hotel, stationed at 51 Brook Street, was an architectural jewel of Art Deco design. Any museum or collector could have easily coveted this masterpiece of construction were it a painting. It hosted a diverse assembly—royalty, affluent exiles, and eccentric bohemians alike—all pacing its corridors in hushed silence, fleeing from their pasts and navigating their futures. The war acted as a magnetic force, pulling at their gilded-age jewelry and providing a sanctuary amidst the European storm.

At midnight, Anna Akhmatova reclined in the hotel's beaux-arts bar refuge, *The Fumoir*, nursing a final nightcap. She revisited the events of the evening. Dining with Franz Krüger had been a revelation, as had been her coincidental encounter with Olaf Hambro. The realization that a wealthy banker-cum-restaurateur desired her paintings and, by implication, also her body provoked a faint smile on Anna's face. It had been an eternity since a man had looked at her with longing, and it stirred memories of the past. She yearned for the insouciant Parisian days of her youth, but then guilt washed over her, a reminder of her friends enduring a merciless siege back home.

"I, too, am drinking to a ruined home and my life in hell," a male Russian voice echoed her *Last Toast* given earlier in the evening.

"Excuse me?" Anna said, pivoting towards the source of the voice.

"Are you reminiscing about Paris? The carefree indulgences of youth, perhaps?" The voice materialized into a man as he stepped into the candlelight, giving Anna a clearer view of his chiseled profile.

There was a peculiar familiarity about the man, but Anna could not attach a name to his face. "Why have you been shadowing me?" she said, her tone reflecting alarm.

The man let out a laugh, "Oh, Anna, relax. I too am a fugitive from the clutches of the NKVD."

"And what crime did you commit?" Anna asked, her voice laced with skepticism.

"I committed the unspeakable—I spoke the truth," the man said grimly as he sat beside her.

"Then we are kindred spirits. Share your name," Anna commanded.

"I am a ghost, Anna, walking the Earth on borrowed time," he said, deftly sidestepping her inquiry. "I see you still favor the Armagnac that Gertrude used to serve at her soirées?" he added, gesturing towards her glass, then lifted his own. "Birds of a feather."

"You know Gertrude Stein?" Anna was taken aback, unnerved by this man's detailed familiarity with her past while she remained clueless about his identity.

The man returned her shock with a knowing smile and then quoted one of Gertrude's most favored phrases - "Nothing is really so very frightening when everything is so very dangerous."

A glimmer of recognition flickered across Anna's face, but her mind warned her it was implausible. This man was supposedly dead, yet here he stood, alive and in front of her. "It cannot be, it cannot be," she muttered in disbelief. "Fyodor?" she finally blurted out.

In spirited conversation, Anna and Fyodor passed the remainder of the night, their companions a trio of Baron Gaston Armagnac bottles. Fyodor unveiled his chilling tale of narrowly evading the NKVD in Paris, a hit squad dispatched by Stalin for Fyodor's audacity to flout Party orders and not return to Moscow. But even more so, it was for his bold public critique.

Fyodor's open letter to Stalin, splashed across the pages of a Parisian newspaper, brazenly called out the Red Tsar for his corruption of the revolution and his ruthless execution of all who impeded his relentless quest for absolute power. This courageous display of civil disobedience, unparalleled since the American Revolution, propelled Fyodor Raskolnikov into the limelight as a revered figurehead of the anti-Stalin resistance movement. It also painted a target on his back, marking him as Stalin's most wanted, at least until his alleged 'death' in Paris.

In return, Anna inquired about Fyodor's 'coincidental' encounter with her during her dinner at Wilton's. She discovered that Franz Krüger was far more than an expatriate art gallery proprietor. He also filled a role akin to an Underground Railroad "Conductor." However, rather than guiding runaway slaves to the North during the American Civil War, Krüger spearheaded an escape network that crisscrossed war-torn Europe. He had the uncanny ability to make people vanish from the public eye and shield them from multifarious perils. This explained Fyodor's presence in London.

"Tell me again about this composition Shostakovich is working on," Fyodor said, fatigue edging his voice as dawn broke over a slumbering London.

"He is crafting a symphony to commemorate the bravery and valor of Leningrad's inhabitants. However, concealed within the musical notation are subtle criticisms of Stalin. If he can manage this without losing his life in the process, it will be a masterpiece," Anna declared, her words punctuated by a yawn.

"Intellect triumphing over brutalism," Fyodor mused. "Brilliant."

"What do you mean?" Anna said, her eyes heavy with sleep.

"As a former diplomat, I have examined authoritarian tactics in depth. As individual liberties incrementally vanish, the aspiring tyrant first has to convince the populace that they are not enslaved. They direct blame toward perceived enemies, vilify intellectuals, ridicule the highly educated, downplay the importance of the arts, and caution against the nefarious intentions of the education system in brainwashing their offspring. These would-be tyrants are purveyors of misinformation and fear. To challenge them, we must ensure people remember their humanity above all else. That is our mission," Fyodor explained, rising to his feet. "Shostakovich has accepted this call. And I will aid him."

Anna mulled over the enigmatic figure in her presence, a specter vocalizing a call to action among the Lalique crystal panels of a room designed to harbor secrets. She had known others who felt as he did, and she, too, used to share his spirit. Could she summon the courage to rise again? Upon returning to her room, her inebriated mind found rest on her pillow, her dreams filled with echoes of Dostoevsky.

'To remain a human being among people,

no matter the circumstances,

never succumbing to despair or losing hope -

that's what life is about, that's its ultimate task.'

Upon waking the following afternoon, Anna discovered a renewed commitment to the cause. Inspired by Fyodor's words and Krüger's advice, she decided to employ her poetry as a weapon, harnessing the power of words to influence public sentiment. Her verses would indeed be louder than bombs.

22

THE INTERPRETER

LONDON- SECOND WINTER OF THE SIEGE

Anna was perched in a room that could barely qualify as a waiting area at the BBC's Broadcasting House in London. The building had been a repeated target of the Luftwaffe's relentless bombing campaign, with parts of the 7th floor already ravaged and several employees tragically killed. Dark days had descended upon London, and England yearned for 'light relief.' This craving explained the recent surge in popularity of numerous variety shows and heartening songs produced to buoy morale on the home front. Sir Basil Nicholls, the Controller of Programs at the BBC, was deeply disturbed by this trend.

Sir Nicholls regarded the BBC's shift in direction with distaste, decrying the 'insincere and overly sentimental performances' proliferating on its broadcasts. He found particular fault with Vera Lynn and her popular *'Sincerely Yours'* show. In truth, he was a misogynist like most men in positions of power. Despite his aversions, however, he had agreed to meet with Ms. Akhmatova at the behest of one of the BBC's most generous patrons, Olaf Hambros.

Franz Krüger had first broached the subject with Olaf Hambros, proposing an irresistible deal. If Olaf could facilitate Anna's appearance on the BBC to discuss current conditions in Leningrad, alongside reciting some of her 'less sentimental poems,' the banker would receive a few of Anna's portraits.

While fluent in Russian and French, Anna was still perfecting her grasp on Italian and English, languages she yearned to master to appreciate the works of Dante and Shakespeare. To ensure no miscommunication, an interpreter accompanied her to Broadcasting House. Despite his relative youth, Anna found the man from the Ministry of Information entirely engaging, even if he tended to be verbose. His chatter, often on the most mundane topics, was incessant, but his familiarity with her early poetry rivaled her own.

"How is it that you have garnered such vast knowledge about such trivial matters?" Anna finally said. Before the interpreter could respond, a secretary informed them that Sir Nicholls was ready to receive them.

The meeting was courteous, and Sir Nicholls listened attentively as Anna proposed a broadcast to raise awareness about the state of the war in the Soviet Union and the appalling conditions suffered by Leningrad's residents due to the fascists' blockade and bombardment. Anna expressed herself in heavily accented, fractured English, only asking for help with certain English words she did not understand. Sir Nicholls listened respectfully before indicating he had heard enough and would notify her should the BBC Board show interest in such a broadcast. Sensing a polite dismissal, the man from the Ministry of Information chose to intervene on Anna's behalf.

"Sir Nicholls, correct me if I am wrong, but has not the BBC been accused of being 'soft on Germany'? Avoiding conflict, as it were? Some have even used the term 'cowardly.'"

"Yes, that is true," Sir Nicholls conceded. "However, I must weigh the risks associated with such a significant deviation from our normal programming."

"What 'risks' do you incur by allowing a graying woman to speak the truth about the fascists on the radio?" Anna said, her fingers tightly interlaced and elbows resting on the programming director's desk.

Sir Nicholls blinked, apparently unused to such candid pushback from a woman. "I...," he started, stuttering. "I could..."

"Lose your job? Get fired? Suffer a bruised ego?" Anna interrupted, challenging him further. "Are you aware of the risks the people of Leningrad are enduring at this very moment?"

"Ah, no, I do not," Sir Nicholls admitted. "However, I do know that His Majesty's Ambassador, Sir Archibald Clark Kerr, submitted a personal request to your People's Commissar for Foreign Affairs, Comrade Molotov, for permission to send a war correspondent to Leningrad to witness the front lines and report on the conditions of its brave citizens."

"And how did Comrade Molotov respond to your ambassador's request?" Anna asked though she suspected she knew the answer.

"It was denied," Nicholls said with a hint of embarrassment. "I cannot disclose more without jeopardizing national security."

"National security? Balderdash!" the interpreter guffawed. "I work in the Ministry of Information, Sir. Molotov's response is common knowledge, even to me. He said, and I quote, 'At present, we cannot authorize your war correspondent, Alexander Werth, to visit Leningrad. We are trying to keep the sufferings endured by the inhabitants of Leningrad from becoming too widely known.'"

Sir Nicholls cleared his throat. "I cannot put Ms. Akhmatova on the radio. It would ignite an international incident and distract from the genuine war effort."

"What, precisely, is this effort aimed at?" Anna said.

"Winning the war," declared Sir Nicholls.

"The English concern themselves only with war efforts that safeguard the remnants of the British Empire," Anna said defiantly. "It is the people of Leningrad who are genuinely winning the war."

"This meeting is concluded," Sir Nicholls announced, dismissing his visitors with a back-handed wave.

"In that case, I shall inform dear Olaf that you declined and that I am merely a distraction to you," Anna said, rising to her feet and preparing to depart.

The prospect of upsetting Anna's affluent banker patron - a substantial contributor to the BBC - filled Sir Nicholls with trepidation. "Wait, please," he said, releasing a heavy sigh. "I might be able to arrange a solitary broadcast, just one mind you, perhaps... in the early morning hours. I doubt many will be listening, but if you wish to recite some of your poetry and discuss your homeland, then so be it."

"I accept," Anna said with a feigned smile. "How does tomorrow evening sound?"

After exiting Sir Nicholls' office, the duo congratulated each other like returning war heroes.

"You were positively brilliant in there, my dear," the interpreter effused, "You vanquished that man like Scylla and Charybdis; even Homer himself would be proud to call you his equal."

"You navigated those turbulent waters as adeptly as Odysseus himself," Anna said, a broad smile lighting up her face. "I must admit something," she confessed, her tone turning solemn, "Your name has slipped my mind. Who are you again?"

"My name? Ms. Akhmatova, my name is Silas Bollerud," he said, taking her hand gently and pressing a kiss to it. "And I would be honored to remain at your service for as long as you are here in England."

⊷⊶⊷ ⊷⊶⊷

"People will question your intentions, Anna, if you ask them to do simple things. To captivate their attention, you must challenge them, task them with something they believe is beyond their capabilities," Silas advised. "Guilt will not motivate the English into action. Instead, appeal to their sense of pride. This is Great Britain, after all. Laud us, extol our virtues, and we will be putty in your hands. It is the same approach I suggested to Churchill when we were crafting his 'Finest Hour' speech."

"You were involved in writing that speech?" Anna said, her face showing apparent disbelief.

"Madam, I am the author of that speech," Silas replied with a hint of indignation. "Well, initially, Churchill and I collaborated on it. We revised over twenty drafts, but ultimately, the final product was my doing."

Anna studied the young man before her, trying to discern if he was serious. "What is the best way to use our broadcast time?"

"Start with a simple introduction. Tell your audience who you are and why they should care about what you are about to say," Silas suggested. His enthusiasm growing, he continued, "Then present the facts of the situation, reinforced with poignant snippets from your poetry. Your poems 'Solitude', 'Prayer', and certainly the 'Wild Honey' stanza from 'Voronezh' would do the trick. By then, they will be hanging onto your every word. Then, you introduce your call to action, capped off with your new poem, 'Courage!'"

"But I do not have a poem titled 'Courage'," she said, a puzzled expression crossing her face.

"I am aware of that fact, but you will write one and deliver it with the force of a North Sea gale," he said confidently.

"I think you may be misunderstanding how poetry works," Anna replied. "The broadcast is in twelve hours. I cannot simply whip up a poem as though it were a batch of potato pancakes."

"You will. I have confidence in you," Silas said. "Trust me. While you concentrate on 'Courage', I will wrap up the rest of the speech."

"Give me 'Courage,'" Anna said, gazing skyward as a dark rain fell over London's streets. Twelve hours later, Anna reentered the Broadcasting House studios, her determined expression reflecting her resolve to sway the English public's opinions and hearts.

"You are finished?" Silas asked, hope lighting his eyes. Anna nodded. "Let me see it," he insisted, approaching her.

Anna pointed to her head. "It is in here, no need to write it down."

"Of course, you need to write it down," Silas objected. "I have never heard anything so preposterous."

Anna smiled. This man might know much about her, but certain aspects of her life under Stalin would always be beyond his comprehension. "Do you know what is worse than a tyrant oblivious to poetry?" Anna asked. "One who is obsessed with it."

Anna noted Silas's reaction. He did not argue or probe for more information; he returned her smile knowingly, returning to her script's final edits. She moved closer to Silas and whispered in his ear, "I understand why you pushed me to do it."

"Do what?" he said, still engrossed in the script.

"The impossible," she said, her breath warming his neck. "You wanted me to know what tonight's audience will feel when I challenge them and try to make them care. You are a very clever man, Silas Bollerud. Were you Russian, you might have been my next husband."

"Be careful what you wish for," Silas said, "It might just come true."

Suspicion flitted across Anna's eyes as she examined Silas. "Are you secretly Russian? Is that why you are so familiar with my poetry?" she teased.

"My grandmother was Danish. My grandfather, George...I never met him. He passed away before I was born," Silas said.

A guarded truth seemed to lurk beneath Silas's words, but before Anna could probe further, the broadcast's producer entered the room and announced, "We are going live in fifteen minutes."

"How did you end up as my interpreter?" Anna asked, scrutinizing Silas.

"I requested it," he said with an air of nonchalance.

"Why? Or rather, 'how'? How did you know I was scheduled to meet with Sir Nicholls? I was only informed of his consent to meet the day before our appointment."

"I was notified," Silas said, leaving Anna's flurry of questions unanswered. "I have connections," he finally admitted under the intensity of Anna's gaze.

"Whom exactly are you connected to? You are barely out of adolescence. How many people could you possibly know that would have been privy to my arrival in London?" Anna persisted.

Silas chuckled at Anna's attempt to belittle his age, a routine she seemed to have adopted. "King Tutankhamun became Pharaoh at age nine."

"And he died at age nineteen," Anna said, struggling to decipher her conflicting feelings for this man.

"Perhaps I am a spy?" he suggested, darting behind a coat rack in the broadcasting studio.

"You are too clever to be a spy," Anna said, her laughter filling the room. "They are also incredibly serious. You smile far too much to be a spy."

A guffaw escaped from Silas before he could stifle it. "People tend to view those they perceive as intellectually inferior as non-threatening unless they meet in a dim alleyway. The young, the foolish, the self-agg randizing... they are always underestimated. It lulls people into a sense of security, making them more likely to divulge secrets they would prefer to keep hidden."

"And what have I divulged to you?" Anna asked, her tone growing severe.

"You are plagued by guilt about the continued suffering in St Petersburg," Silas said honestly, "while you dine in London's finest restaurants and clink cocktail glasses with the ghostly memories of men you once knew."

"Continue," she whispered, her voice barely audible as she edged closer to him.

"You feel damned. Everyone you have ever loved is either dead or languishing in prison. You believe that you do not deserve happiness, that you are incapable of experiencing joy or any emotion. That is why you chronicle the suffering of others in your poetry - '*One hundred million voices shout through your tortured mouth.*'"

Anna stood trembling. The man before her was inside her head. How could he possibly understand her better than she knew herself? To suffer and endure, that was the Russian way. Could this man grasp the essence of the Russian spirit, the depth of Russian suffering? How could a man of Danish blood comprehend anything Russian? As she pondered, the connection dawned on her.

"We go live in sixty seconds," the producer's voice broke through the tense atmosphere.

"I know who you are," Anna finally managed to say. "You said your grandfather's name was George."

"Did I?" Silas answered in a light voice, quietly stepping back towards his chair to retrieve the script.

"You are the grandson of George Alexandrovich of Russia, Tsar Nicholas II's younger brother," Anna revealed, her voice tinged with astonishment. "The Grand Duke, while convalescing from the tuberculosis that had taken hold in his lungs, visited Denmark and must have fathered a child with a Danish woman. Had the first assassination attempt on Nicholas' life succeeded, George would have ascended to the throne before his death, and you, as his descendant, would be the rightful heir to the title of Tsar."

"Does that make me your adversary?" Silas said, passing Anna the script. "As Russia's preeminent living poet, I presume you have studied

Ovid - 'The harvest is always richer in another man's field,'" Silas quoted. "Yet it is not until you set foot in their meadow that you comprehend that beneath the lush greenery lies the same old dirt. Has Russia improved under Stalin's regime? Have you?" His words, though quietly spoken, stabbed her heart like a blade.

"Who do you think you are, speaking to me this way?" Anna said, defiance flaring in her eyes.

"You know who I am, Anna. I could have been an alternative," Silas responded, his voice barely a whisper, "But the Bolsheviks duped your compatriots into assassinating my grand uncle. Now Russia and its people must bear the consequences of that choice. That is your true curse."

"What can I possibly do?" Anna asked, tears welling in her eyes.

"You approach that microphone, you recite the script, and pray fervently that I am a great writer."

23

THE CHRONICLE

LENINGRAD - SPRING 1942

As the harsh, long nights of a first winter under siege receded and the promise of Spring's rebirth warmed the citizens of Leningrad, Joseph Orbeli found himself increasingly drawn to solitude, engrossed in the bound journals of past Versemakers. He was captivated and occasionally indignant as he delved into the content of these diaries. The privilege of reading entries written by the legendary Pushkin himself moved him deeply. Tracing the inked letters on the page with his finger, he could envision the master poet seated at this very desk, in this same room, penning these words. The thought of being Pushkin's successor filled him with awe and humility.

To his surprise, Joseph realized that only some of the journals in this room were the work of past Versemakers. Some were personal diaries stolen or copied from Tsars, Tsarinas, and court members, all stored as part of the historical record. His shock was immense when he opened one such diary, only to discover that it was Catherine the Great's.

The Diary of Catherine painted a vibrant story of passion, treachery, political maneuverings, and calculated assassinations. It unveiled the Empress's secret affair with a young soldier and her extraordinary measures to conceal it from her adversaries. Yet, as Joseph dug deeper—often joined by Tatiana—he uncovered something even more astonishing. Catherine had documented a vast conspiracy involving her court's members and multiple foreign powers for years. Their objective was nothing less than a coup to seize control of Russia.

Reading the intricate, laid-out scheme that revealed itself page by page, Joseph and Tatiana were stunned by the detailed planning, which provided contingencies for every possible scenario. However, they found a crack in the plot—a flaw Catherine had identified and exploited. She had persuaded a prominent conspirator, a nobleman, to switch sides. In return for his betrayal, Catherine had promised him immunity and a place at her court.

Joseph's emotions swung from rage to disbelief as he delved into the journals penned during the lead-up to, and the aftermath of, the revolt against the last Tsar, Nicholas II. Indisputably recorded by Sophia herself, these entries bore witness to the turbulence and treachery that cemented Stalin's iron grip on power and the flagrant perversion of the revolution's once noble ideals.

Joseph's world shifted on its axis when he spotted his brother, Levon's name, embedded within one diary. The brief paragraph, though merely a few lines long, was enough to cause Joseph to reassess everything he thought he knew about his older brother. He was left grappling with the disturbing question - could it be possible?

Delving deeper into the archives, Joseph and Tatiana began to unravel a hidden network of deceit and treachery that had long lingered in the shadows. They uncovered evidence of theft, corruption, and even the cold-blooded murder of Grigori Rasputin. This act, perpetrated by British agents, was intended to end Rasputin's pacifist influence on the Romanovs during the First World War. This war had been optimistically and tragically dubbed 'the war to end all wars.'

It was a disturbingly dark world, a reality they had never envisioned lurking within the Hermitage's walls. Over three centuries of harsh Russian history, numerous firsthand accounts filled the room, captured within neatly ordered, red leather-bound volumes arranged chronologically.

As their inquiry proceeded, they grasped that their unearthing secrets were only the beginning. A far more malevolent force was at work, threatening the Hermitage and the entirety of St. Petersburg.

Engrossed in documents and artifacts late one evening, Joseph felt a startling touch on his shoulder. He turned to find Tatiana with her eyes gleaming in the archives of the candle lit room.

"Joseph, I think I have stumbled upon something significant," she said, her voice quivering with anticipation as she laid a journal beside him.

"What have you found?" he asked, squinting at the open page.

"The Chronicle of the Versemaker is not merely the journals we see surrounding us. It signifies something far more crucial. The Chronicle symbolizes all the identities of the brave souls who dared to document the truth," Tatiana explained with growing excitement.

"I do not follow," Joseph confessed. "Why would anyone be reckless enough to record the names of those who, if discovered, would be deemed traitors and executed for crimes against the state?"

"It is not a written list, Joseph. Look," she urged, pointing towards the journal.

Joseph scrutinized the page again. It listed an inventory of art, lesser-known works by only two artists. "These are obscure paintings by Tropinin and Repin."

"Joseph," Tatiana said, her frustration palpable, "Do I need to paint you a picture? They are portraits—depictions of the men and women who have served as the Versemakers."

He peered again at the cataloged list, attempting to visualize the portraits in his mind. Repin's name was attributed to more than twenty portraits, some familiar to him, others not. Vasily Tropinin had just three works listed, including a notable portrait of Alexander Pushkin.

"You are suggesting that Repin, known for his paintings capturing the backbreaking labor of peasants and farmers and now the Bolshevik's darling, was a subversive?"

"Yes, Joseph. He was one of us."

24

THE DEADMAN

LENINGRAD - SPRING 1942

Joseph Orbeli stood in the courtyard of the Kirov Military Medical Academy, his gaze landing on a statue of Hygieia. The figure was a comparatively recent addition to the academy's grounds, replacing the previous statue of a Scottish baronet who had presided over the facility a century earlier. That statue had been unceremoniously hauled away—another casualty of the Great Purge. Joseph mused that Hygieia, the goddess of health and hygiene, was a fitting, albeit surprising, replacement. The Bolsheviks were not typically known for their admiration of classical Greek culture. He strongly suspected that his brother, Levon, had a hand in selecting this statue.

It was a rarity for Joseph to venture beyond the protective corridors of the State Hermitage Museum, but today was no ordinary day. The appearance of his brother Levon's name in the Chronicle had shaken Joseph, leading him to question everything he knew about Levon's proclaimed loyalty to the Red Army and his devotion to his mentor, Dr. Pavlov. As

218

he stood there, his gaze locked onto the face of the Hygieia statue, Joseph was anxious. What had brought him here? Was it a confrontational urge to address Levon, a desperate attempt to ease his gnawing fears, or perhaps a longing to cleanse the guilt that plagued him — the guilt for doubting his brother's loyalty to their father and to him?

Levon Orbeli's office was nestled within the main building's administrative wing. As a chosen disciple of Pavlov, Stalin himself appointed Levon to lead the academy's cadet program and carry-on Pavlov's groundbreaking research after his passing. Stalin wielded Pavlov's theories on classical conditioning with the precision of a Spartan lance. This provided Levon with a certain level of immunity from, and sway over, Marshal Zhdanov and other party officials in Leningrad.

Upon entering his brother's office, Joseph observed Levon was engrossed in an animated conversation with another man he did not recognize. Over time, the brothers devised a covert code to silently inform each other of the safety of their surroundings - specifically, if the people present were allies and if open conversation was possible without risk. Quoting a Shakespearean tragedy was a subtle warning to tread carefully while citing a line from a comedy signaled an all-clear for unguarded discourse.

"'Away! you starveling, you elf-skin, you dried neat's-tongue, bull's-pizzle, you stock-fish!'" Levon roared on seeing his younger brother.

His reference to the humorous Falstaff provided Joseph with the clarity he sought.

"I did not mean to intrude, Levon. I see you are already engaged," Joseph said with a strained smile.

"Nonsense! Please, have a seat and join us."

"Levon," Joseph began, a hint of regret in his voice, "I believe what I need to discuss is best done in private, despite your Henry IV assurances."

"Brother, do you know who this gentleman is?" Levon gestured to his guest. "Allow me to introduce Fyodor Raskolnikov."

The surprise that washed over Joseph was as clear as Lake Ladoga in springtime. "That is impossible. Raskolnikov was assassinated in Paris three years ago."

"Technically, I 'fell out of a window,'" Raskolnikov said, quoting the official news reports. "But yes, you are correct. The NKVD attempted to murder me after I defied Stalin and failed to return to Moscow."

"I believe, comrade, it was your blasphemous 'Open Letter to Stalin' that led to your 'demise,'" Levon said with laughter.

"This is madness," Joseph blurted out as his shock faded.

"I assure you, Director Orbeli, I am very much alive," Raskolnikov said. "Like my namesake in Crime and Punishment, I did not die. Instead, I was the one who committed murder — figuratively speaking, of course."

The room erupted in laughter. For a moment, Joseph felt this whole scene must be a fabrication of his imagination, a dream. It was an absurd dream, he reasoned.

"Joseph, take a seat," his brother ordered, guiding him by the arm to a chair.

The three men sat in silence, exchanging wary glances for a moment before Levon broke the awkward quiet. "Look, Fyodor has already entrusted you with an immense secret. If it comes out that he is alive in this city, it would likely lead to his actual demise."

"I am not certain that any one in St. Petersburg can even be considered 'alive.' Have you strolled through its streets lately?" Joseph asked.

"Just spit it out," Levon pleaded with his brother, beginning to light his pipe.

Joseph cleared his throat. "I have come across information suggesting that you may have had a hand in the death of Dr. Pavlov's rival, Dr. Vladimir Bekhterev."

Levon stilled, the ignited match suspended mid-air, as his brother's words seeped into his consciousness. "And where did this supposed knowledge originate?"

"From a trustworthy source."

"Nonsense. There are no trustworthy sources in this city," Levon scoffed. "You discovered this in that damn Chronicle, didn't you?"

Fyodor Raskolnikov's eyes widened. "The Chronicle of the Versemaker? Is that the Chronicle you are referring to?" he asked, sitting up straighter.

"Yes," the brothers said in unison.

"The Chronicle is a myth, merely a legend. It is a white whale, a Shangri-La, if you will," Fyodor said.

"It indeed exists. I have held the journals in my own hands," Joseph confessed, still uncertain why he was extending any trust toward this supposed-dead man. "History is written by the victors, and it rarely aligns with facts. The Chronicle was initiated centuries ago to preserve the inconvenient truths about the Romanovs, and now, the Bolsheviks."

"Could I examine the journals myself?" Fyodor asked, his voice laced with anticipation.

"They are to be viewed only by the Versemakers," Levon said with disdain. "And it appears my brother prefers to trust the words of a stranger over those of his own family."

"Then look me in the eye and tell me it is not true, Levon. Swear to me that you had no knowledge of or involvement in Stalin's countless killings. If you cannot, then I must question everything I believed about you."

Levon puffed on his pipe, considering how to respond to his brother's accusations. "Our world is in shambles," he began with a sigh.

"I find it painful to recall the events you mention as I have tried to erase them from my memory for over a decade. Yes, it is true that Pavlov and Bekhterev were academic rivals. Our laboratories were competing for state funding and Stalin's favor. We attempted to discredit each other's work at every turn. Initially, it was just foolish pranks. We spread rumors about the lax controls in Bekhterev's experiments. In retaliation, they deemed our experiments careless and poorly executed. Regrettably, the situation escalated."

"So, you had Bekhterev killed?" Joseph asked.

"No," Levon replied, shaking his head and meeting his brother's gaze. "I never imagined Bekhterev would go through with it."

"Go through with what?"

"It was at the First All-Russian Neurological Congress in Moscow in 1927. Dr. Pavlov and Dr. Bekhterev were each presenting their respective theories of the mind. Although they shared similar beliefs, their methods and the root causes for their conclusions were quite distinct. Bekhterev claimed that he could determine if a person had a weak mind, making them more prone to manipulation. I found this absurd and dared Bekhterev to put 'his money where his mouth was'. If he was so confident in his findings, he should have no hesitation in examining Comrade Stalin to identify his ailments. To my shock, Bekhterev actually did it."

"That is utter suicide," Fyodor said.

"You and I understand that," Levon acknowledged, fear flickering in his eyes, "But I am not certain Bekhterev realized the peril he was stepping into. If he did, then he had more courage than an entire regiment of soldiers because he did not just carry out Stalin's examination; he divulged the truth!"

"What do you mean?" Joseph said. "I have never heard the full account of Dr. Bekhterev's demise."

"After his consultation with Stalin, Bekhterev returned to the Congress and informed a few colleagues that he had 'examined a paranoiac with dry, small hands.' The very next day, Bekhterev was no more," Levon said, snapping his fingers for emphasis.

"One does not need a medical degree to discern that Stalin is a sociopath," Fyodor said. "I knew it and felt compelled to take action. *I shall reveal a truth about you that's worse than any lie,'* he quoted from his open letter.

"Indeed," Levon said. "You were brave enough to expose Stalin's treachery in your letter to the Red Tsar, clever enough to publish it in a Parisian newspaper twenty-four hundred kilometers away."

"Yet, the Red Tsar still managed to reach me and almost take my life."

An avalanche of revelations left Joseph's mind in a whirl. He yearned to believe his brother, but numerous questions were still gnawing at him. "Where was Dr. Bekhterev's body found?"

"It never was," Levon recalled. "Although that is not entirely accurate. I was reading late into the night when I heard a thud at my door. Opening it, I found Bekhterev in a critical condition. There were no visible signs of harm, leading me to suspect later he had been poisoned. He staggered down the hall, never to be seen alive again. His brain was the sole survivor. Bekhterev's remains were cremated the following morning I am told."

"Hmm," Fyodor grunted. "That sounds like Stalin's style. He has a preference for poison. It is cleaner, leaving no blood on his *'dry, small hands.'* That is how he eliminated Lenin too."

Joseph was staggered by the revelation about Lenin's death. To his surprise and that of his companions, he quoted a paragraph from Fyodor's now infamous open letter to Stalin:

'In the Soviet Union, safety is a luxury no one possesses. None, upon retiring to bed, can be certain they won't be arrested by dawn. There is no mercy. Righteous or guilty, hero of October or revolution's enemy, old Bolshevik or non-party member, collective-farm peasant or ambassador, People's

Commissar or worker, intellectual or Marshal of the Soviet Union—all are subject to the blows of your scourge, all are caught in your bloody maelstrom.'

"Never have truer words been written," Levon acknowledged, looking with admiration at Fyodor. "Did you also read Fyodor's account in the Chronicle?" he asked his brother.

"No, I have learned that when confronted with multiple versions of the same story, the truth usually resides somewhere in the middle. I will not forget that again, Levon."

"Then you are perfectly suited to be the guardian of The Chronicle," Levon said, accepting his brother's apology.

"Now allow me to disclose the reason for my miraculous return from the dead," Fyodor Raskolnikov announced with a mischievous grin on his lips. "Shostakovich," he said, his voice teeming with the kind of gusto one typically expects from a Russian at the close of a vodka-fueled evening of traditional merriment.

"Shostakovich?" Joseph echoed, struggling to discern the connection between the two men.

"Yes, the illustrious composer Dmitri Shostakovich," Fyodor confirmed. "My return was prompted by the news that he is crafting a masterwork - a sublime denunciation of our moronic leader, Stalin. Though, admittedly, his critique is shrouded in more clever subterfuge than my own ever was."

"Where have you been residing since your 'demise' three years ago?" Joseph wondered if Fyodor's mind had suffered from his failed assassination attempt.

"In Paris," Fyodor said. "Oh, how I loved Paris - its springtime blossoms, its nighttime illumination, and above all, the opera. But those damned fascists have tainted all of that."

A puzzled look crossed Joseph's face. "So, out of all the locations in the world, you leave Paris and return to our city ensnared by the same vile fascists?"

"Not quite. I journeyed to England first. It was in London that I heard about Shostakovich,"

"Fyodor," Levon intervened, "I believe my brother is struggling to understand how you could possibly be privy to Shostakovich's potential new symphony that critiques Stalin. It is a secret he would guard closely. How then, did you come to hear of it in London?"

"Anna Akhmatova," Fyodor said, flashing a knowing smile. "I ran into her at a restaurant in London."

"That is ludicrous," Levon scoffed. "Anna has been missing for months and has most likely perished from starvation. It is highly improbable that she escaped the fascists' stranglehold on our city, and even less plausible that you spotted her dining in London."

"I believe he is telling the truth," Joseph said. "I assisted in Anna's escape and her transportation to London. I was uncertain if she made it safely there until now."

Levon stared at his younger brother in astonishment. He had not known that Joseph was capable of such feats. "And Anna was the one who informed you about Dmitri's symphony?"

"Indeed, the news of Shostakovich's daring, yet covert act of defiance inspired my return to my birthplace. Despite what the Bolsheviks and fascists have reduced it to, I found myself longing for home."

"You are willing to risk your life for a mere musical composition?" Levon asked, disbelief written all over his face.

"And yet you show so little regard for your own life, boldly coming here. This city is a mausoleum, a place where thousands meet their end daily and your executioners are within an arm's length of your throat," Joseph added.

"It is not about disregard," Fyodor whispered. "It is about overcoming fear. I am liberated. The Bolsheviks, the fascists, the Red Tsar, none of them hold sway over me anymore. I have vanquished their most potent weapon—fear."

25

THE HIVE

With the rising sun, Dmitri Shostakovich began his day, looking forward to observing the industrious bees atop the Winter Palace. Despite being given a teaching position by Director Orbeli, Dmitri continued his rooftop vigils of the hives. Their inspiration fueled his musical writings. Therefore, the presence of another man perched gargoyle-like near the cement hives stirred annoyance within him. Perhaps it is the night watch awaiting relief, he mused. But as he drew closer, Dmitri soon realized this was not the case. The man had been waiting for him.

"Maestro Shostakovich, I presume," the man addressed him, his voice hinting at a past steeped in diplomacy. The speech was cultured and omnipresent and instantly put Dmitri on guard.

"I am Dmitri Shostakovich. And you are?" he said, aiming for courage.

"A friend of Anna Akhmatova," the stranger announced, removing his hat and executing a slight bow.

"I am familiar with many of Akhmatova's friends, but I have not seen you before," Dmitri said, suspicion tingeing his words.

"You are significantly younger than Anna and me. It is not expected for you to recognize an old friend of hers from overseas."

"What do you want?" Dmitri asked, his patience wearing thin. "I need to begin my shift and do not have the luxury of idle conversation with Anna's 'old friends'."

"But you will want to talk to me," the man persisted, "I have what you need."

"To do what?" Dmitri said.

The stranger gestured to the cement structure nearby. "To expand your hive."

"I am not a beekeeper, Anna's friend."

"No, but you are as busy as one, are you not?"

The cryptic exchange with the man, who steadfastly refused to reveal his identity, exasperated Dmitri. Assuming the stranger to be an admirer of his work, Dmitri decided to display his annoyance. "Look, I no longer give autographs. It is perilous to draw attention to oneself in our current world. So, I have work to do, and I must ask you to leave me be."

"I am not seeking your autograph," the man laughed, then paused to reconsider. "Actually, that is not a bad idea, but that can wait until we have discussed business."

"I do not conduct business with men who will not even disclose their names."

"Are you capable of keeping secrets, Maestro Shostakovich?" the man asked, eyebrows raised. "I suppose you must be, as I have heard your 7th Symphony is rife with them."

Dmitri's body jolted with fear. Was this man here to arrest him for a crime he had merely contemplated? Were the NKVD so skilled they could read minds? "I am no criminal," Dmitri said once the choking fear in his throat subsided enough for him to speak.

The man laughed again. "Only one criminal stands on this rooftop, and it is not you, Maestro. But if you permit me to assist you, I could turn you into the greatest one of all."

"Your name," Dmitri demanded.

"I am Raskolnikov," the man replied, his voice grave.

Now it was Dmitri's turn to laugh, "How fitting for you to adopt the name of Dostoevsky's renowned criminal protagonist. And your first name?"

"Fyodor," came the man's simple response.

"Fyodor, Dostoevsky's own first name. You are not the most inventive, are you?" Dmitri mocked, "Only a fool would christen themselves Fyodor Raskolnikov."

"Or a dead man," Fyodor said.

Dmitri's face lit up with shocked realization. The man standing before him was far from a fool. He was a legendary figure who achieved the impossible. "You should name yourself Theseus," Dmitri suggested with newfound reverence, "For you have vanquished the Minotaur and returned from the underworld."

"Fyodor suits me just fine," the man said, his smile returning. "Now, come sit. We have business to attend to, and a new monster to conquer."

Dmitri listened to Fyodor's proposition with bated breath. The audacious plan was so monumental, so intricate that it seemed miraculous it could ever come to fruition. Moreover, it would expose both himself and his family to considerable risk.

"I have recently begun to regain some favor with Stalin," Dmitri said. "Why should I gamble his wrath on a scheme so unlikely to succeed?"

Fyodor regarded one of the stone flowers perched on the roof and the concealed chamber inside it. "What is good for the hive is good for the bee," he said. "A bee risks much when it leaves the safety of its hive, venturing vast distances in pursuit of precious nectar. The honey created from the toil of the worker bee sustains the entire hive, expands it into a larger entity, and in turn, produces more bees. We need more bees, Maestro."

Dmitri pondered the analogy before replying, "You were an impressive diplomat, Ambassador Raskolnikov, but you would have been an even better beekeeper. It is no wonder you defied Stalin's order to return to Moscow."

"The honey is sweeter in Paris," he replied a hint of smugness in his tone.

"Tell me again, how will my symphony galvanize the world to vanquish our two-headed beast?"

"A microfilm of your complete score will be transported out of Russia to Tehran on a different kind of bee, a metallic one, a B-17 bomber," Fyodor explained. "It will then be carried overland to Cairo, flown to Brazil, and set sail for New York. From there, it will journey around the globe. Your fame will skyrocket, and the plight of the Russian people will tug at heartstrings worldwide. Anna is already performing a similar role in London. It is crucial we establish a second front in Europe as swiftly as possible. If the fascists are forced to defend both their front and rear, the siege of our homeland could be lifted, and further loss of life averted."

"But how will you coordinate all these maneuvers from within Russia? Everyone believes you are dead."

"Being a renegade diplomat has facilitated numerous connections. There are many who empathize with our cause," Fyodor assured him.

"This plan can only succeed if I am granted safe passage from Leningrad, ensuring safety for me and my family," Dmitri said. "I cannot compose with bombs raining down on my head."

"Leave that to me, Maestro. I have internal allies who are more than willing to assist," Fyodor replied, his confidence in the plan unwavering.

26

THE COFFINS

LENINGRAD – SECOND WINTER OF THE SIEGE

Joseph chaired the weekly meeting of his department heads, deeply troubled by the sequence of misfortunes that had struck the Hermitage. Over the past month, since the fascists recommenced their reign of terror by shelling the Winter Palace, four shells had significantly damaged the monumental structure. In a single day, three out of the four seventy-millimeter shells had accurately struck their targets. One hit the southern wing of the Winter Palace, detonating in the kitchen facilities, the second exploded before the building's façade overlooking the Admiralty, and the third hit the portico of the New Hermitage. During that brazen aerial bombardment, two of the museum's staff were killed. And now, a fourth high-explosive bomb had detonated overnight in the early morning hours while they slept with unease in their cots within the protective vaults beneath the Hermitage. Joseph listened as his head of security relayed his assessment of the damage.

"Director, as I am sure you felt last night, the Winter Palace convulsed like a feeble vessel amidst a tempestuous sea. A high explosive shell struck the Palace Square directly in front of our structure's façade. The colossal blast radiated throughout all Hermitage buildings. The shockwave traversed the Hanging Garden, surged into the Pavilion Hall, and shattered the remaining windowpanes, even those facing the Neva. Numerous windows are now yawning in vacancy. As the night progressed, temperatures plummeted and a blizzard set in. Hoarfrost formed amongst the shattered glass, creating a rigid crust of ice throughout the exposed rooms."

"Does the frost pose any imminent threat to our facilities?" Joseph asked.

"At this time, no," the man said, "but when spring arrives, the rising temperatures will—"

"—Will cause dampness to be on the offensive," Joseph interrupted his head of security, completing his train of thought. "Very well. Let us concentrate on today's adversary and tackle tomorrow's enemy when the time comes. Our first priority should be boarding up all the windows in the exposed rooms."

"There is another issue, Director, that will hinder our repair efforts," the man confessed, wearing an expression of desolation. "Our head caretaker was killed in the blast."

The remainder of the meeting seemed to pass in a haze. The news of the Hermitage's head caretaker's death, Pasha's death, threw Joseph into a profound emotional descent. Recognizing his distraction, Tatiana tactfully took charge of the meeting. The remaining committee heads gave their reports, then dispersed, facing another day of urgent tasks.

"Joseph, can you look at me?" Tatiana said with tenderness. "Joseph," she repeated, reaching to touch his shoulder when he failed to respond.

Joseph turned to look at Tatiana, but in his mind, he saw the faces of his father and Pasha, who had become like a surrogate father to him. Both were now gone, and he blamed himself for their violent ends. Everyone Joseph held dear had become a casualty of a botched revolution or a disastrous war. As Joseph's gaze settled on Tatiana, he saw her for the first time. "I cannot lose you too."

"Joseph," she said, her concern palpable. "I am not going anywhere. I will never leave."

"And that is what terrifies me the most, Tatiana. That is what...terrifies me...the most," he repeated haltingly. Joseph feared her resolve to stay by his side, at the museum and within St. Petersburg, would be her doom. He believed that anyone trapped within the city was destined for extinction.

The next day brought a message from Marshal Zhdanov's office, instructing the staff of the Hermitage to repurpose their supply of excess wood, initially designated for creating shipping crates, for the construction of coffins. With the besieged city's population of two million, thousands were now succumbing daily to starvation, disease, or bombardment, as Pasha had. Scant wood was left in the city, forcing survivors to pile the dead on street corners like refuse. Every few days, the army would send sleds to collect these mounting piles for disposal in mass graves. Marshal Zhdanov and the city leadership recognized this practice as unsustainable if the death rate persisted. Coffins would enable more efficient stacking and storage of bodies.

"What should we tell Marshal Zhdanov?" Tatiana asked when Joseph failed to issue work orders to the museum staff or respond to the city leadership's request.

"Tell him, 'No,'" Joseph said.

"No?" Tatiana echoed her face etched with disbelief.

"I will not have my staff consigned to the macabre task of building coffins. It is demoralizing and a waste of precious energy. Morale and energy are two commodities we are desperately lacking."

"We cannot merely say 'No,' Joseph. We need to give Marshal Zhdanov a more comprehensive and considered response, or he might visit the Hermitage himself and pile our own bodies on the street corner," she said, fear creeping into her tone.

"Then tell Marshal Zhdanov that our head caretaker, Pasha Kuznetsov, has perished and no one else on our staff has the energy or skill to construct coffins. If the esteemed Marshal Zhdanov wants our wood, he can retrieve it himself and build his own damned coffins," Joseph said, anger flaring in his voice.

"I will deliver your message...with more diplomacy," Tatiana replied, attempting a weak smile.

Joseph grunted, recognizing Tatiana's wisdom. He then retrieved a journal from his office wall safe. Over the past few days, he had found comfort in filling the pages of this book. Writing gave him a semblance of control in a world ensnared in chaos. Heeding his brother Reuben's advice, Joseph was resolved not to let the events of this absurd siege be whitewashed or cleansed by whichever army prevailed, be they the fascists or Bolsheviks. In this case, an impartial observer would pen history – if he were still capable of such impartiality.

⁂

Tatiana observed the man she loved with deep concern. Joseph had been eating almost nothing, surviving primarily on his cherished black tea and honey harvested from the rooftop hives the previous summer. Joseph would often decide to forgo the safety of the underground shelters, choosing instead to sleep in his office or listen to banned foreign radio broadcasts. This space, one of the few remaining lit corners of the Hermitage, was powered by an electricity cable linked to the Tsar's former yacht, which still lay anchored in the Neva alongside the museum. Like the others, their bodies were deteriorating, growing frail and weak. Yet, they persisted, doing their utmost to keep both mind and body active. A shift was necessary if they were to make it to the spring.

"We have received a response from Marshal Zhdanov," Tatiana said, her eyes silently reading over the official message.

"Read it aloud to me, please," Joseph requested, continuing to study the new maps provided by his brother Levon.

"Since you inform me that your staff is unable to engage in the urgent task of constructing coffins, you are hereby ordered to assemble a party of fifty men whose sole task it will be to collect the bodies of any dead found on the streets within a two-kilometer radius of the Hermitage, effective immediately," Tatiana said with a groan.

Joseph shook his head at this added responsibility that fell outside the museum's purview. "And who will collect the bodies of these men when they expire on the streets? This is another impossible task."

"I fear that Marshal Zhdanov views our staff as expendable since we are no longer a living, breathing museum," Tatiana observed.

"Then maybe we should become one again," Joseph said before returning to his map and drawing a scaled two-kilometer circle on its pages.

27

THE METRONOME

LENINGRAD – SECOND WINTER OF THE SIEGE

The monotonous drone of a metronome roused Olga Bergholz from her restless sleep. It was the last remaining companion in a city on the brink of a second winter of starvation. A season where her friends and family had perished or disappeared. Olga had started sleeping in a studio at the Radio Committee building as the effort to trek from her apartment to the studio had become too demanding for her weakened state.

Her physical body was deteriorating, but her memory persisted. She was uncertain how long her voice would hold out for broadcasts, yet she remained resolute in reading her poetry and offering comfort and hope to anyone who might be listening. But the nagging question remained: Was anyone still alive to hear her words?

Olga had shed the fear of censure or arrest. Each passing day injected her words with raw honesty and increasing brutality. She questioned: What could the authorities inflict upon her graver than the suffering she already bore? Death loomed as a potential liberation from her torment.

Like exposed nerves, her poems veered between the stark, horrific reality of the siege and the growing heroism birthed from its heart. No one but her could claim the mantle of the Voice of Leningrad.

Reaching into her pocket, Olga removed a pack of Belomorkanal cigarettes. Before the war, she might have felt ashamed for the trade-offs she had made to acquire them. Now, it was merely a transaction. Lighting a cigarette, her thoughts wandered toward her mentor. What had happened to Anna? She had vanished months ago without a word. She could be dead, yet Olga felt certain otherwise. Anna had escaped. She must have. Olga pictured Anna seated at a quaint café in New York, savoring a cup of hot, sumptuous coffee. She imagined the beverage's warmth flowing down her throat, filling her empty stomach. Shaking off the indulgent fantasy, Olga refocused on preparing for her next broadcast.

She had scrawled her words on wallpaper strips peeled from a neighboring office. Paper had become a scarce commodity. Anything loose and flammable had been repurposed to kindle fires. After her broadcast ended, Olga would feed these wallpaper scraps to the flames, leaving the metronome to fill the city's silence again. Oh, how she yearned for the company of someone, anyone to converse with about life, art, or any topic that veered away from the war. Olga felt trapped by the unending conflict. Death seemed the only respite, but she had to keep living to inspire others to endure.

But who was left? Many had already been mercifully evacuated while thousands perished each day. Why was she left behind? No one championed the revolution more ardently in its nascent years than she did. Her parents were Bolshevik supporters, and she grew up embracing the communist philosophy. She believed that men and women would inevitably need to struggle before attaining a wholly communist society. However, this struggle would be justified by the promise of universal equality and harmonious coexistence. At one point, Olga was prepared to relinquish anything, even her life, to secure a radiant tomorrow for future generations. And yet, was this her reward? She would not die for this.

Like many in her prewar social circle, Olga continued to believe in the principles of communism. It was the individuals, like those entrenched in the NKVD, who ended her unborn child's life in an interrogation room, not the concept of communism, that was flawed. The revolution was hijacked. For the citizens to enjoy the fruits of communism's promise, Stalin had to be overthrown.

With these thoughts in her head, Olga approached the microphone, intent on telling the truth and not giving a damn about the consequences. Three, two, one.

With renewed vigor, Olga opened her broadcast with her now customary greeting. "I am Olga Bergholz, The Voice of Leningrad, a testament to the indomitable spirit that courses through our veins. Let it be known tonight, amidst the chaos and the invaders' ongoing siege, that I am still alive. Our city's heart still beats, resolute in the face of adversity. Life, against all odds, persists within our war-torn streets. We shall not be conquered."

Glancing down at her notes, Olga took a deep breath, addressing not just a city but also a dear friend. "Let me recount yesterday in a poem for you:

> It was a typical morning
>
> When my neighbor knocked
>
> Showing no emotion at all she announced
>
> I just buried my only friend
>
> We sat in my apartment, not talking
>
> Until the sky lightened upon the next day
>
> What could I say to her?
>
> I am a Leningrad widow, too."

Olga swallowed hard trying to remain calm. "Many friends and family have I lost during this siege. My body may be failing, but my memory will persist long after I have been laid to rest." She read three more poems that vividly recalled the gruesome reality that anyone left alive in Leningrad could attest to, if they only had the energy to do so. As Olga's voice dwindled, she ignited the wallpaper scraps containing her notes. Enthralled, she observed the flames waltzing, radiating life-sustaining warmth. Were her words akin to these flames? Did they cast light in the perpetual gloom? Did they bring heat to this mausoleum-like city? Olga found herself indifferent. She was alone, forsaken to endure a fate grimmer than death. Loneliness, she reckoned, would be her hangman.

"I am a voice of one," she confessed to the walls. "And I will die alone."

28

THE BBC BROADCAST

Anna's hands clutched the script with such intensity that her knuckles blanched. Unsettled by the unfamiliar feeling of being ill-prepared, her heart thumped with anxiety. She chided herself for her lack of foresight in not scrutinizing the script earlier. Her unique opportunity to use her renown and the poetic sensitivity she possessed to aid her nation was undoubtedly destined for failure.

She surveyed her surroundings through the studio's window and noticed the viewing gallery below was devoid of spectators. At least there will not be any witnesses at such a late hour, she thought, attempting to find something positive about her situation. As the Variety Repertory Company's final skit, 'Adolf in Blunderland,' neared its end, Anna took a deep, steadying breath and turned to Silas, seated in the corner of the room. In response, he flashed an assuring smile and offered a nod, silently communicating that everything was under control, at least in his mind.

Returning to the pages clutched in her hands, Anna focused on the opening paragraph. As the producer counted her in, she cleared her throat and began to read.

"Good evening, dear listeners of London and beyond. I am Anna Akhmatova. Many of you may not recognize my name, for I am a weary traveler, a self-imposed exile, and above all, an observer of the human condition. Tonight, I am here to share a tale that, regrettably, will resonate all too familiarly with those of you tuning in amidst the cloak of night."

"I am honored to be in England this evening, or should I say, early morning. This is a land that has staunchly resisted the incursion of fascism, repelled the swarm of Luftwaffe bombers, and told that *Adolf in Blunderland* exactly where he can stow his 'Heil Hitler,'" she improvised; light laughter echoed through the viewing gallery, which had begun to fill since the broadcast commenced.

"It is no surprise to me that the valiant people of Great Britain refuse to bow to such aggression. You have a history of standing tall, of answering the call of duty when it resounds. Many of your young men and women have already made the ultimate sacrifice in the defense of their homeland. During the Battle of Britain, 544 RAF Fighter Command pilots — one in six — were killed. In addition, 718 airmen of the Bomber Command, and 280 brave souls of the Coastal Command, also perished. Above and beyond these losses, over 23,000 innocent civilians have lost their lives." Soft sobs filled the viewing gallery, undoubtedly echoing memories of lost loved ones from those dark days.

"Tonight, it would be my honor to recite some of my poems as a tribute to these brave souls who are no longer with us," Anna said while dropping the script to the floor. "This first piece is titled 'To The Londoners.'

'Time, with an impassive hand, is writing

The twenty-fourth drama of Shakespeare.

We, the celebrants at this terrible feast,

Would rather read Hamlet, Caesar, or Lear

There by the leaden river;

We would rather, today, with torches and singing,

Be bearing the dove Juliet to her grave,

Would rather peer in at MacBeth's windows,

Trembling with the hired assassin —

Only not this, not this, not this,

This we don't have the strength to read!'

Anna paused and stared at the enigmatic man who puzzled her more than anyone else she had ever met. Depending on the circumstances, he could be her lover, adversary, or Tsar. He had infiltrated not just her thoughts but also her heart. Gathering herself, she continued to speak from the heart.

Half a world away and two hours closer to dawn, Olga slumped against the unforgiving wall of another studio, weeping. Her tears were not the sorrowful kind, to which she had every right, but rather, tears of joy. Olga had taken to sleeping in Leningrad's Radio House, for the exhausting trek back and forth to her dingy, death-scented apartment was simply too burdensome. Furthermore, the colossal radio receiver housed at the Radio House afforded her the last vestiges of joy in this city gripped by the throes of death.

Olga would tune into the BBC on the radio, craving news of the war from a less prejudiced source. During sleepless nights, she found comfort in humorous programs like 'The Man Who Resembles Charlie Chaplin.' But tonight, she was astounded to hear a voice that felt like divine intervention. "Anna is alive! Anna is alive!" she screamed in the empty room. She savored every word Anna spoke and recited each poem that

Anna had required her to memorize. It was a burst of happiness that Olga had not felt in nearly two years, reigniting her will to live.

And she was not alone in listening. As Anna's words echoed through the early morning ether, her heartfelt tribute to the fallen and her rallying cry to aid the people of Leningrad began to stir the hearts of thousands around the globe. The question lingered, however: would her impassioned plea be enough to spur tangible action? Could it shift the mountain of isolationist sentiment embedded in the United States and challenge the staunch British conviction to preserve an already lost empire?

"It is hard to make sense of a senseless loss or to lose one's sense of things that are hard," Anna said before reciting another poem.

'I, like a river, was channeled by this stern age.

They gave me a substitute life. It began to flow

In a different course, passing my other one,

And I do not recognize my banks.

Oh, how many spectacles I've missed.

'And the curtain rose without me and then fell.

How many of my friends

I've never met once in my life,

And how many cities' skylines

Could have drawn tears from my eyes;

But I only know one city in the world'

"And tonight, my friends, that city is London. You are all that I know. For in your hands, you hold my heart. It is you alone who can grant me life or bestow upon me death. If it is death you choose, opt for the simple path and remain inactive. But, if you choose life, do the seemingly impossible: open a second front in Europe."

⁕ ⁕

A journal tumbled from the lap of Joseph Orbeli as he sat in his office and heard Anna implore the people of London, and indeed the world, to achieve the seemingly unattainable. He was captivated by the voice radiating from the tinny speaker of his clandestine radio. Like Olga, he, too, found a flicker of joy in the early morning broadcasts from the BBC. This was the one moment in his day when he could let his mind wander and his soul dream of a world that still cherished culture and art. A world untainted by purges, where people retired to sleep with sated appetites.

It was a world now so alien to him; it might as well have been on the moon. Where did Anna find the fortitude to continue striving for what was indeed only a mythical better tomorrow, he wondered? She possessed a courage that he found elusive, and her voice—oh, that voice—was as intoxicating as the first bloom of a summer rose.

⁕⁕⁕ ⁕⁕⁕

Anna breathed in a deep, comforting breath and looked through the window to the now overflowing crowd that had gathered below her. Where had they come from? And why had they remained? She pondered as she continued to speak into the microphone.

'I am greeting my third Spring
far from Leningrad.
Third? And I think that it
Will be my last.
But I will never forget,
To the hour of death,
How delightful to me was the sound of water
In leafy shade.
The peach tree has bloomed and the haze of violets

Is sweeter and sweeter.

Who would dare tell me that

I am a stranger here?'

"Allow me to conclude tonight's broadcast by sharing a poem I composed at yesterday's break of dawn. Given that the skies over Leningrad will soon lighten, heralding another day filled with fresh challenges to survive—to endure for one more day, to witness yet another sunrise, and to make it to the gentle glow of another evening—this poem seems fitting. It is for all of us, the entirety of the human race. May we all find 'Courage'," Anna breathed into the microphone, her tear-filled eyes meeting Silas's as he rose in expectation.

'We know what lies in balance at this moment,

And what is happening right now.

The hour for courage strikes upon our clocks,

And courage will not desert us.

We're not bitter without a roof overhead -

And we will preserve you, Russian speech,

Mighty Russian word!

We will transmit you to our grandchildren

Free and pure and rescued from captivity

Forever!'

A hush, born of shock, filled the crowded viewing gallery beneath Anna's feet as her final word reverberated through the darkness—a world already submerged in shadow. Anna's words were the beacon they all needed. They were a rallying cry that many had been too fearful to express. The dye had been cast; the Rubicon had been crossed. Now, would they follow the path of Caesar or Pompey?

Silas stepped forward and navigated his way to Anna, his face etched with an awestruck admiration. Anna pivoted towards him, her eyes swimming with emotion. "Silas," she whispered, her voice muted yet composed. "What did you think of my words?"

"You improvised," he said. "You told me poets never improvise, yet you did just that."

"No, I said poets never improvise their poems. Scripts, however, are fair game. You initiated the process, then the emotion, an overwhelming surge of energy unlike anything I've ever experienced, overtook me."

"More like possessed you," Silas said, his hand enveloping hers.

"Well, 'One hundred million voices do shout through my tortured mouth'," Anna replied with a smile.

"And how many kiss your lips?" he questioned, leaning in to press his lips onto hers.

29

THE FALLOUT

LENINGRAD – SECOND WINTER OF THE SIEGE

Anna's astounding early morning broadcast did reach around the world, including the war-ravaged Soviet Union. However, the reaction in Leningrad and Moscow was muted. In fact, there was no immediate reaction from the political leaders. It was like the broadcast never happened. At least Stalin had refrained from critiquing or praising it. This caused trepidation down the chain of command. How would they respond? Would they respond? All would wait to see.

"Have we received any word from Moscow?" Marshal Zhdanov asked his Communication's Director.

"Nothing," the man said. "The silence is uncanny, but General Popov awaits you in your office."

"Notify me the moment something arrives," he commanded, going down the corridor. As he reached the threshold of his office, he observed Popov pacing like a fretful nurse.

"Take a seat, Markian, and quit that restless pacing. You are going to wear a hole in my floor."

"I assume you have heard about Akhmatova's BBC broadcast this morning?" General Markian Popov asked.

"You swore to me that woman was dead, Markian. Yet here she is in London, with her own broadcast, reciting her trivial poems and airing our dirty laundry to the world. Someone will pay for this, and it certainly will not be me. What am I to tell Stalin if he asks why I rejected the extra provisions he offered Leningrad? I was the one who adamantly refused, assuring him we were well-stocked and prepared for anything the fascists could hurl at us."

"We can still reach Akhmatova in London and silence her for good," Popov proposed, "Before she can stir more trouble for us."

"Our poet, part nun and part whore, will inevitably return to our city by the Neva," Zhdanov said. "She will not be able to resist it. Just like a moth to a flame, she will come back, and that will be her downfall. We need not make any precipitous decisions until I hear from Comrade Stalin. It is always prudent to understand his stance before taking matters into our own hands."

"Do you think he heard the broadcast?" Popov asked, his voice tinged with apprehension.

"Do you honestly believe our supreme leader stays awake to listen to the BBC in the middle of the night? My concern lies in the aftermath if our wayward poet actually succeeds in what she implored the world to do last night. Her performance was reportedly most persuasive, almost aristocratic. If it becomes known that I opposed her actions after they bear fruit, I shudder to think what the consequences would be."

"The likelihood of Churchill and Roosevelt opening a second front based on the ramblings of a forgotten poet, is highly unlikely. Perhaps, however, we should reassess our management of our remaining high-profile citizens regarding their propaganda potential," Popov suggested.

"What are you proposing, General?"

Popov stroked a clean-shaven chin, mulling over their options. "I think it might be time to consider relocating this elite group further east. Make them Moscow's problem. Keeping them in Leningrad has become dangerous when our military situation requires all our attention and we cannot monitor them as closely as before. I do not trust the former Intelligentsia."

Marshal Zhdanov contemplated Popov's proposal. It was sound advice. They could present it to Stalin as a plan to utilize the talents of these poets, musicians, and artists to disseminate their propaganda on Soviet radio broadcasts. In more favorable conditions, away from the fascists' guns, the State could better control and exploit these individuals. "Make up a list."

In the halls of the Hermitage, Anna's words radiated a healing energy akin to warm sunlight. Optimism had made a triumphant return to the cultural heart of the besieged city and, more importantly, to Joseph Orbeli. Anna's broadcast had yanked him from the shadowy depths of despair that had gripped him since Pasha's death.

He reminisced about the beneficial exchange he'd had with his former assistant director, Vladimir, during which they had imparted valuable insights to one another. Joseph had counseled Vladimir, "Keep people engaged, present them with a meaningful challenge, and above all, devise plans for the future." Vladimir, in turn, reciprocated with his insightful nugget of wisdom, stating, "When circumstances become unfavorable, we should not hesitate to adjust our sails against the wind and alter our approach."

With renewed spirit, Joseph began envisioning the future. His initial task was to reinvigorate the Hermitage. He and his staff had been constantly reactive rather than proactive for far too long. Starting from this moment, they would resurrect the Hermitage as a living, breathing museum for the people of St. Petersburg.

During Joseph's subsequent staff meeting, he introduced a brainstorming session on the agenda. Its goal was to generate ideas for programs that the Hermitage and other cultural centers across the city could offer. These initiatives aimed to reintroduce a semblance of normalcy into the populace's lives. "Do no harm and make people's lives better," was Orbeli's marching orders to his staff.

Given the fact that a significant chunk of the Hermitage's treasures were safely stored in the Urals, and the remainder was securely packed up in crates — either tucked away in vaults or piled in the Hall of Twenty Columns — the staff's creativity was put to the test. One of the most favored ideas implemented, inspired by Pasha's memory, was to restart guided tours through the now vacant galleries of the Hermitage. Swelling crowds of soldiers, mothers with their children, and occasionally even city officials would meander through the museum's now dim expanses. They would listen with excitement as the Director of the State Hermitage pointed to the empty picture frames still hanging on the walls. His detailed descriptions of the once-resident paintings were so vivid that attendees could almost visualize them still in place.

Elsewhere in the city, the Leningrad Zoo's less-valuable animals, initially overlooked for evacuation in the war's early weeks, became unexpected stars. Rather than slaughtering these creatures for food during the harsh winter, devoted keepers ensured their survival through extraordinary measures. Taking a cue from the Hermitage, the zoo reopened a few weeks later, elevating a black vulture, a bear, and the crowd favorite, 'Beauty' the hippopotamus, to celebrity status. Beauty became an unofficial symbol of the city's unlikely survival, having defied death due to the remarkable efforts of her caretakers. They lovingly bathed Beauty daily with forty buckets of water drawn from the Neva River, which they subsequently warmed. After her warm baths, liters of camphor oil were massaged into her sagging skin to prevent it from cracking.

Evocative of the legendary Phoenix rising once more from its ashes, the residents of Leningrad persevered through what history would later recount as the most lethal winter of the entire siege, confounding and frustrating the fascist high command. As a retaliatory measure, the enemy intensified their brutal assault on the city's cultural epicenters, unintentionally further bolstering the determination of the Leningrad populace.

This entire sequence was a testament to the power of a single, extraordinary woman, one stirring poem, and a solitary word - 'Courage.' Let it be a standing testament that the impact of an individual should never be underestimated. A dark cloud is but a temporary shroud, not an indication that the sun's light has gone out; similarly, grim convictions should not be misinterpreted as evidence of God abandoning His mercy on those suffering. Like Lazarus, Leningrad had risen from the dead.

30

THE FAUSTIAN BARGAIN

"Maestro, the first clarinet player has collapsed! We cannot continue at this pace," the conductor warned.

"We must make it through the entire piece at least once if we are to have any hope of a live performance. The orchestra has been working on the first two movements for months and they still have not perfected it," Dmitri Shostakovich said, his voice filled with desperation. "And there are two more movements yet to learn."

"We cannot do it. We may have only three minutes of life left before the entire ensemble succumbs," came the chilling reply.

They stood before him, an orchestra of skeletal figures. Their bodies were frail and depleted. Their last breaths and remaining energy were dedicated to bringing Shostakovich's magnum opus to life, even if it meant sacrificing their own lives. The harsh reality of their circumstances, the lack of sustenance and a harsh winter had drained them of their strength. For the past month, they had diligently practiced the intricate movements. Yet, the inability to perform the complete symphony without casualties along the way was a disconcerting reality that loomed over them.

"How many have we lost?" Shostakovich asked, his voice filled with demoralization.

"We started rehearsals with sixty musicians, we are down to forty-seven," the conductor said.

"A baker's dozen," Shostakovich muttered, a tinge of bitterness in his tone. "If only it were as simple to create new musicians as it is to bake fresh loaves of bread. Can we find replacements?" he said, a glimmer of hope in his voice.

"It's not as easy as that," the conductor explained. "Most of our losses have been in the brass section... trombones and cornets. The required lung capacity is diminished in these trying times. I cannot simply transform a violinist into a French Horn player with a wave of my hand."

"We would need a miracle of monumental proportions to achieve such a feat," Shostakovich declared, his voice laced with defeat. "What if I could secure additional rations of food and coal for the remaining orchestra members? Perhaps it would rejuvenate them and enable us to navigate through all the movements at least once."

"Indeed, if we hope to successfully complete it at least once before performing it live, an improvement in everyone's health could have a tremendous impact," the stage manager acknowledged. "However, how do you propose to conjure such a miracle?"

"I believe I may know someone who has the power to strike a deal with the devil," Shostakovich said.

⁂

"Let me make sure I understand," Sergi said, a flicker of an idea igniting in his mind. "Your orchestra members are succumbing to illness and death, and you urgently require provisions and coal to sustain those who remain, if there is any hope of accomplishing your latest musical triumph?"

Shostakovich grunted in confirmation, his mind grappling with the depths to which he had descended to negotiate with this despicable man. Thankfully, Director Orbeli took charge of the conversation on his behalf.

"Sergi, think of it as a virtuous act you can perform for your besieged city," Joseph proposed. "This magnificent symphony will inspire all who have the privilege to hear it."

"I am fresh out of virtuous acts," the black-market operator replied, "but there is something I desire, Maestro, something only you have the power to grant, that might convince me to offer my assistance."

Joseph sighed, "Name your price."

"I want to be a part of the orchestra," he said, his eyes shining with anticipation.

"Good god no, absolutely not," Shostakovich replied with firmness.

"Sergi," Orbeli said with amusement in his voice, "what instrument do you propose to play? You have only one arm."

"Trumpet, piano, gong," Sergi began listing eagerly, "it matters not. I simply wish to stand on that stage, with all eyes fixed upon me, basking in the approving gazes for once."

"Do you possess any proficiency in playing any of these instruments?" Shostakovich asked, his disbelief apparent.

"No, you would have to teach me, Maestro."

Shostakovich rubbed his weary face with a hand, contemplating the Faustian Bargain before him. But what other choice did he have? "We gather for rehearsals at 6:00 PM. If you bring us the supplies, I will find a role for you."

31

THE EVACUATION

LENINGRAD - SECOND WINTER OF THE SIEGE

As the fascist siege continued, the entrapped masses of Leningrad were plagued by real hunger. The pre-blockade food stores had dwindled to mere crumbs. Despite their dire circumstances, the leaders entrusted with defending Leningrad declined the extra supplies offered from Moscow a month into the siege, unwilling to be seen as unprepared. "We cannot eat pride," became the all too familiar refrain among the starving citizens of the city.

Driven to desperation, wallpaper was scraped off the walls, and its potato-based glue was consumed. Leather belts and hats were boiled down into a meager edible jelly, barely enough to quiet the pangs in children's stomachs. Birdseed and even beloved pet canaries found their way to the tables. Pets became an unaffordable luxury. As the situation deteriorated further, unimaginable and ghastly things were consumed out of sheer necessity.

Dmitri Shostakovich sat around the small table in his meager apartment, feeling powerless as he witnessed his family's decline. They were among the fortunate ones, for he and his wife Nina's additional jobs at the Hermitage granted them extra daily rations of bread, a meager 125 grams, weighing no more than a bar of soap. Dmitri's mind wandered, hallucinating about the tangy spray of citrus juice, a distant memory.

The sudden shrill ring of the house telephone jolted him back to reality. A tinge of fear crept into his brain. The phone had remained silent for months, and he was unsure if it still functioned. With vacant eyes and terrified expressions, his entire family stared at the clanging box - were the secret police coming?

Rising from his chair, the composer tiptoed towards the telephone, akin to a prisoner marching towards the gallows. "Hello," he said, his voice hoarse and parched. "Yes, this is Dmitri Shostakovich," he replied to the tinny voice on the other end of the line. "Yes...but there is no way...I understand," he murmured after a moment of reflection. "I will be there."

Turning around, his gaze fell upon his wife and children; their heads hung low in anticipation of bad news. "We are being evacuated tonight," he announced, his voice filled with disbelief. "One suitcase each. Hurry, we must pack and not be late."

A whirlwind of questions erupted from his astonished family as their excitement overflowed, but Dmitri remained oblivious. His eyes fixated on the stacks of his unfinished symphony, neatly arranged across the room. "Evacuated," he whispered, unaware of the fate that awaited him in the coming days. The dead man had worked another miracle.

"What did they say?" his wife Nina asked, shaking him out of his trance.

"Marshal Zhdanov has ordered the full evacuation of the cultural elite. We are all to leave the city in the coming days. Some will depart by air and some across the ice by truck."

"But why now?" Nina asked, bewildered by their stroke of fortune.

Dmitri contemplated his wife's question for a moment before responding. "I fear the war is not progressing favorably, and Stalin wants to ensure the safety of his propagandists, ready to serve his needs. Morale is low, and the war effort desperately requires a boost of positive news."

"Where shall we go?" Nina said, her voice filled with uncertainty.

"Does it truly matter? We are among the fortunate ones escaping this abyss of death. Those who remain are destined to either perish or endure immeasurable grief as they watch their loved ones suffer," Dmitri reminded her, his tone heavy with resignation.

Observing her husband caressing his unfinished composition, Nina asked, "What will become of your symphony?"

"The orchestra has been rehearsing, but I have only completed three movements. It deserves to live on. It will accompany us wherever we are sent," Dmitri declared. "I shall complete it at any cost. It must reach its conclusion."

Lake Ladoga would serve as Dmitri Shostakovich and his family's escape route. Their journey along the ice road, aptly named the 'Road of Life,' across the vast expanse of the lake was laden with hazards. The passage, undertaken solely under the cover of night, was painstakingly slow. Convoys of trucks navigated around areas of thin ice and artillery-pocketed crevasses, occasionally halting. At the same time, men armed with pickaxes and long poles prodded the ice ahead of the lead truck, seeking the safest path across the shifting ice floe. Ultimately, more than 1.3 million residents of Leningrad, primarily women and children, would cheat death and starvation by traversing this 'Road of Life,' leaving behind their city of death.

On this particular night, Dmitri, his wife Nina, and their two children huddled together in the penultimate truck of a column of sixty. The 27-kilometer escape route would be undertaken without headlights to evade fascist detection. As they drove, they passed the remnants of previous failed attempts: abandoned vehicles and charred hulks partially submerged and hastily refrozen in a chilling tableau that echoed Dante's Inferno.

Despite the terror gripping the truck's occupants, each one felt overwhelming gratitude for being among the 'lucky ones' marked for evacuation. More than a thousand trucks had already been lost to the lake's depths, while another two thousand were out of commission. The convoys were dwindling.

Between Dmitri's legs rested his sole suitcase, its contents not clothes but his life's work. His symphony would survive this evacuation to thrive or sink lifelessly to the lake's abyss. Regardless of the outcome, Dmitri was resolute that he would never abandon his family.

Nina gazed at her husband with profound affection. His renown and talent as a composer had been their family's saving grace. She whispered a prayer to a god she did not believe in, expressing gratitude for their deliverance.

"Dmitri," she murmured into his ear.

"Yes," he answered, his eyes closed, endeavoring to dismiss his own doubts about the existence of the Creator as their truck swayed and groaned over the ice.

"Do you think we will win the war?"

He mulled over her question for a long moment, enough for Nina to believe he had fallen asleep. "Dmitri," she said again, nudging his shoulder. "Will we emerge victorious?"

"Regardless of who emerges victorious, our fate remains the same. We are destined to be prisoners in a jail with no bars," he lamented.

The first artillery shell exploded about one hundred and eighty meters to their left, casting a blinding light over the stark, white expanse of the lake. In response, the convoy picked up speed. Death by fascist shells was a far grimmer prospect than the risk of driving over thinning ice. Would their demise come by fire or by ice? Dmitri pondered, his grip on his suitcase tightening just as a second shell screamed over their convoy, detonating closer yet still off its target.

Dmitri soothed his nerves by directing his thoughts to his unfinished symphony. The rumble of trucks speeding over the ice reminded him of the percussive sound of timpani. He imagined a procession of kettledrums, followed by a crash of cymbals as violins crescendo and fall in rhythm with the emotions of the innocents caught in the conflagration. His creativity had been stifled for weeks, but now, in this moment of terror, he could envision the elusive movements and instrument interactions that had hindered him from completing his masterpiece. The fascists had granted him a gift of life veiled as the Four Horsemen of the Apocalypse bearing down upon the damned. He had crossed the river Styx and was prepared to face whatever fate awaited him on the other side. Regardless of the outcome, there would be music.

32

THE REGRET

STATE HERMITAGE - SECOND WINTER OF THE SIEGE

Joseph's evacuation order arrived at the Hermitage, delivered by messenger. He read it alone in his office, a sinking sensation in his chest as the implications of his inaction—the fear that had prevented him from fully loving Tatiana—settled in. God indeed has a twisted sense of humor, he mused, rereading the most striking sentence of the message: 'Be prepared to evacuate yourself, wife, and children if you have any.'

Joseph was ensnared by his regret as though his inaction had unwittingly condemned Tatiana. He found himself speechless later when Tatiana, noticing his pallor, inquired about his well-being. He merely handed her the message, his strength giving way to overwhelming grief as he slumped onto the floor.

"It will be okay," Tatiana tried to reassure him, her voice shaky but determined. "The Hermitage needs someone to keep it functioning. There is no better choice than me," she said, her sense of duty unwavering.

273

"It is not fair," Joseph protested. "Why should I leave and you stay?"

"You are not well, Joseph. Your malnourishment has aggravated your arthritis. You need warmth, tropical air, and the restorative properties of citrus fruits. Once you regain your health, you can return," Tatiana reasoned.

"Even if I were in perfect health, I would still be forced to leave," Joseph said. "This entire situation is a farce. Where is the logic in evacuating the leaders who are keeping the morale of a besieged city intact? It is like expecting acorns to grow without any oak trees."

Tatiana had no response, her mind overwhelmed with the potential consequences of Joseph's departure and the grim prospect of the siege not lifting anytime soon. She did not want him to leave but felt duty-bound to insist. "You must go," she urged, her eyes imploring. "And once you are well, you must return to me, my love. Do you hear me?"

"If I could elope with you this very moment, I would," he confessed after a pause, his tone soft. "You are the sun, the air of my world. I realize now how selfish I have been."

Tatiana regarded the broken man before her, his spirit subdued and directionless. "Come with me," she said in a gentle voice, reaching for his hand.

"Where are we going?"

"To a place of faith - a sanctuary for miracles," she whispered in his ear.

"I have already confessed that my faith is dwindling and miracles to me are merely illusions."

"Hush, close your eyes and allow me to guide you."

With his eyes sealed shut, Joseph entrusted himself to Tatiana's guidance. She navigated him through the endless corridors of the Winter Palace - upstairs and down, across parquet floors and granite staircases, their footfalls the only accompaniment. Upon reaching their destination, Tatiana positioned him, rotating him three times, and whispered, "Open your eyes."

Following her command, Joseph found himself at the brink of a grand sight – the Vatican, or at least Catherine the Great's rendition of a tiny part. "Why have you led me to one of Rafael's Loggias?"

"The Logge di Raffaello, while perhaps perceived as inconsequential within the expanse of the Vatican, serves as an integral part of the ceremonial route leading one toward the redemption of the soul. This corridor needs to be traversed, just as the human soul must navigate through space and time after departing the body in pursuit of eternal life. Catherine the Great constructed replicas of these transient hallways here, to bridge the buildings of the Winter Palace, as they cross our city's canals," Tatiana explained.

Joseph shook his head, the essence of their journey evading him. "I do not grasp why we are here."

"The road to faith is not confined to any physical location; it can be discovered anywhere - in Rome or even in St. Petersburg. Faith finds its home in the human heart, and I believe in my heart that you will return to me."

"I lack such faith," Joseph confessed. "How do you know everything will be alright in the end?"

"Faith is not about everything turning out okay, Joseph. Faith is about being okay no matter how things turn out."

To the east of St. Petersburg lies Lake Ladoga, a formidable sight. In the winter, its vast frozen surface becomes a twisted mass of ice blocks, creating abstract shapes that captivate and instill fear in the hearts of men and women. The swift current beneath keeps the ice sheets in constant motion while the extreme temperatures ensure their solid freeze. Some parts of the lake boast an impressive thickness of nearly four feet, making it strong enough for trucks to traverse or aircraft to land upon.

On this evening, as a frigid wind gusted across the open expanse, Joseph Orbeli found himself seated in the back of a sleek black sedan. His instructions were clear: pack his belongings and arrive at the designated landing zone before midnight. A plane awaited him, ready to transport him to an undisclosed location in the east, likely Moscow. With reluctance, Joseph acknowledged to Tatiana and to himself that remaining in St. Petersburg was no longer an option. His deteriorating health left him with little choice but to leave, even if it felt like a betrayal in his mind.

The absence of a moon allowed the night sky to come alive with a celestial display as countless stars shimmered like pinpricks on an endless black canvas. Outside their vehicles, a handful of men stood motionless, straining their ears for the anticipated sound of an approaching aircraft. A faint drone of propellers unleashed a flurry of activity, signaling the arrival of the plane from the north. Headlights were turned on, casting an eerie glow across the icy surface, outlining a makeshift runway for the incoming pilot.

Once the aircraft touched down, Joseph knew he had no time to waste. The imminent threat of the enemy's artillery loomed over him; their shells poised to rain down upon the illuminated glow of the headlights. The enemy's objective was clear: to shatter the ice runway and send the aircraft plummeting into the frigid depths below. Joseph could not help but find it wasteful, the reckless expenditure of ammunition by the fascist forces. Alas, their cunning had never been their strong suit, Joseph thought to himself.

"Go!" bellowed the Red Army officer, his voice cutting through the icy air. He was responsible for ensuring the plane's safe landing and swift departure. Joseph sprinted towards the aircraft, its engines revving as it prepared for takeoff.

Ice pellets struck his face as he approached, stinging like relentless rounds from a machine gun. Joseph could not help but question the necessity of an aerial evacuation. Indeed, a journey across the frozen expanse by ice road would have been more practical. Yet, he understood that the trucks were gathering on the lake's eastern shore, preparing for their vital supply run across the treacherous ice.

The plane surged forward with an abrupt jolt, catching Joseph off guard as he scrambled to fasten his seat harness. The shrill whine of the engines offered little comfort, drowned out by the thunderous explosions of artillery shells that began to rain down all around them. The sky ignited with bursts of vibrant orange and searing yellow, temporarily blinding Joseph as the aircraft ascended steadily and banked towards the safety of the north, evading the enemy's relentless barrage.

As Joseph's vision cleared, he directed his gaze toward the pilot, only to realize that another passenger was seated inconspicuously at the plane's rear, whose presence had eluded his notice until now.

"Hello, brother," Reuben said, his voice cutting through the turbulence. "Nice of you to join us. Sit back and try to relax. I'm taking you back to our ancestral homeland in Tbilisi, Georgia."

33

THE WORLD DEBUT

MARCH 1943

Situated precisely 1,776 kilometers from St. Petersburg, Dmitri Shostakovich paced a once-opulent hotel's sparsely furnished drawing room. He harbored hopes for an Independence Day of his own, his footsteps echoing like a restless father awaiting the birth of his first child. All his hard work, every ounce of his creative genius, culminated in this one momentous evening. The world premiere of his 7th Symphony broadcast nationwide over State radio held his fate in its delicate notes.

Dmitri's inability to be present at the Bolshoi Theater in Kuybyshev proved both a blessing and a curse. On the one hand, it spared him the anxiety of witnessing immediate audience reactions. On the other hand, it heightened his worries. How would those in attendance receive his composition? How would it be embraced by the nation or by the world? Yet, among these swirling concerns, one question loomed above all: How would Stalin receive it?

The deep hum of the radio's tubes warming up heightened his anxiety, intensifying time's relentless ticking. Dmitri could not help but question the absurd slowness of bringing a mere radio to life. Thoughts raced through his mind, fearing that he might miss the orchestra's opening notes, the herald of his symphony.

Embodying the role of a devoted wife, Nina attempted to assuage his unease. "This is truly exhilarating! The triumphant return of Russia's greatest composer is mere minutes away."

"Or," Dmitri contemplated, "perhaps this marks the culmination of my life's journey."

"Come now," she said with unwavering conviction, "I have faith that everything will unfold in your favor."

"Perhaps it is for the best that we are not present. It will grant us some respite before they ship us back to Leningrad, assuming Stalin sees through my disguise," he admitted, his anxiety escalating.

Nina's expression morphed into a pout as she gazed at her husband. "Well, unless the fascists choose to bomb the theater within the next two minutes, there is no way to halt the proceedings. Why not take a seat and relish in the first live performance of your masterpiece?"

Dmitri acknowledged the irrationality of his thoughts but found himself unable to shake off his pessimism. Positivity had eluded him for far too long, leaving behind only the familiarity of fear.

Vibrant sounds of applause filled the room as the radio sprang to life, jolting Dmitri out of his stupor. The crowd's admiration for the conductor reverberated through the airwaves, magically transporting him to the grand theater. Closing his eyes, Dmitri immersed himself in the music. The delicate sway of violins and the commanding beat of kettledrums marked the beginning of the first movement.

No words were spoken; not even a breath escaped Dmitri's lips during the initial five minutes of the performance. His creation, a testament to the resilience and magnificence of a besieged city, resonated in his ears, akin to the tantalizing sweetness of freshly plucked fruit. It was a moment of sheer glory.

"I hope they are listening in Leningrad," he dared himself to whisper. "I need them to know that they are not forgotten."

The people of Leningrad were not the only ones listening. Emissaries, military attachés, and proponents of a second front in Europe bore witness to Dmitri Shostakovich's awe-inspiring tour-de-force. It ignited a flame of inspiration among the Allies, who were grappling with demoralizing defeats across Europe, North Africa, and the Asian Pacific theaters. As the final notes of the orchestra faded away, immediate action was set in motion to extricate the scores of the 7th Symphony masterpiece from the confines of the Soviet Union and deliver them into the waiting hands of musical ensembles in London and New York. This profound work of art, born from the depths of despair, would become a resounding call to arms, shifting the tides of public sentiment in the United States and unleashing the full might of the Western world against the tyrannical grip of fascism.

34

THE MICROFILM

APRIL 1943

Anna's galvanizing broadcast from London had also moved mountains, but not the ones most needed by the besieged citizens of Leningrad. Public sentiment in Great Britain and the United States had been stirred. Monetary support for weaponry and surplus military equipment began pouring into England and the Soviet Union. This 'Arsenal of Democracy' was pivotal in aiding the European allies to resist the fascist invaders. Still, it fell far short of the second front that Stalin was advocating and Churchill opposed for imperialistic reasons. Great Britain clung to the hope of salvaging its once-great empire, where the sun never set. Consequently, Churchill continued to push for operations in North Africa, India, and Malaysia - practically anywhere but continental Europe.

To overcome this persistent stalemate, internal factions and their international allies, initiated plans to smuggle Dmitri Shostakovich's 'Leningrad Symphony' out of the Soviet Union to disseminate it worldwide. The mastermind behind this operation – was none other than Fyodor Raskolnikov.

A knock at Dmitri's door stirred him from a deep sleep. Now alone, having sent his wife and children to live with relatives further east, he had not entertained visitors in what felt like ages. Consequently, the sound of the knock sparked unease in the composer. "Yes?" he said from behind the locked door.

"I might be a ghost, but I cannot pass through a solid door, Dmitri," came the response.

Releasing a breath of relief, he opened the door to welcome the man who had achieved the improbable to save him and his family.

"It has been so long," Dmitri said, relief lining his voice as he ushered in his guest, "I started to believe you had actually ventured into the afterlife."

"I have journeyed far, but I have returned bearing good news," Fyodor declared, "It is time to dispatch your symphony to the New World." Over the next half hour, Fyodor outlined the logistics of the initial phase of the daunting journey that lay ahead. He would accompany Dmitri's score to Tehran aboard an American plane. The B-17 bomber, primarily used for supply runs between the alternative Soviet capital and the Persian country, presented the perfect cover for their operation. These flights served as training grounds for Soviet pilots, allowing them to familiarize themselves with American aircraft before they entered the war zone. This presented an ideal opportunity for Fyodor to depart the Soviet Union with his invaluable cargo bound for New York and London without drawing unwanted attention to his mission.

"You are personally going to accompany my composition?" Dmitri said, a hint of longing tinting his voice.

"You could join me, Maestro. Imagine the acclaim and prosperity that await you in the New World. You could follow in the footsteps of Columbus."

For a few suspended moments, Dmitri entertained fantasies of what life might be like in such a world, a career free from the constraints of Soviet oppression. His reputation had weathered the fury of Stalin for over a decade. Wealth, fame, and nearly his sanity all had been casualties of a sociopath who paid scant attention to the professed ideals of the revolution. If Dmitri remained, he would never again experience the artistic freedom to pen his thoughts and feelings unrestrained. Yet to depart meant admitting defeat, forsaking those bound to stay. "My family—" he began.

"There is no time to wait for them, my friend," Fyodor interjected, a note of sorrow in his voice. "The plane departs tonight. I may be able to arrange their exit from the country at a later date."

"Then I shall stay," Dmitri declared. "I will not abandon my family."

"I will secure your escape along with your family's, Dmitri, or die trying," Fyodor promised with conviction. "Of all people, you deserve to savor the sweet honey of your labor."

Dmitri nodded in silent resignation, acutely aware that the average life expectancy of a worker bee was a mere thirty days, even during the sweet, abundant summer months. "Safe travels," he bid his friend before closing the door behind him. He would never see Fyodor again.

35

THE URALS

AUTUMN 1941

The turbulent departure of Vladimir Levinson-Lessing from Leningrad in the early months of the war starkly contrasted with his relatively uneventful arrival in Sverdlovsk, nestled in the Ural Mountains. The five-day journey via train was a dizzying, monotony-interrupted series of eastward sprints, marred by exasperating detours off the main line to make way for a relentless stream of troop transports heading in the opposite direction. Elements of the 22nd Army were repositioning to the Western Front, a move likely leading to a grim encounter with the fascists' elite Panzer Divisions.

Upon arrival at his destination, Vladimir observed a 'security force' composed of aged men well past their prime and adolescent boys pretending to be soldiers. This sight prompted a disheartening realization: This was the elite force tasked with guarding the art. The nearly deserted, eerily silent city offered a stark contrast to the vibrant buzz of Leningrad. Despite this, Vladimir felt sure Joseph Orbeli had chosen this place for these very characteristics.

The dearth of able-bodied manpower and discernible organizational leadership had led Vladimir to another alarming realization: he was inadvertently in charge. His innate caution and aversion to physical labor were attributes typically deemed unsuitable for a leader in this situation. Vladimir's tendency to blend into the crowd rather than stand out was more comfortable for him, and as a result, his initial tenure in this new role was marked by inaction.

For the first month, little transpired apart from the train cars being relocated to a fenced-in yard while Vladimir perused and edited the manifest lists. The modest workforce under his supervision remained oblivious to the priceless treasures concealed within the rail cars. Furthermore, there needed to be a suitable location to safely store these invaluable items in Sverdlovsk, even if he could offload them. The city's limitations were starting to become a distinct issue.

Consequently, Vladimir decided to sidestep the issue. He identified an advantage in keeping the artwork crated and mobile, ready to evacuate immediately should the fascist army prove more successful than Napoleon had been. Vladimir cleverly transformed a limitation into an opportunity. "Perhaps I am suited for this leadership role," he pondered.

While Vladimir was managing the dire circumstances, his quiet world was disrupted a few months later by the unexpected arrival of Sergi Agron.

"What on earth are you doing—or rather, not doing?" Sergi exploded at him.

"Waiting," Vladimir responded truthfully, echoing the guidance of his mentor. "I was instructed to escort the cargo to the Urals." He glanced around, "Is this not the Urals?"

"Yes, these are the Urals, you idiot. Why have you not unloaded the cargo from the rail cars?"

"I was not given such orders," Vladimir answered again with frankness.

"You are the one in charge!" Sergi rolled his eyes in disgust. "Where is your workforce? We must act swiftly. Any delay could prove deadly."

"For whom? Us?" Panic began to seep into Vladimir's voice as he imagined the fascist hoard descending on them.

"For your comrades at the Hermitage," Sergi said grimly.

The notorious leader of Leningrad's Haymarket Underground achieved more on his first day of arrival in Sverdlovsk than Vladimir had managed in four months. He coordinated, reprimanded, and even threatened bodily harm to the underwhelming workforce of elderly men and 'pretend soldiers.' He showcased to Vladimir what genuine leadership entailed and how even a one-armed man could move mountains. Having accomplished all his tasks in under a week, Sergi readied to depart, leaving behind the underwhelming 'leader' of the boyish troops.

"I intend to leave in the morning," Sergi announced over dinner one night.

"I had assumed you would be staying on with me," Vladimir replied nervously, "Where will you go? What will you do?"

"I am a trader. I barter for what one man possesses in excess in exchange for what he covets most," Sergi clarified. "I repeat the process until I obtain all that I need. Then, I shall return to Leningrad."

"Why did you come here first then?" Vladimir said, his mind teeming with confusion.

"To acquire what I desire most," Sergi said menacingly. "If you have impeded my pursuit, I will return to give you a sound thrashing. When I leave tomorrow, crate number One-Five-Eight-Three will accompany me."

"Where will you take it?" Vladimir asked. "No place in Russia is safe. It faces threats from both fascists and Bolsheviks."

"To London," Sergi said. "A man of Romanov blood still lives and breathes there. The contents of crate One-Five-Eight-Three belong solely to him now."

Vladimir nodded his understanding. "And what shall I do in the meantime while you are away?"

"You will excel in what you do best—doing nothing," Sergi reprimanded. "When the time comes, you will pack up the remaining crates and return to Leningrad. Do you comprehend?"

Vladimir stuttered, "How...how will I do that?"

"You do the exact opposite of what we have already accomplished. You cannot possibly be this inept? Now I understand why Director Orbeli sent you away. You would have done more harm than good had you remained in Leningrad."

Vladimir mulled over Sergi's words. Was he indeed 'sent away' because Joseph deemed him a liability? Was the crucial task of guarding the art merely a diversion? In that moment, Vladimir Levinson-Lessing resolved to overcome his fear and prove to himself and others that he could be 'an asset.' He drew inspiration from the advice he had once given Joseph at the war's outset: 'When circumstances become unfavorable, we must adjust our sails and adapt our course.' Determined not to see his ship wrecked on the hidden shoals of war due to indecision, he vowed to be prepared, to navigate around every obstacle that might arise. Thus, he embraced his role as a leader of men and vowed to no longer be afraid.

36

THE SQUALL

LENINGRAD - AUGUST 1943

The world's response to his newest symphony exceeded Dmitri's wildest dreams, surpassing even his most audacious imagination. Once again, he was reborn and basked in the adulation of his peers. Yet, beneath the surface of his newfound glory, unrelenting guilt lingered, stemming from his perceived abandonment of the people of St. Petersburg. His symphony, simply titled "Leningrad," publicly manifested this remorse. To attain true inner healing, Dmitri knew that his creation had to resound within the anguished walls of its birthplace. It was a necessity, a vital step towards redemption. If no one remained alive to conduct his magnum opus, he resolved to find a way back into the doomed city, leading the skeletal orchestra himself or sacrificing everything in the attempt. The call of his symphony was an unyielding force that would not rest until it had echoed through the very heart of St. Petersburg.

Stalin also found great satisfaction in Shostakovich's creation, yet his response lacked the depth of emotion that one would expect from an average person. There was no room for genuine sentiment within the tyrant—only calculated possibilities. The Red Tsar perceived Dmitri's masterpiece solely in its shrewd utility. He saw the potential for propaganda, the means to manipulate hearts and minds. Stalin recognized the psychological impact it could have on the fascist invaders surrounding Leningrad and intended to wield it as a potent weapon of war. He aimed to crush the spirits of the barbarian aggressors and fortify the revolution's message of unwavering dedication and sacrifice.

Therefore, it was no surprise to Marshal Zhdanov, the leading party official in Leningrad, when he received the written communiqué from Moscow. The directive was clear: The Leningrad symphony was to be performed in its entirety at the earliest possible opportunity by a dedicated ensemble of local musicians. The performance would be broadcasted over the radio, amplified by an awe-inspiring wall of speakers of such magnitude that it would resonate through the air, piercing the consciousness of the deluded warmonger in Berlin. The message was unequivocal: his aggressive war efforts were doomed. Zhdanov bore the weighty responsibility of ensuring the uninterrupted execution of this historical performance, employing all military means to fend off any potential interference from the fascist forces. The decree was resolute: success must be achieved at all costs.

The plan unfolded with remarkable clarity: Lieutenant General Govorov, entrusted with commanding the Leningrad Front's artillery corps, would spearhead the implementation of Zhdanov's orders. On the fateful day in August, a jarring Soviet military offensive, codenamed 'Squall,' would unleash an hour-long thunderous barrage of artillery, silencing the guns of the fascist invaders with shock and awe. It would be precisely at this moment, as the Leningrad Radio Orchestra commenced their awe-inspiring performance of Shostakovich's Symphony No. 7, that the titanic speakers would amplify the musical triumph, bombarding the German forces with a second onslaught of sound. This unorthodox orchestrated assault would deliver an unrelenting psychological blow, leaving no doubt that, despite enduring months of a harrowing blockade, the indomitable city and its defiant citizenry would never surrender or succumb to the savage attempt to starve them into submission.

Despite his impassioned objections voiced directly to the Politburo, Dmitri Shostakovich was denied re-entry into the besieged city of Leningrad. His life was deemed too precious to be jeopardized for a single performance. Instead, the composer would be compelled to experience the concert through the radio waves again, much like the thousands of others eagerly awaiting its transformative notes. However, Dmitri retained the authority to handpick the conductor who would navigate the treacherous path of interpreting his masterwork. That man was Karl Eliasberg, a figure more akin to a living skeleton than a robust individual, mirroring the emaciated state of Leningrad's remaining inhabitants.

Ravaged by dystrophy, his organs withering away, Eliasberg struggled to summon the strength to traverse the distance to rehearsals. Yet, a superhuman determination ignited within him, infusing his frail frame with a single-minded spirit that inspired the motley assembly of makeshift musicians enlisted for this momentous occasion. Unyielding in his commitment, Eliasberg also proved to be a stern taskmaster, withholding extra rations from orchestra members who missed or arrived late to rehearsals. Privately, he viewed the upcoming concert as an insurmountable challenge, akin to breaking the German blockade.

"Marshal Zhdanov," Eliasberg gasped between labored breaths, "I have serious doubts about the musicians' ability to accomplish this miracle."

"They must," came the harsh decree from the political leader of Leningrad, "or perish in the attempt."

"They lack the energy and mental acuity necessary to tackle such a complex masterpiece. The 7th Symphony is intricate and not easily grasped by performers who are wasting away."

"You must suppress any dissent and find a way, maestro. You have nine days. Those are your orders," Zhdanov said with the finality of an executioner, abruptly departing the theater after assessing the progress of the rehearsals.

From the shadows of the balcony emerged a voice akin to that of a fallen angel. "Zhdanov is a self-serving imbecile who cares only for his personal well-being."

Eliasberg looked up to see the infamous black market crime boss. While he appreciated Sergi Agron's extra rations for the orchestra, Eliasberg despised the previously arranged agreement that obligated him to include this despicable man in the performance.

"We need to discuss my solo," Sergi said as he descended onto the stage.

"What about it?"

"Somehow, there is always someone dying or collapsing just before my grand performance," Sergi complained. "It is incredibly inconsiderate," he added callously.

"What would you have me do?" the maestro said, rubbing his throbbing temples. "The performers are still malnourished, and the Pushkin Theater has no running water. If we do not starve to death first, we will surely collapse from thirst."

"Perhaps we could request a change of venue?" Sergi suggested.

"And who should we approach, and why would they care, Sergi? You witnessed Zhdanov's foul mood firsthand. He is not inclined to sympathize."

"To motivate a man like him, you appeal not to his heart, but to his stomach. I can make it in Zhdanov's best interest to move us to a superior theater, one that is cooler and has running water," Sergi said. "He will not be able to refuse without risking the loss of my special deliveries of caviar and boar's meat. Tell me, where would be a suitable venue for our concert?"

"Tell him to relocate the performance to the Grand Philharmonia Hall," Eliasberg said, a half-smile creeping across his face. "There, we just might have a chance to pull off the performance."

"And my solo," Sergi reminded him.

⁂

The Leningrad Philharmonia Hall slowly filled with an audience radiating restrained energy. Each concertgoer had managed to endure two brutal winters under the fascist siege, seasons marked by death and starvation. They had gathered to celebrate this improbable survival and to witness the city premiere of Shostakovich's 7th Symphony. A musical piece he had dedicated to the city he cherished. It represented a hopeful breath of life in their summer of renewal. Some had heard the world premiere of Shostakovich's 'Leningrad' on the radio five months prior, but most had not; they were preoccupied with burying their dead and scavenging for sustenance. Tonight's performance offered a chance to experience a resurgence, to envision a world free of war and hunger.

Levon Orbeli claimed his seat among the fifteen hundred, perusing the theater from his elevated position in the stage-left balcony. Levon observed the varied cross-section of audience members below. Ironworkers, engineers, and academics huddled in harmony while party members and revered old men in uniforms adorned with a cascade of medals looked on from above. A thought occurred to Levon, a nod to Aristotle: 'A common enemy unites even the bitterest of foes.' Regardless of their unique circumstances, social status, or personal beliefs, they had found common ground tonight. Such unity is possible, Levon thought to himself, when the stakes are high enough, and the ego is sufficiently humbled.

The audience greeted tonight's conductor, Karl Eliasberg, with polite applause while the assembly of musicians, their clothing torn and disheveled, raised their instruments in tribute. Eliasberg reciprocated their displays of affection, bowing with stoic grace, yet he could not help but wonder if the crowd's adoration might morph into disdain before the night was over. Under his direction, the orchestra had managed to execute the intricate composition just once in rehearsal. The magnum opus, spanning a grueling eighty minutes, would present a formidable challenge. Could they rise to the occasion?

Precisely on the hour, as if timed to the minute, the ominous rumble of distant Soviet artillery abruptly ceased. The deafening silence was promptly replaced with a discordant surge of feedback as the wall of speakers directed towards the fascist lines sprang to life. Eliasberg took a deep, steadying breath, raised his baton, and initiated his auditory assault against the besiegers.

The introductory strains of Shostakovich's first movement burst into the air - at first inspiring and proud. They delivered a powerful punch against an unseen enemy before subtly transitioning into a delicate evocation of peaceful, bygone summers and the tranquil life that characterized their city before the advent of two oppressors - fascists and Bolsheviks. This idyllic past lingered in the theater for seven minutes, wafting through the space like a honeybee on a leisurely tour of a field of Forget-Me-Nots. Each note released a sweet scent as intoxicating as the cherished fragrances of childhood. Yet, the spell of this utopian interlude shattered as swiftly as it had been conjured by the auditory introduction of 'invaders.' The persistent 22-measure 'ostinato,' reminiscent of Ravel's 'Boléro,' suffused the air within and beyond the theater with a repetitive drum line - a march. It signaled the approach of a looming enemy, though the direction of their advance - east or west - was left ambiguous.

Levon gasped at the realization of the manifold meanings hidden within Shostakovich's complex score. He continually held his breath in the wake of each fresh revelation. The music was the most inspiring sound Levon had ever heard. His eyes welled with tears, memories rushed forward in a relentless assault, and all the while, the orchestra pressed on. They spurred one another to continue performing just as the entire populace of Leningrad had encouraged each other to persist in the face of adversity. There was no doubt in Levon's mind that the people of Leningrad would overcome all their oppressors.

The fascist foot soldiers, hunkered down at the city's gates and barraged by the resonating music, also grasped this truth. Their high command in Berlin, too, swiftly recognized their misjudgment. However, it was only the Party leaders, ensconced high above in the Tsar's erstwhile gilded theater box, who remained obtuse to the fact that this symphony heralded not just the triumph over the current foe but also the Bolsheviks' inevitable downfall and the termination of the revolution. The true victors would be the indomitable human spirit, graced by the divine and manifested as Shostakovich's 7th Symphony.

Therefore, the response from the audience, both those gathered in the theater that night and those tuning in worldwide, was predictably overwhelming. For more than an hour, people in the theater remained standing, applauding, shouting, their emotions spilling over, even after the final refrain had faded into the night's ether. This stalwart declaration, a refusal to succumb to immeasurable suffering, possessed such unyielding strength that it would never be forgotten. It was forever etched into the collective soul of humanity.

Breathless and swelling with pride, Levon navigated through the teeming crowd, making his way onto the stage to personally congratulate the victorious musicians. Scanning for a familiar face to share his joy with, he bumped into an ecstatic Sergi Agron.

"Did you hear my gong solo? My illustrious gong sounded the alarm!" Sergi shouted over the thunderous applause of the enthralled crowd.

"My brother told me you were a man of many surprising talents, but not until this very moment, did I believe him," Levon said, bear-hugging the one-armed man.

"I told them, as sure as rain, I told them," Sergi said, tears streaming down his cheeks. The surge of emotion, acceptance, and acknowledgment for something noble was more than Sergi envisioned. A man universally seen as a personification of evil was, for the first time, being loved. The grace of the divine had redeemed him through the power of music.

The Soviet bombardment of the German forces outside the gates of Leningrad that night followed by the musical onslaught of Stostakovich's masterpiece had earned the Russian people a decisive psychological victory. The protracted siege, now two years old, continued onward as the fascists tightened their grip and resolved to starve the city of Leningrad until no one was left alive to resist.

Thousands of kilometers away, Dmitri Shostakovich collapsed into his leather chair, drained of every last ounce of energy. Throughout the eighty-minute performance, he clenched his jaw, wrung his hands, and paced in anticipation of the worst. The pure joy Dmitri felt at the orchestra's triumph was immeasurable. His success, he realized, was entirely due to the relentless efforts of others. Achievements are not forged in isolation. The dedication of a supportive community—friends, family, and associates—propels one to the finish line, despite one's doubts and human frailties. Dmitri knew he was a fortunate man.

He fell to his knees, his gaze turned towards the heavens, expressing gratitude to Joseph Orbeli for saving his life. Firstly, by offering him a job that allowed him to sustain his family and then later by sparing him the inevitable agony of being incinerated by an unexploded bomb. He thanked the unknown voice on the other end of the phone line that informed him of his evacuation. He honored the driver of the convoy truck who navigated his family out of danger on the 'Road of Life,' and he extolled the virtues of a 'dead man,' Fyodor Raskolnikov, who had given his musical creation life beyond the borders of the Soviet Union. Without these individuals, future generations would not have remembered Dmitri's work, energy, and essence. He did not consider himself deserving of this gift of immortality, but others saw him as worthy and insisted on bestowing it upon him. For that, he felt truly blessed.

37

THE HOMECOMING

SOVIET REPUBLIC OF GEORGIA - AUTUMN 1943

Joseph Orbeli's forced evacuation to his ancestral homeland, a vast 2,600 kilometers south of Leningrad, had spared him from a fate much darker. The subtropical climate of Tbilisi, nestled at the crossroads of Europe and Asia, offered Joseph a reprieve from the cold and relentless malnutrition that haunted those still trapped in Leningrad. Yet, even in this haven, guilt gnawed at him—an unrelenting shadow cast by his abandonment of Tatiana.

Reuben, his eldest brother, endeavored to soothe Joseph's physical and emotional wounds through intellectual engagement. They immersed themselves in discussions about Reuben's research along the Caspian Sea—examining the tragic similarities among civilizations and the causes of their demise. They dined in Tbilisi's restaurants, strolled through the local gardens, and luxuriated in public steam baths, all to heal Joseph's battered body. However, the emotional scars remained raw, demanding a

305

subtler remedy. To address this, the brothers relocated to Reuben's dacha in the serene hills of Mestia, 450 kilometers northwest of Tbilisi.

In Mestia, Reuben retreated to the rolling alpine hills, where he normally conducted his scholarly writing in solitude. As an archaeologist, he was a skilled detective of the past, sifting through layers of forgotten history to unearth the sorrowful declines of once-great nations, cities, and peoples. His research led him to a stark realization: humanity is fated to repeat its mistakes because so few study history or learn from its lessons. Thus, his urgent plea to Joseph at the outset of yet another senseless war: "Document the impending tragedy I fear will befall our city. Chronicle it, hide it and preserve the truth at all costs. He who controls the archives controls the story of our people."

One morning, as the sun bathed the landscape in a soft golden hue, Reuben greeted Joseph at the top of the Svaneti tower attached to his stone house. These defensive towers, constructed between the 9th and 12th centuries, commanded breathtaking views of the snow-capped peaks to the north. Reuben had spared no expense renovating the tower, converting the uppermost floor into a cozy study with access to a rooftop observatory. As he handed Joseph a steaming cup of salep, he remarked, "You're up early."

"I'm still struggling to sleep through the night," Joseph confessed, gratefully accepting the warm drink. He gazed out at the serene landscape and murmured, "It's hard to believe there's a war still raging."

Reuben placed a reassuring hand on Joseph's shoulder. "These peaks have long shielded this land from a multitude of aggressors as well as Russia's cold."

"In all the months we've been together, I've never properly thanked you for saving my life, Reuben. I owe you a debt I doubt I can ever repay."

Reuben moved to an expansive bookshelf resting against a cracked wall. "Debts are like children—begotten with pleasure but borne with pain," he said, pulling out a volume of Molière's plays. "I'm just thankful you're still here."

Joseph nodded, his thoughts drifting back to Tatiana and those still struggling in the Hermitage. "I have no children, no wife. To me, pleasure and pain are inseparable—curses."

"I can only imagine the horrors you've endured, Joseph. I was in the dark until Levon's letter arrived, asking for my help to get you out of St. Petersburg. Stalin has kept the truth about the fascists' victories and our people's suffering from the world. No one knows the desperate conditions in our beloved city."

Joseph's mind flashed back to his initial encounter with Sergi Agron and the chilling offer to sell him the sugary dirt from beneath the burned-out Badaev warehouses as a substitute for food. He recalled Sergi's contemptuous smile as he said, "A glass from the first meter of soil will cost you one hundred Rubles. Deeper layers are only fifty."

"Nobody is aware? More like nobody cares!" Joseph's head pounded, and though he longed to speak more, his rage left him speechless. Instead, he saw only the emaciated bodies stacked like frozen firewood on street corners.

Reuben stroked his long gray hair, trying to fathom his brother's torment. Sadness filled him as he pondered the relentless cycle of humanity's self-destruction. "There have been thirty-two advanced civilizations that have collapsed over the past 5,000 years, and I've excavated the remains of most. Debt, war, and resource depletion have doomed them all, and we are next."

Joseph looked at his brother, whose deep-seated eyes bore witness to countless seasons spent in the field documenting the death throes of civilizations like the Sumerians, Babylonians, and Hittites. "Is this your way of cheering me up?"

"No," Reuben said, his voice solemn. "It's my way of sobering you up. We are a violent race that willingly sow the seeds of its destruction. This is why it's crucial to record our history accurately. We will never change our foolish ways unless the consequences are clear and irrefutable."

"Your words, Reuben, remind me of when I presided over the 3rd International Congress of Iranian Art at the Hermitage in 1938. Has it only been five years? I had the pleasure of meeting the remarkable Will Durant. Are you familiar with his writings?"

Reuben responded with his characteristic playful arrogance—something Joseph had sorely missed. "Oh, please, the real question is whether Will Durant is familiar with my writings!"

Joseph continued, recalling Durant's insightful observations that had stayed with him as conditions in Russia worsened. "Durant once said, 'From barbarism to civilization takes a century; from civilization to barbarism takes but a day.'"

Reuben nodded in somber agreement. "Indeed, since the Bolsheviks came to power, they have steadily eroded the elements that define our civilization—truth, beauty, adventure, art, and peace. Everything is vanishing." Reuben debated his next move before deciding his brother needed to know the truth. "Ah, that reminds me," he said, rummaging through his coat pockets. "A letter from Levon arrived for you."

Joseph took the envelope from Reuben and read the letter aloud, each line sinking him deeper into despair.

'Dear Brother, I write with alarming news. The situation in Leningrad has deteriorated from nightmarish to apocalyptic. It's as if Hades himself has claimed our city. The food shortage has worsened as the fascists

tighten their grip. Packs of ghouls, which I've named 'coffin wolves,' roam the city at night, feasting on corpses and preying on those unfortunate enough to be out alone. In these grim circumstances, I must tell you that Tatiana has vanished. I spoke with your chief of security at the Hermitage, who informed me that no food deliveries have arrived in over a month. Driven by desperation, Tatiana ventured out to find her father. She's been missing for a week, and our worst fears are surfacing. I have my armed cadets searching for her. I promise you, Joseph, if Tatiana is still alive, we will find her.'

Joseph folded the letter with a heavy heart, struggling to come to terms with his guilt over Tatiana's fate. "The last bastion of civilization teeters on the edge," he echoed Durant's ominous prophecy. "I must return to St. Petersburg, Reuben. Will you help me?"

Reuben looked at his brother with a heavy heart, knowing that a return to that city might lead to Joseph's death as well. Yet, how could he deny Joseph the relief from his mental anguish that he so desperately sought? "I know someone with a plane who can take you back."

"Who?"

"A foolish old man with a soft spot for hopeless love stories."

38

THE REDEMPTION

LENINGRAD - AUTUMN 1943

Joseph Orbeli defied all odds as he slipped through the gates of Leningrad, his steps cautious and heavy with despair. In less than 72 hours after receiving his brother's letter, Joseph had navigated his way back to the war-ravaged city, racing to Levon's office to pore over reports of ongoing searches for Tatiana. The city was being combed, block by block, building by building; no corner was left unchecked. While Levon's armed Corps of Cadets diligently scoured the city, Joseph set out on a desperate quest to find the woman he loved.

Where would a woman of faith seek refuge in a world turned upside down? Joseph wondered. A church seemed the logical choice. With that thought guiding him, he made his way to The Church on Spilled Blood—the place where Tatiana had once asked him to pray with her, and where his refusal to marry her had cost her the chance to evacuate as his wife.

As he stepped into the vast, solemn space of the church, Joseph's eyes scanned the empty expanse of what had once been a sacred haven. When he saw no sign of Tatiana, he called out her name, only to be met with the hollow echo of his voice. The stale air seemed to hold a faint trace of incense, a ghost of the past. Joseph took a moment to collect his thoughts before lifting his eyes to the soaring vault of the sanctuary, his voice trembling as he addressed God.

"Why do people only turn to you in their darkest hours?" he whispered. "Is it because their prayers go unanswered? Shouldn't we be grateful for each day we're given, for another sunrise? I've turned away from you myself, not just because of unanswered prayers, but because you've forced me to endure another day in this hell," he said, bitterness sharp in his voice. "Another day without my father. Another day without my wife and unborn child, whom you took from me, turning what should have been joy into profound sorrow years ago. How can people maintain unwavering faith when you allow such suffering to persist, even among your most devoted followers?" Tears welled in Joseph's eyes as he drew a ragged breath. "So here I am again, begging for a miracle. Give me a chance at happiness. Allow me to make amends."

Joseph fell to his knees, overwhelmed by grief. His sobs were raw and unrestrained, each cry a release of the agony that had consumed him for too long. When his tears finally subsided, he began to hum—a hopeful

Ukrainian New Year's Day song that his wife used to sing to their unborn child as they lay together at night, dreaming of a future that would never be. His voice cracked as he sang, "A little swallow flew...Where is my little swallow now?"

"Do not take her. Do not dare take Tatiana!" he yelled out to the heavens. "I cannot endure another loss. If you must take someone, take me instead. I am unworthy of your mercy. My heart is shattered, and my soul is drained, mourning a life we never got to share. The thought of her absence, of dreams never realized, tears me apart. I beg you, take me in her place!"

The gentle patter of rain on the enameled roof of the bell tower was the only answer Joseph received. It seemed that God had once again chosen to not answer his prayers. With no sign of divine intervention, Joseph rose from the cold floor, his resolve hardened. He would find Tatiana, or he would die trying.

❧ ❦

After leaving The Church on Spilled Blood, Joseph found himself wandering like a white martyr pilgrim, navigating an endless maze of the expansive avenues and slender riverside paths of Leningrad. He arrived at the entrance to St. Isaac's Cathedral as if guided by an invisible hand. Could

Tatiana along with the peace and comfort he sought be nestled within these holy walls? After a simple step over another threshold, Joseph found himself transported back in time.

St. Isaac's Cathedral was perhaps the most eminent house of worship in Leningrad. This mountain of faith presents a formidable silhouette. Named after St. Isaac of Dalmatia, Peter the Great's patron saint, its construction spanned four decades. The cathedral's foundation rests upon twenty-five thousand ingeniously placed wooden piles driven into the marshy land beneath. An astounding one million gold rubles were invested in its edification in the early 19th century. Like all houses of worship in this once splendid Tsarist capital, it was repurposed as a museum — more accurately, a storage facility — shortly after the revolution. The Bolsheviks stripped the cathedral of its ornamental riches, but they did not eradicate the awe-inspiring stained-glass windows or the exquisite frescos gracing its walls and ceilings. For this, Joseph was grateful.

The cathedral's towering flying buttresses and malachite columns silently welcomed Joseph. He noted the transformations since his last visit over two decades ago — back then, he had come to grieve his father's passing; today, he returned to mourn what felt like the loss of his soul. The cathedral's once golden dome now wore a dull gray coat to divert attention from fascist bombers and artillery. A sighting scope had been installed on its skylights, enabling the detection of the invaders' concealed heavy gun positions. "From civilization to barbarism needs but a day," he muttered softly.

Ambling through the vast chamber, Joseph's footsteps echoed back at him, resonating with the voices of angels and archangels that the Bolshevik infidels had somehow spared. He eventually found himself before the Holy Doors, guarded by two towering Lapis Lazuli columns shielding the sanctuary and the treasured image he yearned to gaze upon once more. Sensing a presence behind him, Joseph pivoted and saw Levon.

"Did your spies lead you to me?"

"You are too predictable, Joseph. I just knew you would find your way here."

"Then help me open these doors," Joseph pleaded. "I need to see Him."

The brothers exerted themselves to move the massive, forty-foot-tall, gilded paneled doors. Their joint effort bore fruit as they beheld what lay beyond - the large, vibrant stained-glass window depicting the 'Resurrected Christ.'

Joseph's gaze was absorbed by the majestic image. "Do you still believe in salvation?"

Levon hesitated, uncertainty creeping into his mind. "Our father considered this the most stunning window in all of Europe and Asia. Do you know why it held more allure for him than those at Sainte-Chapelle, La Sagrada Família, or even at the Nasir al-Mulk Mosque?"

Joseph shook his head, his thoughts consumed by the man he so profoundly revered, whose strength and wisdom he now yearned for more than ever.

"It is because it resides here, in St. Petersburg," Levon said.

Joseph exhaled a deep woeful breath, his voice lost, unable to meet his brother's gaze.

"And do you know why St. Petersburg will endure this merciless siege and the ravages of the Bolsheviks' rule? It is because you, Joseph, are once again here, in St. Petersburg."

"I am a flawed human being. I am not deserving of your praises."

"We are all flawed," Levon replied. "That is why God sacrificed His own Son for humanity. And that is why our father sacrificed himself – to spare his sons."

"An omnipotent, benevolent God cannot exist amid all the evil and suffering that has gripped St. Petersburg. If He truly existed, He would not have permitted our father's death, the demise of my wife and child, or the impending loss of Tatiana," Joseph whispered, pain straining his voice.

"To endure hardship and persevere is the Russian way," Levon reminded him.

"Then I no longer care to be Russian. I no longer wish to be part of the human race—a world where there is no God and, by default, there is no 'truth, beauty, adventure, art, or peace.'"

"You sound like Reuben."

"No, I sound like a sane human being living in an insane world," Joseph countered, "a world devoid of miracles."

Levon gazed at the 'Resurrected Christ' above him. What words of wisdom could he impart to Joseph that might offer him solace? Then, Dostoevsky's words came to him. "To remain a human being among people, despite the circumstances, never succumbing to despair or losing hope—that's what life is about; that's its ultimate task.' As Levon's words faded into oblivion, a cadet approached him with a message.

"Tatiana is alive, Joseph! They found her...by the grace of God, they found her!"

Joseph and Levon, followed by a cadre of cadets, rushed along the left bank of the Neva River as the sun began to dip below the horizon. Slowing their steps, the group entered the hallowed grounds of the Smolny Cathedral with its adjoining Convent of the Resurrection. The peculiar history of this holy place was not lost on Joseph as he gazed up at the comforting blue and white structures that defined its perimeter.

The convent was once the home of Elizabeth, Peter the Great's daughter, who took refuge here after being denied succession following her father's death. Elizabeth fully intended to become a nun, but fate intervened when the Royal Guard rebelled, overthrew the 'infant emperor' Ivan VI, and cleared the way for Elizabeth's reign. She continued the policies of her father, financing the construction of Peterhof Palace, the Winter Palace, and the Smolny Cathedral. Unlike the Bolsheviks, Elizabeth enhanced and modernized Russia. She was the last true 'agnatic ruler of the House of Romanov.' Now, two hundred years later, Elizabeth's place of refuge served as a safe haven for another woman of faith.

"What are you doing here?" Tatiana said in a weak whisper, disbelief in her eyes as Joseph entered the infirmary. "You should be a thousand kilometers away from this mournful place, eating lemons and limes."

"I have a wedding to attend," he said, kneeling beside Tatiana, gently stroking her hair.

Taken aback and overcome with emotion, Tatiana sunk into her pillow, moaning in agony. Joseph pulled back, worried and bewildered by her response to what he had envisioned would be a tender reunion. Was she critically ill? Was she spurning him? He did not know. But he realized, at that moment, he could not bear to be apart from her ever again.

"Tatiana," Joseph said, trying to reassure her. "Tatiana, please."

Struggling to believe he had returned, Tatiana's eyes met Joseph's. Was her fever causing her to hallucinate? "Why would you risk your life to return to this graveyard of a city?" she moaned. "There is no life left here."

"I returned for you, my love, I cannot endure another moment apart."

"Then you are in love with a ghost, I am already gone."

"Hush," he murmured soothingly. "I will never leave you again, and together, we will cultivate a life filled with love, laughter and art." He paused and then added, "Under the merciful grace of God, however undeserving I may be."

Tatiana buried her face into Joseph's shoulder, her emotions overwhelming her again. If only she still had the strength to weep, she would have shed tears of joy. But her weakened state had stripped her even of that comfort. "I would be content with a lifetime of sleep," she confessed before losing consciousness in Joseph's arms.

39

THE EXPAT

LONDON - SPRING 1944

"I must return to Russia," Anna announced one evening as she and Silas ambled alongside the Thames. "My son is still imprisoned there. I cannot go on living this fairy tale not knowing if he is dead or alive. I need to bear witness to his fate and the fate of Leningrad. My poetry must speak for those who can no longer speak for themselves."

"Would my plea for you to stay change anything?" Silas posed the question more for himself than for her, well aware of her imminent reply. "I, too, must depart from London, you could accompany me."

"And where would we go?"

"America. The arduous task you have asked of the British people can only be fulfilled with assistance from the United States."

"They are already present here," Anna observed, "why journey further?"

"Only America has the capacity to defeat the fascists, provided I can convince them of the urgency to do so," he explained.

"Were you ordered to go?"

"No, but the Prime Minister has implored me to undertake this final task for King and Country."

"Whose king and whose country? Your true homeland lies eastward, not westward. Your family's honor demands retribution," she reminded him.

"And who was it that decimated my family, Anna? I'll tell you who, it was the silent capitulation of the Russian people. There has been too much bloodshed under the pretext of patriotism and brotherhood. I will not be responsible for anymore."

A wave of guilt rushed over Anna. "Will you return to London after this task has been completed?"

Silas contemplated Anna's question as they continued their mournful stroll through the foggy night. As the chimes of Big Ben echoed through the air, marking the late hour, he halted and turned to face her. "I will not return; neither to England nor to Russia. Upon completing my mission, I intend to remain in America, to carve out a new existence, under a new identity."

"In Washington, DC?" Anna asked, not knowing what else to say.

"In the serene expanses and granite notches of the White Mountains, in a far-away place known as New Hampshire," Silas declared. "A new 'Winter Palace' awaits me there."

Despite not recognizing it during their shared decision to depart London, Anna, and Silas would spend many more months in each other's company. However, an irrevocable shift had occurred between them. An unvoiced melancholy hung over their forbidden love, a love doomed never to reach its apex or to bloom in any sun-drenched garden along the Neva. They would be exiles from one another, Anna forever remaining an unreachable land in Silas's heart. It was a pain the French referred to as '*ladouleur exquise*,' and Silas would never fully recover from it.

Silas lingered alone on the Portsmouth dock, his gaze fixed on a departing fishing boat carrying Anna back to her homeland. With the Leningrad siege lifted months earlier, she was returning to a country both exploited and cursed, first by a force promising liberation, then morphing into a cruel jailer. The Bolshevik reign only worsened the economic turmoil, food shortages, and corruption. Violence, too, had exponentially escalated.

Two and a half decades earlier, the Bolsheviks had not only arrested Tsar Nicholas II and his young family but also orchestrated their gruesome execution—an agonizing affair that spanned over twenty minutes. Yet this bloodshed failed to sate their thirst for vengeance. They persisted in hunting and ruthlessly exterminating any individual harboring the Romanov bloodline.

Due to these chilling realities, Silas could not accompany Anna back to Leningrad. Every fiber of his being yearned to remain by her side, but setting foot in Russia would be akin to slipping his neck into a noose. His current stay in London was tenuous at best, given the ever-present threat of Soviet agents fervently hunting down Romanov descendants who had evaded Bolshevik retribution.

Silas stole one last glimpse of the woman he was destined never to see again as the fishing boat traversed the breakwater. Reaching into his trench coat, he retrieved an ornate ebony box adorned with a double-headed eagle; the Romanov family seal. Silas stoically placed Anna's latest poem, 'Courage,' inside it. This piece would find its final resting place among his grandfather's jests, a fitting addition considering how fate had made a mockery of him. Anna and Silas had lost not just each other but also their courage.

A week later, Silas found himself on yet another dock observing another ship preparing to embark. The sea was not foreign to him. Three years prior, as part of Churchill's staff, he had embarked on a different transatlantic journey to Newfoundland. This distant memory prompted a smile from Silas. He had swindled much of Churchill's cash during that voyage, persistently triumphing over his superior in countless backgammon matches. His tendency to lavishly tip the ship's cooks and wardroom attendants using his winnings further irritated Churchill. Silas anticipated this voyage would be less cheerful.

"Fine ship," a voice remarked beside him.

"Hello, brother," Silas replied, "Good to see you punctual for once," he added with a playful jibe.

Despite knowing it, Horatio Bollerud feigned interest in the ship's nameplate. "Ah, the HMS Courageous will be our trireme across the vast sea to a new land, a new life. Quite the auspicious sign."

A grimace flickered across Silas's face. "You need not accompany me to America. I no longer require a nanny."

"Indeed, but at some juncture in life, we all need caregivers, Silas.

"Even so, I am physically capable and mentally sound."

"Ah, but it is your heart that needs mending," Horatio reminded him.

Facing the biting wind, Silas gazed eastward. Had he made the correct decision, letting her go? Turning his attention back to the ship's stern, he watched as crate number One-Five-Eight-Three was lowered onto the deck of the aging British warship. "Hard to believe some things from the family survived. I presumed it all lost long ago, Horatio."

"A peaceful mind begins when we cease declaring, 'I have lost it,' and instead proclaim, 'It has been returned to whence it came,'" Horatio interjected.

"Another morsel of your fraternal wisdom?"

"No, another morsel from Epictetus," Horatio corrected him. "Do you know what else he said? 'It is not what happens to you, but how you react to it that matters.' We will board this ship, sail for America, and never look back."

"'History repeats itself, first as a tragedy, second as a farce,'" Silas quoted. "That is why we must ensure our history is properly chronicled and never forgotten. For without memory of yesterday, we are hopelessly adrift in a tempest called ignorance."

40

THE RETURN

LENINGRAD – JUNE 1944

In January 1944, the fascist Army Group North was finally routed and driven away from Leningrad. The blockade had been shattered. For 872 agonizing days, the citizens of Leningrad had endured a relentless siege. Over a million residents perished from starvation, while another million and a half, mostly women and children, were evacuated across the ice. Just outside Leningrad's gates, along the once tranquil banks of the Neva River, more than 100,000 Soviet soldiers and an equal number of Germans fought and died over a parcel of land no larger than one square kilometer—roughly one-third the size of Central Park in New York City.

Five months later, on the first day summer, Anna leaned against the scarred and pockmarked brick wall of the Radio Committee Building, noting how it mirrored her battered exterior. Anna was no stranger to love or suffering, yet the emptiness she felt within surprised even her. Had she erred in returning? Could this mistake prove fatal? With each passing day, death crept closer, devouring time already past. It was winning a war that individuals did not realize they had already lost. Thus, fearing death or anticipating it was irrational in her mind. It was part of each day, each hour, ticking away steadily like a metronome.

Seeing her weathered friend and confidante exiting the building filled Anna with immense joy and inconsolable sadness. Olga, too, experienced a similar flood of conflicting emotions when she recognized the figure before her was not a mirage but a tangible presence offering a true promise of life. They stared at each other for a long moment, savoring each other's existence before erupting into tears.

Olga found her voice first, "What are you doing here? Are you out of your mind?"

"I would only be out of my mind if I had not returned to you and the city I love by the Neva," Anna replied, her voice weak.

They embraced, leaning against the supportive wall of the building, each confessing they had thought the other dead until they heard their spectral voices late at night on the radio waves. The unexpected strength those words gave each of them was profound. As they strolled arm in arm along the city's canals, like in the old days, they shared their trials and tribulations of the past three years.

Olga listened, incredulous, as her friend spoke of her improbable romance with a man of royal descent. This man had made her question everything she had valued and known, not only about the revolution but about herself. He had instilled in her the confidence to attempt the impossible and had given her 'Courage.'

In turn, Anna paid close attention as Olga recounted her battles with loneliness and self-doubt, her regrets, and the lengths she had gone to for survival and to maintain her nagging cigarette habit. Olga voiced her self-deprecating views of the poetry she had written during the siege and its worthiness to be included in the annals of history.

The ease with which they carried on these deeply personal conversations after years apart spoke to their profound kinship and shared experiences of loss and redemption. They had missed each other's company terribly and vowed never to separate again. To this end, Anna moved into Olga's apartment, attempting to gauge the potential repercussions of her unsanctioned return from the city's leaders. Regardless of the consequence, Anna vowed to accept it with grace and unwavering resolve.

As she waited for her fate to unfold, Anna relentlessly embedded line after line of her ongoing magnum opus—a poem that would eventually become her *"Requiem"*—into Olga's memory. Olga had devoted years to this task and often became irritated with Anna when she demanded relearning previously memorized sections. *"Requiem"* was more than words on a page—it was a living, breathing entity. If Anna revised it in her mind, she expected Olga to adapt accordingly.

"I have reworked the beginning," Anna informed her friend, "to reflect my time in London, my experiences with Silas, and my subsequent return home."

A slight frown creased Olga's face, her disapproval apparent.

Reading her friend's reaction, Anna reassured her, "Do not fret, it is only four lines. But it is crucial that you, and the others I have chosen as my memory bearers, grasp these changes. I firmly believe that this poem—my life's testament—will not appear in print until after I am gone from this world. That is why it is so vital. Do you understand?"

Olga peered at her friend with affectionate eyes. "Proceed," she said, "Relieve your soul. I am here to bear witness to your pain."

With a gentle touch, Anna caressed Olga's face. Foreheads touching, she began to recite the fresh lines.

'No, not under the vaults of alien skies,

And not under the shelter of alien wings—

I was with my people then,

There, where my people, unfortunately, were.'

Anna did not have to wait long for her judgment from the leaders of her people. Considering the alternatives, she got off relatively easily, according to others' estimations. Anna was unceremoniously ousted from the Writer's Union, her membership revoked. She was forbidden to write or perform any of her poetry in public or private venues, and she was sentenced to work as a manual laborer on one of the many restoration projects undertaken to repair the siege's damage.

While working on one of these projects, Anna unexpectedly ran into Joseph Orbeli. She had not seen him since he had helped orchestrate her silent exit from the city en route to London years before. He was tending to the apple trees bordering the fountain pools at Peterhof Palace. As she neared him, she heard him chatting as though he was conversing deeply with an unseen companion.

"Hello," she greeted tentatively as she came within earshot, unsure of his reaction to her presence.

Joseph turned, gazing upon her with the sunburned countenance of a man who finally freed himself from his demons. No longer the prim and proper authority figure responsible for thousands, he was now a solitary man, determined to live each day with intention. He extended his hand, placing something in hers.

Anna glanced at her palm, a silver medal gleaming up at her. On its face was a solitary word: 'Courage.' She looked at Joseph, her eyes reflecting her surprise.

"Silas inspired the idea of presenting medals to all of the siege's heroes," he began, mentioning a name Anna had been trying desperately to forget, catching her off guard.

"How do you know Silas?" Anna managed to ask amidst her shock.

"Have you not heard? Versemakers know everything," Joseph replied, his faint smile accompanied by a wink.

"How did you know I would..." Anna began but cut herself off.

Joseph turned to pluck an apple from a nearby tree. Biting into it, he savored the flavorful but bittersweet juice. "Do you know the best time to plant an apple tree?" he asked, handing the fruit to Anna.

Shaking her head, she bit into the ripe fruit, signaling her lack of knowledge.

"Yesterday," he answered. "The tree of knowledge allows us to remember yesterday. That is the forbidden fruit that generates or averts all of our world's woes. Always remember yesterday, Anna," he added before turning away and continuing his conversation with his invisible confidant.

As Anna turned to view the Gulf of Finland shimmering in the distance, she thought of the man she loved but could not have. Somewhere to the west, this man without a country was journeying forward without her.

I delighted in deliriums,

In singing about tombs.

I distributed misfortunes

Beyond anyone's strength.

The curtain not raised,

The circle dance of shades -

Because of that, all my loved ones

Were taken away.

All this is disclosed

In the depths of the roses,

But I am not allowed to forget

The taste of the tears of yesterday.

41

THE END

"I did not know the Hermitage still had a store of silver," Levon Orbeli remarked, his fingers caressing a medal that suspiciously resembled the Cross of St. George.

"There are many things about the Hermitage you do not know," Joseph said, his tone terse, hoping to divert his brother's attention.

"It is curious how you managed to present silver medals to all the survivors of the siege who served the museum," Levon probed further, a hint of skepticism in his voice.

Joseph shrugged his shoulders. "Sometimes miracles simply happen."

"I distinctly recall a similar feeling when you hosted the 3rd International Congress of Iranian Art in 1938. Each of the participants, nearly two hundred, received silver medals from you as well. That should have depleted the Hermitage's silver stores. Quite a coincidence, don't you think?" Levon pressed on.

"As our grandfather used to say, 'coincidence is God's way of remaining anonymous.' It is better not to dwell on such matters."

"In my eyes, you have always had unwavering faith, Joseph. I admire that about you, but unfortunately, I do not possess it."

"People often misconstrue faith," Joseph replied, thinking of Tatiana's words and the Hermitage's Raphael Loggias. "Faith is not about everything turning out okay. Faith is about being okay no matter how things turn out."

Levon smiled, reassuringly touching his brother's shoulder, surveying the sparsely furnished office. "I think I would like a cup of black tea. Would you mind making me some from our family's silver samovar?"

Joseph paused his rummaging through the crate in his office, turning to face his brother. "I am sorry. The samovar was lost during the blockade, most likely stolen during my absence."

Levon rested his hands back on Joseph's shoulders, meeting his gaze. "You are a terrible liar, Joseph, but you have the heart of a saint. I hope history remembers all that you have done here during the blockade. You are a true patriot, not just of Mother Russia, but of humanity as a whole. You deserve medals more than I do."

Tears welled up in Joseph's eyes. "Knowing that future generations will be able to gaze upon the art in the Hermitage is all the gratitude I need."

"If you say so," Levon grinned, donning his coat as he prepared to leave. "Reuben was right."

"About what?"

"He believed you would make an excellent guardian of 'the family chronicle,'" Levon answered enigmatically, dropping a letter from Reuben on Joseph's desk before darting out of the room.

Joseph stood alone in his office, his brother's heavy boots retreating down the hallway. Reflecting on his tumultuous journey, he saw the faces of dear friends and dedicated employees his mind. He struggled to comprehend the magnitude of what his beloved city on the Neva River had overcome. Neither the fascists nor Joseph Stalin had been able to crush their spirit.

Exhausted, Joseph sank into his office chair, the weight of the world he had shouldered for nearly nine hundred days finally catching up with him. He idly traced his fingers over Reuben's letter, caught between hope and curiosity. A smile spread across his face as he began to read:

'My Dear Joseph,

I trust this letter finds you well and in good spirits amidst the familiar surroundings of our youth. My years spent researching on the shores of the Caspian Sea have proven fruitful. Now, I find myself embarking on even more challenging pursuits. Enclosed, you will discover a draft of my first epic poem. I am sure that even Homer would look upon it with envy.

Please add it to the 'family' archive for posterity. You are undoubtedly the most fitting person to curate such significant pieces. I look forward to discussing it in much greater detail upon my return. Your loving brother, Reuben.'

"It is ready," Vladimir's voice echoed from the hallway.

"Tell me again how many crates made it back from the Urals?" Joseph inquired.

"All of them," Vladimir replied with a twinkle in his eye. "One thousand five hundred and eighty-TWO, to be precise."

A faint smile found its way onto Joseph's lips. Decades of relentless effort and deceit had finally paid off. Despite the Bolsheviks' persistent attempts, some of the Romanov's belongings, which had not been stolen or surreptitiously acquired, had been returned to their rightful heir. In the grand scheme of life, it was a minor victory, but to Joseph Orbeli, it held immense significance. He exhaled deeply, expressing gratitude to God.

"Thank you, Vlad. Your assistance has been invaluable not only to me but also to many others you may never know. I owe you a debt of gratitude I doubt I will ever manage to repay."

"Your appreciation just now is all the repayment I require," Vladimir said, his heart swelling with pride. "Before you go outside, there is something else you must see first," he said, ushering his childhood friend out the office door.

Draped in his overcoat, Joseph, with Vladimir accompanying him, strolled through the vast corridors of the Winter Palace, now bustling with activity. Carpenters and throngs of workers scuttled about like bees mending a ravaged hive. The initial crates of returned art and historical treasures had begun to be unveiled. Portraits now adorned both walls of the 'Hall of Russian Painters.' To Joseph's surprised, all the artwork bore the signature of just two artists – Repin and Tropinin. As he turned towards Vladimir, ready to chide him for this breach of protocol, his eye was caught by a previously unseen portrait. He approached it cautiously and gasped as a dim memory resurfaced - he heard Sophia's tender voice from years past in the Dionysus Room, "Would you allow me to paint your portrait, Joseph?"

"It is as if Repin himself brushed your image," Vladimir marveled. "Sophia was truly a master painter."

"I do not understand," Joseph stammered, rapidly scanning the other portraits along the walls. He then realized that Sophia's self-portrait hung adjacent to his. "Is it—," he started to utter before halting.

"Yes, Joseph, it is Repin's own Chronicle of the Versemakers. Before Sophia's passing, she made me vow that they would all hang together at least once in the Hermitage. I have fulfilled that promise," Vladimir declared solemnly.

Joseph looked again, identifying the portraits of some of the most renowned political figures, writers, and composers in Russian history: Pushkin, Sergi White—the first Prime Minister of the new Russian government, and even Tchaikovsky graced the walls.

"Only a smattering of Repin's portraits have ever hung in the Hermitage at a given time," Vladimir explained, "To the untrained eye, they seem less intriguing than his depictions of physical labor, which the Bolsheviks find so captivating."

"Thank you," Joseph uttered, turning away and wiping a tear from his eye. He then continued his solitary journey, making his way outside. He ventured towards the remnants of the once grand Carriage House, an early casualty of the invader's bombardments. There, Joseph spied the sole surviving carriage of the Romanovs—Catherine the Great's personal conveyance. He tried to remember why he had selected this carriage for evacuation and ultimate preservation as Tatiana polished a piece of ornate gold trim, restoring its gleam.

In perfect harmony, they worked to hitch a duo of courtly horses to the imperial coach. Grasping the reins, the stable coachman led the stately animals by foot, with the carriage in tow, to the Palace Square. Tatiana sat upright, the very picture of majesty, in the golden carriage while Joseph sat beside her. The rhythmic clip-clop of the horse's hooves punctuated the foggy morning air.

Then, the horses broke into a trot, traversing the square and completing triumphant laps, just as the royal carriage's original occupant had done nearly a hundred and fifty years earlier. The sight was immensely joyful and heartbreakingly poignant, a past that echoed ominously into the future. Three centuries of harsh Romanov rule had given way to something far worse.

Later that evening, Joseph sat ensconced in his home study, poised to inscribe the final entry detailing the siege of Leningrad into the Chronicle. Tatiana, his wife, approached him, cradling their child, who slept peacefully on her shoulder. She kissed Joseph's cheek tenderly before she withdrew, moving to tuck their infant daughter into bed.

Joseph took a deep breath, eyeing the red leather-bound copy of *Eugene Onegin* perched next to its twin, the Chronicle. He paused and then unfolded the journal, uncertain of what he would inscribe or how he would distill his thoughts. He resorted to the strategy that had served him best over the years - he committed himself to telling the truth.

'The war is over. The fascists have been defeated. Life, music, and art have all returned to St. Petersburg. Even the birds have resumed their predawn songs. The city breathes anew, the shadow of death momentarily dispelled—until the inevitable rise of another war. Break the cycle, bite the apple, and learn from the past. It is our only hope.'

THE END

Author's Note

One of this book's aims is to serve as a cautionary tale, highlighting the perils of allowing lies to go unchecked and the importance of speaking truth to power while defending our freedoms. As Salman Rushdie powerfully noted, *"A poem cannot stop a bullet. A novel can't defuse a bomb...But we are not helpless...We can sing the truth and name the liars."*

Although the majority of my novel is set in the Soviet Union during World War II, it draws unsettling parallels between the rise of Bolshevism and the increasing political extremism in the United States. The tactics used are strikingly similar: both employ divisive strategies to pit "us" against "them," saturating the public with falsehoods until the line between truth and fiction blurs beyond recognition.

This novel is timely due to some notable anniversaries. The 80th anniversary of the end of World War Two will be acknowledged in 2025. The 50th anniversary of Shostakovich's death will also occur in 2025. And most importantly to me, the 60th anniversary of Anna Akhmatova's passing will occur in 2026. As an American, I desire to increase awareness of Akhmatova's poetry, Shostakovich's compositions, and Obeli's heroics in evacuating and protecting the Hermitage's art. These are unfamiliar names to most Americans and these heroes of history should have wider acclaim in the Western Hemisphere, in my opinion.

Most of the characters in my book are historical figures or amalgamations of historical individuals who, like all of us, experienced the breadth of human emotion. The rest of the characters sprang entirely from my imagination. In this author's note, I aim to delineate between the two while clarifying what events are based on fact and what is entirely fictitious.

A reader who is also an astute student of history may have already identified some inconsistencies in my novel. The timing of some historical events portrayed in *The Chronicle of the Versemaker* have been shifted in order to better facilitate my narrative. For example, the timing of both Joseph Orbeli's and Dmitri Shostakovich's evacuations from Leningrad happen a year later in my novel than when they occurred historically. Consequentially, this also caused a shift in when Shostakovich's Leningrad Symphony was debuted worldwide and then when it was performed in Leningrad. Please remember my novel is a work of historical fiction. It is not intended as a non-fictional account of the siege or those who endured it.

However, in portraying the historical figures in my novel, I have tried to adhere to the historical record whenever possible and capture the essence of these individuals' personalities and known deeds. This endeavor is complicated because the Soviet Union was a society shrouded in secrecy throughout its relatively short sixty-nine-year existence, traditionally unforthcoming with information about its people, actions, or history. The overwhelming amount of misinformation purposefully disseminated by the Soviet state and its sanctioned media is astounding. It has caused incalculable harm to the knowledge and understanding of its people and the world's appreciation of the rich Russian cultural history that predated it.

The political Soviet reform movement of the 1980s called *perestroika* and the policy reforms initiated by Mikhail Gorbachev, known as *glasnost*, led to increased openness and transparency in the historical record. However, finding and examining the limited documents and other primary sources available, particularly for non-Russian readers, remains daunting.

Given these constraints, my objective was to craft an engaging narrative about the valiant efforts of Joseph Orbeli and Russia's once-acclaimed pre-revolutionary cultural elite as they endeavored to safeguard the treasures of the State Hermitage. They faced imminent threats of German invasion from the West and persistent Soviet liquidation of the museum's treasures from within.

Historically, the Hermitage has been evacuated three times: in 1812 upon Napoleon's invasion, during the First World War, and finally during World War II. Realistically, only the third evacuation was indispensable, and it most likely averted much of the art's destruction.

Before proceeding, I would like to describe the book I initially intended to write before it evolved into the final story you have just read. *The Chronicle of the Versemaker* is the second full-length novel I have penned. In my debut, *The North Country Confessional*, I introduced a supporting character named Silas Bollerud, who was personified as "junk mail"—full of incessant chatter and unyielding nonsense that never stops coming. The overwhelmingly positive response from readers to this character exceeded any other creation of mine.

Crafting Silas and his windbag dialogue in my first book was an absolute delight, and deepening the seriousness of his character in this book was even more gratifying. I originally intended for *The Chronicle of the Versemaker* to serve as a prequel to my first novel with Silas as the main protagonist, focused on his early life in war-torn Europe: "Did I ever tell you what I did in 1944?" After crafting around 10,000 words of this initial draft, it became clear that this was not the story I yearned to write or needed to tell. A more significant, larger narrative clamored to be penned and debated. So, I took Vladimir's advice and "did not hesitate to adjust [my] sails against the wind and alter [my] approach." Perhaps the original 10,000 words will make it into a future novel someday.

As I delved into extensive historical research on World War II, I stumbled upon the intriguing lives of Joseph Orbeli and his two older brothers. All three were exceptional experts in their respective fields, with stories so fascinating they alone could have crafted an exciting narrative. However, I ultimately chose to pivot the core of my tale around Joseph and the art of the Hermitage. Additionally, my novel takes its name from an obscure Alexander Pushkin poem that resonated with me during a college literature class at Arizona State University in Tempe over three decades earlier.

I believe, at the core, every human being harbors a deep-seated desire for creativity; expressing oneself affirms being alive. Creativity, in any of its myriad forms, also serves as a pathway toward our quest for immortality. Humans also harbor a simultaneous fascination and fear of death. Religion has traditionally served as a mechanism to comprehend mortality and a tool for exercising authoritarian control. We unfortunately see evidence of this in the United States today.

My journey with faith, reflected in my writings, is complex. While I consider myself a spiritual individual, I do not find it necessary to partake in congregational activities or strive to save others' souls from eternal damnation. My spiritual leaning gravitates towards the inherent interconnectedness and unity of all things. On this planet, we are all interwoven threads in the tapestry of life; however, our actions seldom reflect this profound reality.

Let us delve into the characters featured in this book. As I have already noted, the Orbeli brothers were historical individuals. Joseph, as Director of the State Hermitage, was a renowned expert in 'Oriental Arts' which I interpreted as being an expert of Persian culture. Remember, the Hermitage did host the 3rd International Congress of Iranian Art in 1938. Levon Orbeli, on the other hand, served as one of Dr. Pavlov's research assistants. Pavlov is famously known for his research on conditional responses (for instance, 'bell rings, dog salivates'). Upon Pavlov's demise, Levon continued his groundbreaking work, becoming one of the Soviet Union's foremost scientists in Physiology. Reuben Orbeli has earned the moniker 'father of underwater archaeology.' All three Orbeli brothers shared Armenian heritage, while Joseph Stalin originated from the neighboring Caucasus region of Georgia. The brothers, in a sense, "breathed the same air as Stalin," which potentially lent them a certain kinship with him. This connection offered the brothers some degree of protection from Stalin's notorious paranoia and the subsequent Purges.

Anna Akhmatova was an amazing individual, often hailed as Russia's most illustrious poet, surpassing even Alexander Pushkin in the esteem of some—including my own. The poems cited in this novel genuinely belong to Akhmatova and stand as a testament to her literary prowess. Most of the poems chosen for my novel were penned during the war years: The Last Toast (1934), To The Londoners (1940), Courage (1942), The Moons at Zenith, the 5th stanza, "I am greeting my 5th Spring" (1944-1956), Third (1945), and The Last One (1964). I curated each of these selections to align with my story's plot. The beautiful English translations of Akhmatova's poetry came from The Complete Poems of Anna Akhmatova, translated by Judith Hemschemeyer, edited and introduced by Roberta Reeder. Copyright © 1989, 1992, 1997 by Judith Hemschemeyer. Reprinted with the permission of The Permissions Company, LLC on behalf of Zephyr Press, zephyrpress.org. I highly recommend this 948 page book to readers who want to explore her poetry further.

Contrary to my narrative, Anna never broadcasted on the BBC during wartime. Her first visit to London was not until 1965, when she received an honorary doctorate from Oxford. Sadly, she passed away just six months later. If Helen of Troy's face famously "launched a thousand ships," then Anna Akhmatova's words had the power to unleash two hundred thousand boots onto the blood-soaked beaches of Normandy two years earlier had the world only been allowed to hear her voice. However, it should be noted that the Allies did not have enough landing craft built to allow for an earlier landing in France. I encourage anyone who is interested in learning more about WW2 to visit The National WWII Museum in New Orleans. It is one of the finest repositories of artifacts and information dedicated to the global conflict.

Anna's fictional romance with Silas draws inspiration from rumors of her alleged affairs with a British diplomat and suspected spy named Isaiah Berlin, who was stationed at the British Embassy in Moscow, and another lover of hers, an 'Englishman' artist named Boris Anrep. Mr. Anrep, although born in Russia, spent most of his life in London.

Though Anna was not typically considered a 'physical beauty,' it is accurate that she held an alluring charm for many men and women. Her poetic prowess rendered her as enchanting as Aphrodite. Her words put me under a spell, and I would have loved to have met her. Her poetry speaks for those who had no voice.

Amedeo Modigliani was a talented artist and sculptor, yet his work remained relatively obscure during his lifetime. He shared an intimate relationship with Anna and painted/sketched her on multiple occasions. Modigliani died of tubercular meningitis, at the age of 35, in Paris. However, no historical record of him bequeathing any of his art to Anna upon his demise could be found. This plot point is purely fictional, intended to develop the story further.

Similarly, Sir Basil Nicholls, the Controller of Programs at the BBC, was a real person who had deep reservations about the direction the BBC took during the war years. His disdain for the sentimental love songs and variety shows that dominated the BBC's airwaves was well known, with Vera Lynn's popular 'Sincerely Yours' show drawing particular criticism. Nicholls was ultimately dismissed from his role when a guest, Christopher Stone, wished the King of Italy a 'happy birthday,' adding, "I don't think any of us wish him anything but good, poor soul." This remark, seen as a slight to the King, prompted the Ministry of Information to swiftly terminate his employment.

Dmitri Shostakovich was a talented composer, famed for his 7th Symphony, aptly titled 'Leningrad.' This seminal wartime composition, symbolizing resistance to fascism and totalitarianism, enjoyed widespread popularity in both the Soviet Union and the Western world during World War II. However, its popularity diminished in the West in the decades following the war's end. The symphony is replete with hidden meanings and intricate musical nuances, making it a remarkable work of art.

Shostakovich faced denunciation twice in his lifetime. Initially, it was Stalin who condemned him, followed by another reproach post-war, according to the Zhdanov Decree, which declared that his work contravened the prevailing Soviet cultural doctrine. Despite this, the Soviet propaganda machine repeatedly employed Shostakovich and his music.

The interest in his compositions saw a resurgence when two of his works were used as theme music in the 1980 Moscow Summer Olympics

(Festive Overture, Opus 96) and the 2004 Athens Summer Olympics (Opus 76a: Finale). Shostakovich undoubtedly remains one of the greatest composers of all time.

Tatiana is a fictional character. As the daughter of crime boss Sergi Agron and the granddaughter of literary giant Leo Tolstoy, she encapsulates the complexities of familial ties and the struggle many face when reconciling, or attempting to repair, the damage wrought by the human frailties within our lineage. Tatiana is a mirror for Joseph. She is also the young girl sketching in the Dionysus Room when Joseph, by then the newly appointed Director of the Hermitage, and Sophia are discussing their extensive plans. "And now, the girl on the cusp of womanhood continues the tradition by creating a copy of a copy. Through the hand of God, she becomes a mirror, crafting something new and not so new for you." Does their conversation pertain solely to art?

Zhdanov, as mentioned above, also known as Marshal Zhdanov, was an actual historical figure. His infamous Zhdanov Decree mandated artists to conform to the Communist Party's ideological line or face persecution. He famously branded Anna Akhmatova as "part nun, part whore." Though some translations might substitute "harlot" for "whore," the derogatory sentiment remains unequivocal. Furthermore, Zhdanov audaciously attempted to provide "musical advice" to Shostakovich. Rumor has it he even went so far as to demonstrate musical notes on a piano, purporting to show the Maestro how to compose "State-approved" music. Although this is most likely untrue, Zhdanov was a considerable ass in my opinion and a persistent hindrance to all artists trapped within the Soviet Union.

The character of General Markian Popov, portrayed as Zhdanov's primary military officer in the novel, is a historical figure. Throughout World War II, Popov commanded various armies across numerous fronts. Multiple promotions and demotions marked his military career before he ultimately ascended to Chief of Staff of the Leningrad Front. Remarkably, he was among the few experienced military leaders to survive Stalin's purge of the military ranks.

The character of Olga Bergholz (Berggolts) is a historical person. She famously became the "Voice of Leningrad," broadcasting her poetry across the airwaves to provide solace to the besieged city's inhabitants. Her stalwart presence made her a symbol of defiance and the heroic survival efforts of the city's residents. Despite being a protégé of Anna Akhmatova, Olga never achieved the same level of fame or recognition. Interestingly, Olga's parents were devoted members of the Bolshevik party, raising her to believe in Lenin's claim that women deserved full equity and that the revolution would not be a genuine success until all women were "freed from the yoke that had kept them subordinate and oppressed for centuries." Stalin's rise to power and his rumored poisoning of Lenin ended any notion that women would be equal partners in Soviet society. Olga, like millions of other Russians, became disillusioned and fearful of this new, sociopathic liar who had hijacked the revolution and was determined to destroy all who did not bow down in reverence to him.

While Pasha is fictitious, the golden fountains and meticulously maintained grounds of Peterhof Palace exist. I have been lucky to know several individuals who embody characteristics akin to Pasha's — people who immerse themselves in books and love engaging in thought-provoking discussions over long meals and wine. I believe our world could benefit from more individuals like Pasha. As Eleanor Roosevelt aptly stated, "Great minds discuss ideas; average minds discuss events; small minds discuss people." I cannot help but think that the dissolution of multi-generational households in favor of the American ideal of individual homeownership — the quintessential white house with a picket fence — has inadvertently fostered a rise in more narrow-minded perspectives. This shift appears to have isolated us from our past and one another.

Vladimir Levinson-Lessing was a real person. He served as a loyal associate to Joseph Orbeli at the Hermitage. He was selected to lead the Eastern Branch of the Hermitage, accompanying the evacuated art to the Ural Mountains. In our adult lives, we all need friends like Vlad, harking back to our childhood. They are the ones who provide us with unvarnished truth when we veer from our authentic selves or lose sight of our origins.

Fyodor Raskolnikov was a diehard Bolshevik politician who played a significant role in the October Revolution. A fervent believer in the movement's ideals, he worked tirelessly as an editor of the Bolshevik newspaper Pravda and as a party organizer, spreading its influence. His unwavering dedication led to his ascent within the party, earning him the ambassadorship to Afghanistan — the first country to acknowledge the new Russian Soviet Republic. Later, he served in diplomatic capacities in Estonia, Denmark, and Bulgaria. An eloquent public speaker, Leon Trotsky once lauded him for delivering a speech that Trotsky described as "the most distinctive expression of the proletarian side of the argument," despite his opposition to it.

Raskolnikov watched with growing dismay as Stalin solidified his power, exterminating rivals and perverting the revolution's avowed ideals. Sensing his imminent downfall, Raskolnikov defied an order from Stalin to return to Moscow. Instead, he defected and moved his family to Paris. There, he penned his astounding 'Open Letter to Stalin,' systematically cataloging all the ways Stalin had betrayed the revolution. This fearless confrontation with the 'Red Tsar' is one of the finest examples of 'speaking truth to power' I have encountered. Because of its significance, I have included Raskolnikov's full letter in the appendix of this novel so that you can read it yourself if interested.

Raskolnikov allegedly died after 'falling out of a window' in a Paris hospital. It is suspected that his fall was an assassination orchestrated by Soviet agents at Stalin's behest. In this novel, however, Raskolnikov survives the assassination attempt. This twist is entirely fictitious and is employed solely to facilitate my narrative.

Sergi Agron is fictional, but Leningrad's Haymarket Underground is based on historical facts. Sugar-drenched clumps of Badaev dirt were sold to the starving masses during the blockade and traded for diamonds, silver tea sets, and other valuables that could not satiate hunger. Organized crime thrived during the siege as the general populace dwindled. Sergi symbolizes how often individuals veer toward darkness when deprived of love. This loss can lead to a fundamental shift in character, but in the end, redemption is possible even for the most villainous among us.

Franz Krüger is a fictional character, yet his actions in the novel draw upon the real-life exploits of Franz Zatzenstein-Matthiesen, a young art dealer contracted by the Bolsheviks. His task was to appraise the Hermitage's art collection and compile the 'forbidden list'—items that were never to be sold. The real-life Franz did indeed relocate to England and was associated with Colnaghi's of London, a firm utilized in the art sold to former U.S. Secretary of the Treasury Andrew Mellon. When Mellon passed away in 1937, his will instructed that his art collection be given to the U.S. government to establish the National Gallery of Art in Washington, DC.

The famous Titian's *Venus with a Mirror*, mentioned in the novel, is real and is currently displayed at the National Gallery of Art.

Calouste Gulbenkian was a historical figure. He was the founder of the Iraq Petroleum Company and amassed considerable wealth. In a notable trade, he exchanged barrels of oil with the Soviets, receiving in return numerous Hermitage paintings. These works of art would eventually find a home in the Calouste Gulbenkian Museum in Lisbon.

Every painting, work of art, descriptions of the Winter Palace, and other locations mentioned in my novel are authentic. Peter the Great did build secret underground passages during his reign. One passage led from the Summer Garden to the Summer Palace of the emperor. Real works of art include *Venus with a Mirror*, all the paintings purchased by Andrew Mellon, all the statuary in the Hermitage's Dionysus Room, Van Dyck's *The Madonna with Partridges*, Repin's *Barge Haulers on the Volga*, Rembrandt's *Return of the Prodigal Son*, Hau's *The Cabinet of Italian Schools*, and Catherine the Great's Golden Carriage. As far as I know, none of the art pieces or treasures housed in the State Hermitage are forgeries.

London's people, locations, and establishments featured in my novel are real, including Olaf Hambro, a regular at 'Wilton's.' This banker acquired the esteemed restaurant with a simple declaration: 'Put this place on the bill.' The restaurant has remained under his family's ownership, though it relocated in 1984.

The character of the Hermitage's main forger and Versemaker is based on the Countess Sophie of Merenberg, a historical figure. However, the historic Sophie had no known connection to the Hermitage and was not a forger. The Sophia of my story only shares a different spelling of her name and some backstory with the historical Sophie. The notion of my fictitious Sophia being a forger, and the plotline involving preserving the Hermitage's art from liquidation through the creation of forgeries, stemmed from my readings in contemporary fiction. *The Art Forger* by B.A. Shapiro and *The Swan Thieves* by Elizabeth Kostova inspired me to include a woman forger and gifted artist in my story and to weave the creation of forged artworks into the narrative. The Bolsheviks did sell priceless works of art to sustain their revolution. Thomas Hoving, former director of the Metropolitan Museum of Art, estimates that around 40% of paintings on sale at any given time are fakes. So, is truth indeed stranger than fiction?

This leaves us with all the Versemakers - Past, Present, and Future. In my novel, Reuben tells Joseph, "History is typically written by the victors, rarely is it accurate. The conquered lose not just their land, freedom, and sometimes their lives, but most devastatingly, they lose their voice." I staunchly believe safeguarding the truth is pivotal to our species' survival. As Rousseau reminds us, 'The falsification of history has done more to impede human development than any one thing known to mankind.'

As a public school teacher, I endeavor to instruct my students on the significance of seeking answers to their most probing questions and then scrutinizing the responses they receive. "Do not believe everything you hear or read," I caution them. Teachers, despite what one U.S. political party wants you to believe, do not teach students "what" to think, we teach students "how" to think, analyze, and critically consume information. That is why we and our unions are so dangerous in the eyes of some.

The unexamined allegiance to any single philosophy, religion, political party, or cult of personality poses significant risks. Isaac Asimov eloquently stated, 'When stupidity is considered patriotism, it is unsafe to be intelligent.' The courage to voice the truth in the face of power is imperative. Silence offers tacit consent to the evildoers in our world. While the grass may appear greener on the other side, this can be a deceptive illusion, carefully cultivated through a constant stream of manipulative narratives.

Our media plays an instrumental role in disseminating lies and fostering beliefs in these falsehoods peddled by ill-informed demagogues masquerading as political leaders. Such leaders require followers; hence educating our children to consume information critically from an early age is crucial. This can counteract and potentially reverse the damaging influence of vested interest groups whose only concerns are wealth, power, and preserving the status quo.

The media must take drastic steps to identify lies in real time and prioritize disseminating the truth. Is it such an insurmountable task to deny those with malicious agendas the platforms from which they peddle their deceit? Moreover, the era of sensationalizing violence – the 'if it bleeds, it leads' approach – must end. This trend inflicts lasting harm on our children and desensitizes society to the true horrors of heinous acts, such as school shootings. I have a deep respect for those who put their lives on the line to uphold the law and protect our citizenry. However, with a sense of dread, I also watch as SOME of those who vowed 'to protect and serve' apply oppressive force against the marginalized, threatening the same treatment to anyone who dares challenge the ruling doctrine. There is no place in law enforcement for these individuals and they should be rooted out as expeditiously as possible. The evening news resembles a modern-day Roman Coliseum. Onlookers respond with a binary verdict – a thumbs up or thumbs down. But I implore you to consider, who among us is equipped to take on the role of Caesar and determine our collective destiny? Your vote matters, choose wisely.

Our world needs observant individuals who can bear witness, document, and share our unvarnished collective history. The tradition of engaging in thoughtful discourse at the dinner table, where consequential ideas were pondered and exchanged, has seemingly dwindled. Contemporary dialogues often focus on trivial matters such as events, people, the weather, or idiotic things we see on social media. The mantra 'Keep them fed, keep them entertained, and you will keep them in line' served the Bolsheviks well, and I fear it is a tactic that may prove effective for many of our current leaders too.

I would like to remind readers that a country's figurehead does not necessarily embody the heart or spirit of a nation's people. The unfolding events and ongoing war in the Ukraine and Russia are alarming, especially given the assumption that the Russian populace is indifferent to these horrifying occurrences. Egregious war crimes are being committed in Ukraine, and the world needs to hold Russia's leadership accountable without unjustly condemning its people. As history has hopefully taught us, its nature is cyclical; war resolves nothing except determining who gets to narrate it in our history books.

"Make people's lives better and do no harm." That is the catchphrase, the tagline, and the synopsis. I aspire for the story of Joseph Orbeli, Anna Akhmatova, Dmitri Shostakovich, and all other characters featured in *The Chronicle of the Versemaker* to act as a catalyst for thought-provoking, respectful discourse among people of diverse backgrounds and perspectives about the pressing issues and grand ideas that demand serious discussion within our broader communities. You can disagree with your neighbor and not hate them. Civility must return. Speak your truth and in turn listen to what is spoken back to you. One person can make a

difference, while two create momentum. We only need to find common ground.

I am deeply grateful for your time and attention dedicated to reading this unconventional yet, I hope, impactful novel on 'Courage.'

Craig C. Charles

August 1, 2023

APPENDIX

RASKOLNIKOV'S OPEN LETTER TO STALIN

***This letter, dated August 17, 1939, was first published in the Paris émigré newspaper *Novqya Rossya* on October 1, 1939.**

"Stalin, you have proclaimed that I am an 'outlaw'. By so doing you have given me the same rights—or, more precisely, the same lack of rights—as all Soviet citizens, who under your rule live as outlaws.

For my part, I answer you with complete reciprocity: I return to you the entrance ticket into the 'realm of socialism' you have built, and break with your regime. Your 'socialism', which, now it has triumphed, can find room for those who built it only behind prison bars, is just as remote from real socialism as the tyranny of your personal dictatorship is without anything in common with the dictatorship of the proletariat.

It is *of* no help to you *if* the respected *Narodnaya Volya* revolutionary N.A. Morozov, decorated with an Order, affirms that it was for this 'socialism' that he spent twenty years of his life under the vaults of SchhIsselburg fortress.[1a]

The elemental growth of discontent among the workers, peasants and intelligentsia called imperatively for a sharp political maneuver comparable to Lenin's turn towards the New Economic Policy in 1921. Under the pressure of the Soviet people you 'granted' a democratic constitution. It was received by the whole country with sincere enthusiasm.

An honest implementation of the democratic principles of the constitution of 1936, which embodied the hopes and aspirations of the entire people, would have meant a new stage in the extension of Soviet democracy.

But, in your mind, every political maneuver is synonymous with cheating and deception. You have cultivated a kind of politics without morality, authority without honesty, socialism without love for mankind.

What have you done with the constitution, Stalin?

Fearing free elections as a 'leap into the unknown' that would threaten your personal power, you have trampled on the constitution as though it were just a bit of paper, you have transformed elections in a miserable farce of voting for a single candidate, and you have filled the sessions of the Supreme Soviet with hymns and ovations in honor of yourself. In the intervals between sessions you quietly annihilate the 'ingratiated' deputies, laughing at their immunity and reminding everyone that the master of the Soviet land is not the Supreme Soviet but yourself.

You have done everything you could to discredit Soviet democracy, just as you have discredited socialism. Instead of following the line of the turn indicated by the constitution, you are suppressing the growing discontent by force and terror. Having gradually replaced the dictatorship of the proletariat by the regime of your personal dictatorship, you have opened a new stage which will enter into the history of our revolution as 'the epoch of terror'.

Nobody in the Soviet Union feels safe. Nobody, when he goes to bed, knows if he will escape arrest during the night. There is no mercy for anyone. The righteous and the guilty, the hero of October and the enemy of the revolution, the old Bolshevik and the non-party man, the collective-farm peasant and the ambassador, the People's Commissar and the worker, the intellectual and the Marshal of the Soviet Union—all are equally subject to the blows of your scourge, all are whirled in your bloody devil's roundabout.

Just as, when a volcano erupts, huge boulders crash thunderously into the mouth of the crater, so whole strata of Soviet society are being broken off and are falling into the abyss.

You began with bloody measures against former Trotskyists, Zinovievists and Bukharinists, then you proceeded to exterminate the old Bolsheviks, then you destroyed the Party and non-party cadres that grew up during the civil war and bore on their shoulders the task of carrying through the first Five-Year Plans, and then you organized a massacre of the Young Communist League.

You hide behind the slogan of struggle against 'Trotskyist-Bukharinist spies'. But it is not since yesterday that you have held power. Nobody could have 'insinuated' himself into a post of responsibility without your permission.

Who put the so-called 'enemies of the people' into the most responsible positions in the state, the Party, the army and the diplomatic service? Joseph Stalin.

Who planted the so-called 'wreckers' in all the crevices of the Party and Soviet apparatus? Joseph Stalin.

Read the old minutes of the Politbureau: they are filled with appointments and postings of none but 'Trotskyist-Bukharinist spies', 'wreckers' and 'diversionists'—and beneath them flaunts the signature: J. Stalin.

You make yourself out to have been a trusting simpleton whom some carnival monsters wearing masks have led by the nose for years on end.

'Seek out and prepare the scapegoats,' you whisper to your henchmen, and those who are caught and doomed to be sacrificed you load with the sins you have yourself committed.

You have fettered the country by means of fearful terror, so that even a brave man does not dare to cast the truth in your face.

The waves of self-criticism 'without respect of persons' die away respectfully at the footstool of your throne.

You are infallible, like the Pope! You never make a mistake!

But the Soviet people know very well that you are responsible for everything, you, the smith who is forging 'universal happiness'!

With the aid of dirty forgeries you staged trials in which the Preposterousness of the accusations surpasses the mediaeval witch-trials you learnt about from your seminary textbooks.

You know that Pyatakov did not fly to Oslo, that Maxim Crorky died a natural death, and that Trotsky did not derail any trains. Aware that that is all lies, you spur on your minions: Slander away: from slander something will always stick.'

As you know, I was never a Trotskyist. On the contrary, I waged an ideological struggle against all the oppositions, both in the press and in broad meetings. Today as well I do not agree 100% with Trotsky's political position, with his program and tactics. While differing with Trotsky on points of principle, I regard him as an honest revolutionary. I do not believe and never shall believe in his 'compact' with Hitler and Hess.

You are a cook who prepares highly-spiced dishes that are ''digestible for normal people.

At Lenin's tomb you swore a solemn oath to fulfill his testament and to preserve the unity of the Party like the apple of Your eye. Perjurer, you have violated Lenin's testament. You have calumniated, dishonored and shot those who for many years were Lenin's companions in arms: Kamenev, Zinoviev, Bukharin, Rykov and others, of whose innocence you were well aware. Before they died you forced them to confess to crimes they never committed and to smear themselves with filth from head to foot.

And where are the heroes of the October Revolution? Where is Bubnov? Where is Krylenko? Where is Antonov-Ovseyenko? Where is Dybenko? You arrested them, Stalin.[1]

You corrupted and befouled the souls of your collaborators. You compelled your followers to wade, in anguish and disgust, through pools of blood shed by their comrades and friends of yesterday.

In the lying history of the Party written under your direction you robbed the dead, those whom you had murdered and defamed, and took for yourself all their achievements and services.

You destroyed Lenin's Party, and on its bones you erected a new 'Party of Lenin and Stalin' which forms a convenient screen for your autocracy. You created it not on the basis of a common program and tactics, as any party is built, but on the unprincipled basis of love and devotion towards your person. Members of the new Party are not obliged to know its program, but instead they are obliged to share that love for Stalin which is warmed up every day by the press. You are a renegade who has broken with his past and betrayed Lenin's cause!

You solemnly proclaimed the slogan of advancement of new cadres. But how many of these young promotees are already rotting in your dungeons? How many of them have you shot, Stalin? With sadistic cruelty you exterminate cadres that are useful and necessary to the country, because they seem to you dangerous from the standpoint of your personal dictatorship.

On the eve of war you disrupt the Red Army, the love and pride of our country, the bulwark of its might. You have beheaded the Red Army and the Red Navy. You have killed the most talented commanders, those who were educated through experience in the world war and the civil war, headed by the brilliant Marshal Tukhachevsky. You exterminated the heroes of the civil war, who had reorganized the Red Army in accordance with the most up-to-date military technique, and made it invincible.

At the moment of the greatest danger of war you are continuing to exterminate the leaders of the Army, and the middle-ranking and junior commanders as well.

Where is Marshal Bhicher? Where is Marshal Yegorov? You arrested them, Stalin.

To calm anxious minds you deceive the country by saying that the Red Army, weakened by these arrests and executions, has become even stronger than before.

Although you know that the law of military science demands one-man command in the army, from the commander-in-chief down to the platoon commander, you have revived the institution of political commissars, which arose in the early days of the Red Army and the Red Navy, when we did not yet have commanders of our own, and needed to exercise political supervision over military specialists drawn from the old army. Out of distrust of the Red commanders you are introducing divided authority into the Army and undermining military discipline.

Under pressure from the Russian people you are hypocritically reviving the cult of the heroes of Russia's history -Alexander Nevsky and Dmitri Donskoi, Suvorov and Kutuzov—in the hope that in the coming war they will help you more than the Marshals and Generals you have executed.

Exploiting your distrust of everybody, genuine agents of the Gestapo and the Japanese intelligence service fish successfully in the troubled waters you have stirred up, palming off on you quantities of false documents to blacken the best, most talented and honest people. In the poisoned atmosphere of suspicion, mutual distrust, universal spying and omnipotence of the People's Commissariat of Internal Affairs to which you have handed over for rending the Red Army and the whole coun-try, any intercepted 'document' is accepted—or a pretense is made that it is accepted—as indisputable proof. By slipping to Yezhov's agents forged documents which compromise honest members of the mission, the 'internal service of the ROVs', in the person of Captain Voss, has managed to destroy our Embassy in Bulgaria, from the driver M.I. Kazakov to the military attaché Colonel V.T. Sukhorukov.[2]

You are annihilating the most important conquests of Oc-tober one after the other. On the pretext of combating 'fluctuation in labour-power' you have abolished freedom of labour, enslaved the Soviet workers and bound them to the factories. You have ruined the country's economic organism, disorganized industry and transport, undermined the authority of the manager, the engineer and the fore-man, accompanying the ceaseless leap-frog of dismissals and appoint-ments with arrests and hounding of engineers, managers and workers whom you call 'hidden wreckers, not yet exposed'.

After making normal work impossible, you have, on the pretext of combating 'absenteeism' and 'lateness' on the part of the workers, forced them to work under the whips and scorpions of harsh and anti-proletarian decrees.

Your inhuman repressions are making life unbearable for the Soviet working people, who for the slightest offense are dismissed from their jobs, with a record that damns them, and evicted from their homes.

The working class bore with selfless heroism the burdens of intense labour, undernourishment, famine, meagre wages, cramped living-space and lack of necessities. They believed that you would lead them to socialism, but you have betrayed their trust. They hoped that, with the victory of socialism in our country, when the dream of humanity's brilliant minds about a great brotherhood of mankind had been accomplished, all would live in happiness and ease.

You have taken away even that hope: you have proclaimed that socialism has already been fully built. And the workers, bewildered, ask each other, in whispers: 'If this is socialism, then what, comrades, did we fight for?'

Distorting Lenin's theory of the withering away of the state, as you have distorted the entire theory of Marxism-Leninism, you promise, through the mouths of your illiterate, primitive 'theoreticians', who have occupied the places left vacant by Bukharin, Kamenev and Lunacharsky, that the power of the GPU will be maintained even under communism.[3]

You have deprived the collective farm peasants of every incentive to work. On the pretext of combating 'the squandering of collective-farm land' you have abolished their individual plots of land, so as to force them to work in the collective-farm fields .[4]

As the organizer of famine you have done everything possible, by the brutality and cruelty of the unscrupulous methods that are typical of your tactics, to discredit Lenin's idea of collectivization in the eyes of the peasantry.

While hypocritically calling the intelligentsia 'the salt of the earth' you have deprived the work of the writer, the scholar and the artist of even the minimum of inner freedom. You have forced art into a straitjacket in which it suffocates, withers and dies. The frenzy of the censorship, inspired by fear of you, and the understandable servility of editors who answer for everything with their heads, have led to sclerosis and paralysis in Soviet literature. A writer cannot get into print, a playwright cannot put his plays on the stage, a critic cannot express his personal opinion, unless he has received the official seal of approval.

You stifle Soviet art by demanding that it display courtier-like bootlicking, but it prefers to stay silent, so as not to sing Hosannas in praise of you. You are introducing a pseudo-art which hymns with boring monotony that famous 'genius' of yours which sets one's teeth on edge.

Untalented scribblers glorify you as a demi-god, 'born of the Sun and the Moon', and you, like an Oriental despot, delight in the incense of their crude flattery.

You pitilessly crush Russian writers who, though talented, are not to your liking. Where is Boris Pilnyak? Where is Sergei Tretyakov? Where is Alexander Arosev?[5] Where is Mikhail Koltsov? Where is Tarasov-Rodionov? Where is Galina Serebryakova, whose crime was to be Sokolnikov's wife? You arrested them, Stalin!

Following Hitler's example, you have revived the mediaeval burning of books. I have seen with my own eyes the long lists, circulated to Soviet libraries, of books that are to be subjected to immediate and unconditional destruction. When I was ambassador in Bulgaria in 1937 I found in the list of forbidden literature to be burnt which was sent to me my own work of historical reminiscences, *Kronstadt and Petrograd in* 1917. Against the names of many authors was written: 'All books, pamphlets and portraits to be destroyed.'

You have deprived Soviet scholars—especially those working in the humanities—of that minimum of freedom of scientific thought without which the creative work of research becomes impossible. By means of intrigue, troublemaking and persecution, self-assured ignoramuses are preventing scholars and scientists from working in the universities, laboratories and institutes.

Outstanding Russian men of learning, of world-wide fame, like Academicians Ipatiev and Chichibabin,[6] you have denounced to the whole world as 'non-returners', naively supposing that thereby you defame them, but you only disgrace yourself, by making known to the whole country and to world public opinion the shameful fact that the best scholars and scientists flee from your paradise, leaving to you the 'benefits' you confer: flats, motor-cars and tickets of admission to the dining-room of the Council of People's Commissars.

You are exterminating talented Russian scholars and scientists. Where is Tupolev, the best Soviet aeroplane-designer? You have not spared even him. You arrested Tupolev, Stalin!

No field, no corner is left in which one can tranquilly carry on the work one loves. The theatrical director, remarkable producer and outstanding artist Vsevolod Meyerhold did not engage in politics. But you arrested him too, Stalin!

Although you know that, given our poverty in cadres, every educated and experienced diplomat is particularly precious to us, you have enticed to Moscow and destroyed nearly all the Soviet Union's ambassadors, one after another. You have thoroughly destroyed the entire apparatus of the People's Commissariat of Foreign Affairs. Destroying here, there and everywhere the gold reserve of our country, its young cadres, you have exterminated talented and promising diplomats in the flower of their lives.

At a terrible moment of war-danger, when the spearhead of fascism is aimed at the Soviet Union, when the struggle over Danzig and the war in China are merely preparing places *d'armes* for future intervention against the USSR, when the principal object of German and Japanese aggression is our motherland, when the only possible means of preventing war is for the Soviet Union to enter openly into the international bloc of democratic states, concluding as soon as may be a military and political pact with Britain and France, you waver, hesitate, vacillate like a pendulum between the 'axes'.

In all your calculations in politics, both external and internal, you proceed not from love for the motherland, which is alien to you, but from animal fear of losing your personal power. Your unprincipled dictatorship blocks our country's way forward, like a rotten log.

You, 'the Father of the Peoples', betrayed the defeated Spanish revolutionaries, abandoning them to the will of fate and leaving other states to look after them. Magnanimous saving of human lives is not included among your principles. Woe to the conquered! You have no further need of them.

You have callously doomed the Jewish workers, intellectuals and craftsmen fleeing from Fascist barbarism, by shutting against them the doors of our country, which could hospitably offer refuge in its immense spaces to many thousands of immigrants.

Like all Soviet patriots, I got on with my work while closing my eyes to many things. I kept silent for too long. It was hard for me to break my last ties—not with you, your doomed regime, but with the remains of

Lenin's old Party, of which I had been a member for nearly thirty years, and which you destroyed in three. It was agonizingly painful to be deprived of my motherland.

More and more, as time goes by, the interests of your personal dictatorship will come into irreconcilable conflict with the interests of the workers, the peasants, the intelligentsia, the interests of the whole country, which you mock, as a tyrant who has risen to personal power.

Your social basis is shrinking day by day. Feverishly seeking support, you lavish hypocritical compliments on the 'nonParty Bolsheviks', you create new privileged groups one after another, you heap favors upon them, you feed them sops, but you cannot guarantee these new 'caliphs for an hour' not only the retention of their privileges but even their right to live.

Your crazy bacchanal cannot last for long. The list of your crimes is endless! Endless is the roll-call of your victims! It is impossible to enumerate them.

Sooner or later, the Soviet people will put you in the dock as a traitor to socialism and the revolution, the chief wrecker, the real enemy of the people, the organizer of famine and of judicial forgeries.

F. Raskolnikov August 17, 1939

Endnotes

[1a] N.A. Morozov (1854-1946), a leader of the Narodnaya Volya terrorist organization, spent the years 1882-1905 as a prisoner in SchltIsselburg fortress. After the October Revolution, he was given the Order of Lenin and the Order of the Red Banner, and made an Honorary Academician. Raskolnikov refers to the statements in praise of Stalin made by Morozov in his old age.

[1] In another version of the 'Open Letter', the following words appear at this point: 'Where is the Old Guard? You shot them, Stalin.'—B.P.

[2] ' 'ROVS' are the initials of the Russian name of the 'Russian General Military Union', the organization of the ex-soldiers of the White Armies living as émigrés in Europe. In 1927 Captain K.A. Voss, chief of staff of the head of ROVS in Bulgaria, formed an internal service' for the alleged purpose of carrying on secret intelligence work against the USSR. In 1938, however, after a number of incidents had aroused suspicion that Voss and his associates were actually double agents, the ROVS leadership dissolved this 'internal service'. Voss is said to have worked for the Gestapo in Russia during the German invasion

[3] In another version of the letter, the following words appear at this point: 'There is nothing to stop you announcing tomorrow that communism has been established. Crude vulgariser that you are, you have

done everything possible to discredit Lenin's theory of the building of socialism in one country.'—B.P.

[4] In another version of the letter, the following words appear at this point: 'In your mockery of the collective-farm peasants, you have gone so far as to impose a meat-tax levied not per head of cattle but per hectare of land.'—*B.P.*

[5] Alexander Aroscv (mentioned above, p.356, as Muralov's deputy in Moscow), gave particular offence to Stalin as a writer by his book, Km-ni (The Roots), published in 1953. The novel depicts the workings of the Bolshevik underground organization in Tsarist times. 'The character of Vano, a silent, sullen man, eternally smoking a pipe, was apparently intended to represent Stalin. Vano's pride suffers because he is merely one of many instead of the top man, and this injured pride breeds distrust, bitterness and contempt for others.' (V. Zavashilin, Early *Soviet* Writers, 1958, p.2'0.)

[6] V.N. Ipatiev (1867-1952) and A.E. Chichibabin (1871-1945), both distinguished organic chemists, 'failed to return' from visits abroad in 1930. Ipatiev's autobiography, *The Life of a Chemist* (1946), describes the experiences which led him to 'defect'.